I0611534

AN IDEAL WORLD

RAY HOBBS

Wingspan Press

Published in the United States and the United Kingdom
by WingSpan Press, Livermore, CA

The WingSpan name, logo and colophon are the trademarks
of WingSpan Publishing.

ISBN 978-1-59594-992-9 (pbk.)
ISBN 978-1-59594-975-2 (ebk.)

First edition 2020

Printed in the United States of America

www.wingspanpress.com

1 2 3 4 5 6 7 8 9 10

This book is dedicated to the memory of the late Stanley Walker, concert pianist and teacher, whose kindness and example are gratefully remembered by those he taught and inspired.
    RH

I wish to acknowledge the assistance of my brother Chris, who, as ever, has acted both as soundboard and as a regular source of ideas, as well as fuelling my enthusiasm throughout the writing of this book.

RH

Part One

1

A West Riding Town

September 1959

It wasn't the homecoming George had anticipated in the final weeks before his discharge. Delays between Portsmouth and Waterloo, and an overcrowded train from King's Cross to Leeds had resulted in a joyless journey, blighted further by gusting wind and rain that obscured the view from his carriage window and pelted him with unrelenting malice on his arrival. Home was only a short walk from Cullington station but he was soaked by the time he reached the gate.

He'd never considered himself more deserving than any other young lad obliged to forfeit two years of his life in his country's service, but he felt nevertheless that the day should have been somehow special. He'd emerged from the Royal Navy Signals School skilled in all aspects of radio communication and had played his part in the Cold War, monitoring Soviet signal traffic in the North Atlantic despite persistent seasickness, the monotony of the task, and the ceaseless ribbing of his 'real navy' shipmates, and now, having removed the piece of loose mortar from beneath the kitchen windowsill, he realised the key was missing. His father must have left in a hurry and forgotten to leave it there. Exasperated, he thrust the mortar back into its seam and checked the places where they had left the key before the cavity beneath the windowsill had seemed a better idea.

The string was no longer behind the letterbox, and the cat

flap yielded nothing more than a cruel reminder that, unlike their young master, Fred and Ginger could enter the house whenever they wished.

Returning to the front of the house, he peered through the sitting room window. According to the clock on the mantelpiece, it was a little after half-past four. His father wouldn't be home until six and there was nothing to be gained from hanging around so he stowed his kitbag in the narrow lean-to shed where they kept the garden tools, and walked the hundred-or-so yards to the telephone kiosk opposite the Commercial Hotel.

As he unbuttoned his coat, he feared for a moment that he might not have the right change, but he found the four pennies he needed. He knew the number by heart.

The dialling tone sounded for several seconds before the receptionist came on the line.

'Beckworth General Hospital.'

He pressed the button to release the coins and asked to be put through to the nurses' home.

'Hold the line, please.' There was a click and, after a few seconds, a woman's voice answered, 'Nurses' home.'

'May I speak to Staff Nurse Barker, please?'

'Who's calling?'

It was more a challenge than a question, and George recalled the woman from his last leave: bleak, humourless and with wrinkles of disapproval created by a permanent scowl. 'George Barker,' he told her. 'I'm her brother. I've been away, so I don't know what shift she's on. I just thought I'd phone on the off-chance.'

'Just a minute.' There was the soft, double thud of the receiver being placed on a blotter or similar object, and then after a few seconds, she spoke again. 'Staff Nurse Barker is on duty until six o'clock. You'd better try later.'

'Thank you.' He decided to spend the next hour in the Cosy Café. At least it would be warm and dry.

———◆▸◀———

Two hours later, after a bath and a change of clothing, he sat down to eat.

'I've started leaving the key in the shed,' said his father. 'It just slipped my mind to tell you.' Nodding in the direction of George's plate, he said, 'Elsie made us the pie. It was kind of her, wasn't it?'

'Yes, it was. It's really nice.' Elsie was his father's girlfriend, which seemed an odd thing to call a woman in her forties but it was the only title George could call to mind. She'd always been quite pleasant, and he had nothing against her other than the natural unease he felt at seeing her take his mother's place. It wouldn't be long, he imagined, before she and his father got married and she moved in with him, and he didn't know how he would cope with that. So much had happened in his absence, that home was already like another place.

'It was a bad business, Barrett's closing when they did,' said his father, 'but I see Wilkinson's are advertising for a cost clerk. It was in the *Evening News* last night, so you've come home at the right time.'

'Right, I'll have a look at the advert later.' George had worked at Barrett's from leaving school. They had made the fabric that was used to cover bus seats, but it seemed they'd finally lost the battle against the manufacturers of synthetic covers. Wilkinson's, on the other hand, were store fitters and it was difficult to see a time when they might be short of work.

'I'd apply for that job if I were you, George. There'll be others after it as well, so don't let the grass grow under your feet.'

'All right, Dad.'

'Well, you might show a bit of enthusiasm. Jobs don't grow on trees, you know.'

'I know.' George smiled at the mental picture of leafy boughs bent under the weight of countless job advertisements.

'What do you find so amusing?'

'I was just thinking how lucky I am to come home and find a job vacancy waiting for me.'

'Well, don't count your chickens yet.' He was a difficult man to please.

Beyond the necessity of employment, George had little interest in Wilkinson's or any other company. His father had channelled him into accounts because that was the only livelihood he knew, and he still expected George to share his enthusiasm for double-entry bookkeeping.

'It's the greatest shame you didn't work harder at junior school. If you'd passed the eleven-plus, you might have been doing your accountancy training now, on your way to a bright future. You could have had your National Service deferred as well. As things are, you'd likely have got out of it altogether.'

'Well, I'm glad I did it.'

'Why?'

'Because I'm not a shirker. I did my duty when the time came and I learned a lot because of it.'

'You learned a lot? What did you learn apart from the bloody silly language sailors use and how to read dots and dashes? Listen, George, my generation had soft ideas like yours twenty years ago, and you know what happened to us.' He jabbed the air with his knife, as he often did when holding forth on a pet subject. 'We were led across France by a shower of idiots and eventually herded on to the beach at Dunkirk for the Navy to rescue.' He sighed with disgust. 'And you talk about doing your duty.'

'Aye well, the Navy brought you home, didn't they? Somebody was on the ball.'

'Don't get clever with me, lad.' It was his father's stock retort when he knew he'd lost an argument.

The meal continued in silence until his father announced, 'Elsie's coming over later. She's been saying how nice it'll be to see you.'

'I'll be back some time. I'm going to the nurses' home first.'

'Good.' For once, something evidently pleased his father. 'Give my love to our Norma when you see her.' He picked up the empty plates and carried them into the kitchen. As he did so, there was a knock on the door. His father opened it, and George recognised the visitor's voice immediately. It was Sandra from next door, come to welcome him home, and it looked as if she'd put on her best frock for the event.

'Eh, George, I'm right glad to see you,' she said, fastening her arms round him. 'I've been that worried, I don't mind tellin' you.' She stood on tiptoe and reached upward to give him a noisy kiss on his chin.

'I was never in any danger, Sandra,' he assured her.

'I don't know, George. The sea can be dangerous, you know. It's deeper than you think.'

'Well, I'm safe now.' Her naïve concern was touching. She was older than him by two years but her mental age was reckoned to be about eight. She'd had a tough time growing up with some of the other kids because, as well as being slow to learn, her flat features and almond-shaped eyes marked her out as different from the others. Happily, George's mother had encouraged Norma and him to play with her when they were little, and they'd all grown up together.

'Come and sit down,' he said. 'I'm going to see Norma later on but I've got time for a chat and you can tell me about this new job you've got.' Norma's letters had kept him well informed.

'I'm working at the ice cream factory,' she told him. 'It's all right but they're dead mean. They don't let you have any ice cream.' She made it sound like the ultimate act of cruelty.

'I should hope not. You'd eat ice cream all day if you could, and you'd get so fat, you wouldn't be able to get through the doorway, and then you'd have to stay at home until you lost weight.'

The idea made her laugh until George had to give her his handkerchief to mop her cheeks. Then, as her laughter subsided, she said, 'You're daft, you are, George. You're as daft as a brush.'

'That's right. Anyway, what do you do at the ice cream factory?'

'I make tea and I push the tea trolley 'round. Everybody's ever so pleased to see me.'

'I'm not surprised. Tea's always welcome, and I expect they all like you anyway.'

'Aye, they do.'

That didn't surprise him either. She'd been the first to welcome him home properly on a particularly unpleasant day, and her reception had been unquestionably genuine.

———— ▶◀ ————

Norma poured him a cup of tea from the huge teapot in the corner of the nurses' sitting room. 'It's not horribly stewed,' she said, 'but it's not wonderful either.'

'I'd have been glad of it this afternoon.' He told her about his arrival and the missing key.

'I wondered why you weren't in uniform, and I wanted to show you off to the others as well. Come and sit down anyway.' They took their tea to a couple of worn and sagging chairs. Around them, off-duty nurses sat reading, watching television or just talking. If any of them had glanced in George's and Norma's direction, they might never have known they were siblings. George had inherited his father's dark hair and strong jaw-line, whereas Norma's fair colouring and high cheekbones were a pleasing reminder of their mother. They were both tall, but they bore no further physical resemblance.

'Elsie and the Old Man are going for a drink later,' said George. 'I've been invited but I don't fancy it.'

Norma smiled sympathetically. 'It hasn't been the best homecoming, has it?'

'Not until now. I certainly didn't expect a dressing down with the steak-and-kidney pie.'

'What was it about?'

George closed his eyes briefly at the memory of his conversation with his father. 'National Service, the eleven-plus, not taking employment seriously enough....' It was a familiar list and it wearied him.

Norma nodded, leaving her sympathy unspoken. George's contemporaries often complained about their sisters, but his relationship with Norma had always been easy and they'd grown even closer since their mother's death. He knew all about the tension that had caused her to leave home.

'Anyway,' said Norma, 'we're being far too serious on your first day home. What are you going to do tomorrow?'

'I'll find a job if I can.'

'So soon?'

'There's a costing job at Wilkinson's joinery. I'm going to call at the Ex-Servicemen's Club as well, just in case.'

'Do you think it's worth a try?' She sounded doubtful.

'You never know.' Playing the piano at the club had been George's evening job for almost five months before he was called up, and it held far more appeal for him than a job as a cost clerk. It was also considerably more lucrative.

Norma looked as if she were about to say something sensible but was distracted as the door opened and another nurse entered the room.

'Price,' said Norma, 'come and meet my little brother George. He just stepped off his boat this morning.'

'Ship,' he corrected her, 'well, barracks, actually.' As he spoke, he felt absurd, arguing about ships and boats when his sister was trying to introduce him to a very attractive girl.

'How do you do, George?' The girl took his hand and he noticed that hers felt soft and smooth despite the demands of her work. 'What are you going to do now you're on dry land?' A lock of dark hair had come loose from beneath her cap, and George was unaccountably fascinated by it.

'We were just talking about that. I used to work in the accounts office at Barrett's but they've closed down, so I'm out of work. I'm going to start looking in the morning.'

'Oh well, good luck. I hope you find something soon.'

'Thanks. What's your first name, by the way?' The nurses' practice of addressing one another by surname always seemed to him pointless and unfriendly, and he'd already decided he wanted to be on friendly terms with her.

'It's Jeanette.' She took the seat next to George and crossed her legs, noticing as she did so that a ladder had started in her left stocking. 'Oh, look at that,' she said. 'One pair left and I've got a date on Friday.'

'We're all in the same boat,' said Norma. 'Pay day can't come soon enough, and it's a bugger when so much of it has to go on stockings.' For George's benefit, she explained, 'It's an occupational hazard. They seem to catch on anything. It's what keeps us poor, that and NHS wages, and it doesn't help the course of true love either.' She added, 'Price is going out with one of the junior housemen.'

9

He nodded resignedly. As he understood the hierarchy, a junior houseman was a fleeting presence at the bottom of the medical ladder, unlike a senior houseman, who was part of the establishment, like Norma's boyfriend David. Unfortunately, however, the knowledge was of no use to George. He couldn't compete with a doctor, even one deemed lowly in the eyes of his colleagues. He could only hope his luck would improve when he went job hunting.

2

Cullington Ex-Servicemen's Club had always seemed out of place beside the blackened sandstone buildings that sandwiched it on Westgate. With its red-brick exterior and metal-glazed windows, it bore closer resemblance to a school than a social club; in fact, its style was almost identical to that of George's old secondary school in Albion Street.

He padlocked his bicycle to one of the staples set into the back wall and walked round the building to the front entrance, where a diminutive man with a neat white beard sat behind a card table. In front of him was a large book for signing guests in. George showed his membership card and the man nodded, showing no sign of recognition. George couldn't recall him either. Maybe he had known him before the beard had rendered him incognito.

'They've just opened t' bar,' the gnome told him, jerking his head towards the interior.

'Thanks.' George went through to the bar, where he was gratified to see someone he recognised. ''Morning, Jack,' he said.

'Hey up, it's young George Barker back from the wars.' The steward shook his hand. 'What'll you have, George?'

'A pint of bitter, please, and whatever you're having, Jack' After two years on National Service pay, George wasn't exactly wealthy but the gesture was within his pocket.

'I'll just have a half. Thanks, George.' He pulled one and a half pints and put them down on the bar. 'That's two bob,' he said.

George handed him a shilling, a sixpenny piece and two threepenny bits.

'Na then, what have you been getting up to?'

'Not much, just training and then off to sea. I'm glad I did it but it's good to be back all the same.' He looked around him at the familiar furniture, curtains and old photographs. 'I really came to see if there's any work going.'

'Piano playing, do you mean? I'm afraid not, George. I'm not saying the bloke who's doing it now is anything like as good as you, but it looks like we're stuck with him for a while.'

'Oh well, it was worth a try.' George hadn't been particularly hopeful, so he wasn't too disappointed either.

'I'll tell you where they need somebody, though.'

George looked up again. 'Where's that?'

'The Gladstone Liberal Club. I used to work there so I know most of the members. Mind you, it's an organist they're looking for. Can you play one of them things?'

'Yes. Who's the concert secretary there?'

'A bloke called Gilbert Finch, and according to members I've talked to, he calls himself "Entertainments Secretary." For some reason, he thinks it sounds more impressive. It's worth remembering 'cause he sets a lot of store by himself.'

'Thanks, Jack. I'll go and have a word with them.'

'You can phone them from here if you like.' Jack took the receiver from the wall telephone and dialled the number. After a word with his opposite number, he handed the phone to George. 'The steward's name's Arnie.'

'Hello, Arnie?'

'Hello. What's your name?'

'George, George Barker.'

'I hear you're looking for a job as an organist, George.'

'That's right. I used to play here before I was called up.'

'Aye well, we do need an organist. We've been without for more than a month. We've had to suspend concert nights and use gramophone records for dancing. Our members are getting very impatient at seeing the organ stand idle after it cost them so much.'

'You can't really blame them.'

'No, that's true. Anyway, I'll phone Gilbert and see if we can arrange a meeting. It shouldn't take long. I'll call you back in a minute or two.'

A few minutes later George learned that he had a meeting with Gilbert Finch that evening at six o'clock. Then, with his customary optimism restored, he rode home to write his application for the job at Wilkinson's.

———•◄•———

George read a good deal, and had often wondered about the 'commanding presence' favoured by some authors. He'd heard and received many commands during the past two years, but the all-important 'presence' seemed elusive, except at the one admiral's inspection he'd experienced, when as far as he could discern, the presence had been created by intensive preparation and an abundance of gold braid.

Gilbert Finch had neither, but he looked like a man steeped in his own authority. He looked quite imposing too, being tall and heavily built, with a frown that was clearly intended to intimidate.

'So you're the lad who's come about the organ job.' He spoke without removing the cigarette that dangled from between his lips.

'That's right, Mr Finch. I'm George Barker.'

'I know.' The Concert Secretary nodded and smiled to himself as if at some fact known only to him. It was only half a smile, as well, as if his face had mastered the technique, but his eyes were still leafing through the instructions. 'I've been on the blower to the Ex-Servicemen's Club. They seemed pleased enough with you. Mind you, this is a different kind of club to what you're used to.'

'What do you mean?' George was temporarily fascinated by Finch's cigarette, which had burned down, and its glowing end was now perilously close to his lips.

'Look around you.' Finch robbed the moment of its drama by taking the cigarette from his mouth and stubbing it out in an ashtray.

George had already noticed the polished tables and upholstered chairs. The bar room was certainly more lavishly appointed than the one he'd left at lunchtime, and he imagined that the rest of the Victorian building must be similarly furnished.

'We get top-class artists working here and that's why we've taken our time finding an organist. We want a first-rate organist, not some clueless kid.'

Thanks to his brief military service, George was acquainted with loutish authority; he had been snarled at angrily, impatiently and sometimes for no better reason than that four hundred years of tradition demanded it, so he was unimpressed by Finch's posturing. Also, he noticed that a group of men had gathered at the bar and were watching them expectantly. He asked, 'Don't you want to hear me play?'

'All right, come with me.' Finch led him to a pair of double doors at the end of the bar and opened them to reveal an extensive concert room. Like the bar, the seats around the tables, were covered with dark-red plush fabric, and its velvet curtains were of the same shade.

'Can you play a Hammond B Three?'

'I've played a C Three, so I imagine so.'

'All right, don't be cocky. Let's see what you can do with it.'

For all his apparent confidence, George had played a Hammond organ only once, and for a mere thirty minutes, in the piano and organ department of Gledhill's music shop, but he reckoned he could cope. He slid on to the bench, switched on the organ and arranged the drawbars to set the registration that would give him the sound he wanted for 'Catch a Fallin' Star.' It was one of Perry Como's hits from the previous year and he imagined it might go down well during a free-and-easy night at the club. After the first eight bars, he glanced at Finch, who seemed unmoved, so he put in a bridging sequence and changed to 'Magic Moments.'

Finch interrupted him. 'That's all very well, but can you read sheet music?'

"Course I can.'

'Not so much of the "'course I can." I told you before about being cocky.' He opened a cupboard beside the organ and took out a piece of music apparently at random. 'Let's hear you play that.'

George took the music. The title meant nothing to him and the cover suggested that it might be a sentimental Edwardian song, so it was little wonder it was lost on him. He played a few bars before Finch interrupted him.

'Can you play it in a different key?'

'What key do you want it in?' In his last two years at school, George had played the piano in morning assembly, and one of the staff had frequently complained that the hymns were pitched too high for her. His efforts to accommodate her had made him quite adept at transposition.

'What key is it in?' Clearly, Finch knew nothing about music.

'D.'

'Play it in E.'

George obliged. It was part of the job anyway. Some artists brought their dots with them in the right keys, some brought the music but wanted it transposed into a different key, and the worst kind might even hand him a cigarette packet with a song title and the laconic instruction *2 flats* scribbled on it in pencil.

'We have dancing on Thursdays,' Finch told him. 'Can you play a waltz?'

'What kind of waltz?'

'How should I know? Any bloody kind.'

George played a few bars of 'La Ronde.'

'Quickstep.'

George obliged, noticing at the same time that the group of men who had been at the bar were now at the back of the concert room.

'Foxtrot.'

George responded to each gruff demand and each time he was rewarded with a burst of enthusiastic applause from the growing number of members in the room.

'Cha-cha-cha.'

As George began 'Tea for Two,' one of the members decided that the audition had gone on long enough. 'Give the lad the job, Gilbert,' he said. 'He can play as well as any of 'em. Anyroad, you know you can't tell one tune from another.'

'All right,' said Finch, ignoring the criticism, 'I pay four guineas a night and I want you here, smartly dressed, five nights a week. It's bingo on Monday nights and games on Tuesdays so you're not needed then. All right?'

'Fine. Thanks, Mr Finch.'

'One more thing. Members will buy you drinks and that's up to them, but if I catch you the worse for it while you're on the job you'll be out on your arse. Right?'

'I don't drink when I'm working.' George had learned that lesson early in his career.

'Well, see that you don't.' He stood up to bring the audition to an end. 'Right,' he said, 'can you start tomorrow night? It's a dance night, ballroom and Latin. I might be able to lay my hands on a drummer but I'm not promising.'

'I can start tonight if you like.'

Finch nodded abruptly. 'Six-thirty, then. It's a free-and-easy tonight. Off you go and get changed.'

3

The free-and-easy night lived up to its name and George had no problems; in fact, he achieved instant popularity with the members, if not with the Entertainments Secretary. Gilbert Finch was nevertheless a man of his word and, for the following evening, he managed to secure the return of the drummer whose services had been rendered superfluous by the departure of George's predecessor. Bernard was a few years older than George, and a draughtsman by day. His immaculate fair hair and chevron moustache might have suggested vanity, but he was relaxed and good-natured. He was also a welcome source of information.

'I'll tell you why Finch is such a miserable bugger,' he said. 'It's because he's easily the worst concert secretary they've ever had. He was the reason the last organist packed the job in. Mind you,' he added, 'it has to be said that Trevor was wet behind the ears. He was young and he'd led a sheltered life. He was clever all right, a university lad, and he could play jazz as well as classical, but it narked him that nobody took him as seriously as he took himself. Do you know what I mean?'

'I think so.' George had met a few of that kind.

'All the same, Finch had his knife into the lad from the start just because he was clever. He has to feel superior, you see, and that's why he looks permanently disappointed. I mean to say, how many ham-fisted half-wits can he meet in the course of a day?' Nodding towards the crowd, he said, 'Talk of the devil. He's coming over.'

Finch's habitually grim expression told them nothing until he spoke.

'Are you two going to talk the night away? Members have come here to dance, you know.'

'We've been having a break,' Bernard told him, 'and we've been planning the second half. We've only just met, and already we're working together like a well-oiled machine.'

'I'm glad to hear it but I still think it's time we heard some more music.'

'We're getting there, Gilbert.' Unruffled, Bernard picked up his sticks and wire brush.

'Well, I'll leave you to get on with it.' Then, almost as if he felt obliged to explain himself, he added, 'I have to keep an eye on things. I'm Entertainments Secretary, when all's said and done.'

'Oh, we know well enough what you are,' Bernard assured him.

'Right.' Finch gave Bernard an uncertain look before leaving to re-join the other members.

George was puzzled. 'What is it about you? He treats me like dirt, and you've got him eating out of your hand.'

'Not exactly, but he's wary of me. The secret is to stand up to him. He just can't handle it.'

'Can't he?' George wanted to believe him.

'Mark my words, young George, if you lie down he'll walk all over you, like most bosses I know.' Bernard glanced in Finch's direction as he spoke, and said, 'And he'll have a legitimate moan if we don't get started.'

'Okay.' George switched on the microphone. 'Let's have a gentle foxtrot now, ladies and gentlemen: "Love Walked In".' Members moved readily on to the dance floor, happy that they had an organist once again.

———— ▸◂ ————

With his first four nights' earnings, George was able to contribute four pounds ten shillings towards the housekeeping expenses, a gesture Arthur Barker could hardly fault, although he still insisted that it would be better if his son found a proper job. George knew there was no point in arguing, and he had to see Norma, so he left the house as soon as he could.

As he pedalled up the steepest part of Moorside Road to the hospital, he wondered how long it might be before he could afford transport of a more luxurious kind. The old pushbike had served him well for more than five years but he couldn't use it to go anywhere in decent clothes, and he was always at the mercy of the weather. He'd held a driving licence since he was seventeen, although it had come almost as an anti-climax after years spent driving and tinkering with an ancient Standard on the bit of scrubland that was part of Ellison's poultry farm. Roy Ellison, Stanley Holmes and he had taught themselves to drive with the aid of an ancient motoring handbook and occasional bits of advice from old man Ellison in his soberer moments. George recalled that they had also become quite proficient at driving in new fence posts, having hit the same one several times when they were learning.

He left his bike padlocked in the staff shed, took a white cardboard box from the saddlebag and walked into the lobby, where one of the porters sat smoking his pipe.

'Well, if it isn't Popeye the Sailor Man.' His wit was rudimentary.

'Not any longer.'

'What are you doing, then? Writing your memoirs?'

'Not yet. I'm playing the organ at the Gladstone Club in Cullington.'

'Well, I never.' The porter took his pipe from his mouth but no witty remark ensued. Instead, he said, 'You'll be here to see your sister, I expect?'

'If she's here.'

''Alf a mo.' The porter disappeared into the nurses' sitting room and re-emerged with Norma. 'There you are, love,' he said, 'your brother's waded ashore just to see you.'

Norma smiled indulgently and then more enthusiastically at George as she accepted a kiss and escorted him to the sitting room. 'Herbert doesn't get any better,' she observed, 'but he's honest and reliable.'

'It makes up for a lot,' agreed George, distracted for the moment by a burst of immoderate laughter from a group of nurses watching TV.

'They're watching *Emergency – Ward 10*,' Norma told him.

George was puzzled. 'But it's not a comedy,' he said.

'It's not meant to be, but it has its comical moments for us. D' you fancy a cup of tea?'

'Yes, please. I left home early.'

'Oh dear.' Norma poured tea into two cups. 'What was it about this time?'

'He told me I needed to get a proper job, and I'd just given him four-and-a-half quid for my keep.'

'Four pound...? He never got that much from me.' She poured milk into the two cups and handed one to George. 'Mind you,' she added, 'I wasn't earning much more than that.' She waved towards a group of empty chairs. 'Let's sit down before the decent ones get taken, and then you can tell me about your new job.'

'It's okay,' said George. 'The concert secretary's a pain in the neck, but I'm working with a drummer who can handle him. His name's Bernard – that's the drummer, not the concert secretary – and he's a good bloke.'

'Bernard?' Norma thought for a moment. 'What's his surname? There used to be a Bernard at school who played the drums. He was a bit older than me.'

' "Fair"-something. I believe somebody called him that.'

'Fairbairn?'

'That's right. Is he the same one?'

'Yes, he was two years ahead of me.' Unlike George, Norma had passed the eleven-plus and gone to the grammar school. 'Music was all he ever thought about. He was always getting into trouble for neglecting his work.'

'Well, he did all right in the end,' George told her. 'He's a qualified draughtsman now.'

'Is he married?'

'Yes.' George discovered that on Friday night as they left the club and Bernard had said, 'Must go. It's nooky night.' He added with a grin, 'If she's in a good mood I sometimes get seconds on Saturday.' It wasn't the kind of thing George would discuss with Norma, but he'd been wondering if marital sex was always rationed to the extent that it had one night of the week labelled and reserved for it. He could only wonder because his experience was so far limited to an embarrassingly brief and fumbled episode with a Wren in Rosyth.

'Has he any children?'

'Who?'

'You're miles away, George. I'm asking you if Bernard Fairbairn has any family.'

'None that I know of.'

'He was always popular with the girls.'

'He would be.' George nodded, thinking of his friend's good looks and easy manner. It seemed to come naturally to some blokes.

'Hey, guess what,' said Norma, changing the subject.

'What?'

'We're putting on a pantomime. It's Cinderella, and I'm going to be Prince Charming.'

'Great. You were brilliant in Jack and the Beanstalk at Sunday school.'

'That was a long time ago, but thanks. This one's for the kiddies who'll be in hospital over Christmas. We're doing it on Christmas Day. You'll come, won't you?'

'Course I will. Who else is in it?'

'Who else do you know?' She pretended to search her memory in a way that George found profoundly embarrassing. He'd obviously given himself away.

'There's Price,' she concluded predictably. 'She's the prettiest, so they've cast her as "Cinders".'

George needed a change of subject, and it was with a rush of relief that he remembered his errand. 'I brought you these,' he said, handing her the box of cakes he'd been carrying so carefully.

'I wondered why you were clutching it.' She took the box from him and opened it.

'They're cream cakes,' he told her somewhat unnecessarily.

'I can see that, but you shouldn't, George. These must have cost a fortune.'

'Not really.'

'Five of them,' she announced. 'Are you expecting company?'

'Not really. I just thought you might be.' He added lamely,

'There was half-a-dozen, but I gave one to Sandra next door. She was there when I got home.'

'Good for you, George. Anyway, being alone is difficult in this place, so I'm sure I'll have no difficulty sharing them. Thank you.' She leaned over and kissed his cheek just as the *Emergency – Ward 10* theme signalled the end of the programme. The group of nurses who had been watching it began to disperse, and Norma called out, 'Have you a minute, Price?'

Jeanette turned away from the TV set and spotted Norma and George.

'Hello, George,' she said, joining them. 'How's the job hunting?'

'He's got a great job,' Norma told her. 'Look what he's brought.' She held up the box of cakes. 'There's one for you.'

Jeanette blinked. 'Is that right, George?'

George squirmed, hoping madly that his face wasn't as red as it felt. 'Yes,' he managed to say, wishing he could think of a smooth line to follow it.

'That's really good of you. Thank you.'

'You can give him a kiss if you like,' said Norma. 'I did.'

'All right. Thanks again, George,' she said, kissing him lightly on the cheek.

He heard Norma say, 'I've been telling him about the pantomime, Price.' He hoped desperately that she wouldn't embarrass him any more than she had already.

'Oh yes. Your sister's got the part of Prince Charming, being the tall one with the legs. I'm Cinderella. Are you going to come and support us, George?'

'Yes, I'll come.'

'Good. Now, what's this job you've got? It obviously pays well,' she said, taking the cream horn from the box Norma offered her.

'Oh well, I'm just playing the organ in a club.'

'Just playing the organ? How many people can do that? It's a shame he's not playing for the pantomime, isn't it, Staff?'

'Yes, Dr Beatty's rather hit-and-miss, but we can't have everything, and he's better than some pianists I've heard.'

'George,' said Jeanette, 'you can come here again. This cream horn is yummy.'

'You're welcome.' Again, he wished he could think of something smooth to say, but such was the effect she had on him that he felt gauche and inarticulate.

'Everyone should have a brother like George,' said Norma, just to embarrass him even more, although he reflected later that at least he was popular, and that was a good start.

4

George was surprised, if not as delighted as his father might have wished, to be called by Wilkinson's for interview, and subsequently offered the job. According to Arthur Barker, his son was typical of a generation that expected everything and appreciated nothing, and that he'd learned precious little from years of rationing and shortages. Realising that argument was pointless, George simply polished his Oxford brogues, pressed his grey flannels and blue, window-pane check sports jacket, and reported to Mr Patchett, the Chief Clerk, at eight-twenty on the appointed day. The job paid nine pounds a week, and he could earn that in two nights at the club, but he was nevertheless prepared to make an effort. There was just a chance the job might lead to something better, although he'd no idea what that might be.

He spent the first hour in the Costing Office, reading about the Wilkinson Code, a system of rechargeable, capital and revenue works orders, cost centres, cost units and cost elements that he found familiar enough, even with the elaborate house labels Wilkinson's had given them. It was all basic stuff, so it wasn't long before his attention began to wander. He'd already met some of the staff that morning and, from behind the book he was supposed to be reading, he was able to observe them at work.

There was Neville, the junior, a seemingly quiet lad who'd left school only recently and was still finding his way in the busy office. There were two women, but one, a rather pretty girl, was engaged, and the other was married and well into her thirties, so there was no joy to be had there. In front of them sat Michael

Burchett, the trainee accountant. He was a lanky, awkward youth with untidy hair and a condescending attitude that George already found irritating. To be fair, it was a first impression, but it was no less distinct for that, and it seemed he would soon have an opportunity to test it when the coffee trolley arrived, because with it came a visit from Michael.

He approached George's desk and, inclining his head towards the book, said, 'Gripping reading, isn't it? Are you clued up about costing now?'

'I've done quite a lot of costing.'

'Oh? Where were did you work before this?'

'I was at William Barrett's for three years before I was called up.'

'I see. The army, was it? I thought you had that look about you when you arrived. You know, smart and well-behaved.' He took a cup of coffee from the trolley without a word and spooned sugar into it.

'Thank you.' George smiled at the girl behind the trolley. 'Milk, but no sugar, thanks.' Returning his attention to Michael, he said, 'Actually, I was in the Navy.'

The information seemed to amuse Michael, who grinned and folded his arms in a parody of a hornpipe.

'How old are you?' George's patience was about to desert him. He might tolerate that kind of thing from senior staff but not from a conceited kid like Michael Burchett.

'Eighteen.'

'In that case you should be called up soon.'

'Not on your life. Thanks to Wilkinson's and the Institute of Cost and Works Accountants, I got deferment. By the time I reach the end of my training, National Service will be a thing of the past.'

'It's a pity. It would have been good for you.'

Michael gave him a pitying look. 'Everyone says that but it doesn't mean a thing. It might suit some.' He nodded in Neville's direction. 'He'd be all right in the forces, having someone to tell him what to do all the time. I prefer to think for myself.'

'Most of us do.'

His reply seemed lost on Michael, who said, 'I'd better get

along. I just thought I'd stop by and make sure you have everything you need.'

'That was big of you. Thank you.' George was thankful to see him go. Even reading about the Wilkinson Code was better than listening to a bumptious clown who thought he knew everything and who'd probably been known as 'Bird Shit' at school. If he hadn't, he should have been.

He was allowed to do some work for the rest of the day, which brought him into contact with the other occupants of the office, a pleasanter experience by far, and he was in a more contented mood when he arrived home that evening.

He found Elsie cooking sausages and mash with onion gravy, one of his favourites.

'It'll be ready in five minutes,' she told him. 'I know you'll want to get off to the club.'

'Thanks, Elsie, I appreciate that, but I'm not at the club tonight. I'm going to the Reserve to see some of my old mates.'

'What's the Reserve, when it's at home?'

'The Royal Naval Reserve wireless training centre.'

'I thought you were done with all that.'

'I like to keep in touch.'

'Well, dinner will be ready soon.'

'Great.' He was looking forward to it. However he felt about the situation, Elsie was an excellent cook. He joined her in the kitchen to feed the cats, a job his father had left to him since the death of his wife.

'How was your first day?'

'It was okay, thanks, Elsie. They're a decent lot, most of them.'

His father stopped by the kitchen doorway to say, 'I reckon you'll do all right there if you put your mind to it.'

'I'm doing my best, Dad.'

'I should hope so.'

'George,' asked Elsie, tactfully changing the subject, 'why do you call that cat "Ginger" when it's black and grey with white bits?'

'Ah well,' he said, putting the cats' dishes on the floor, 'we named Fred after Fred Astaire, so when the other one came she had to be called "Ginger" after Ginger Rogers.' The names had been his mother's idea, but he thought it wise to keep that to himself.

The matter still seemed to be puzzling Elsie. 'But why,' she asked, 'did you name a cat after a film star in the first place?'

'When he's finished eating,' said George, pointing to Fred, 'watch him walk across the floor. There's only one man in the world who can move as gracefully as that.'

'I can't say I've ever watched Fred Astaire,' she admitted, 'not properly, anyway.'

'George has,' said his father. 'I sometimes think he lives in a world of make-believe.'

'Aye well, I'm ready to serve up now.'

From George's point of view, it was a timely interruption. He just hoped he could survive the meal without his father highlighting any more of his shortcomings; in fact, as they sat down to eat, he reflected that the time was coming when he would have to follow Norma's example and leave the family home.

———◆◆———

The training centre occupied the top floor of an office building outside the town centre. It had been a regular haunt for George before he was called up; in fact, he'd joined at sixteen and served two years as a junior. He had been required to attend a minimum of one night per week, and he'd been able to do that as well as working at the Ex-Servicemen's Club. Weekends had been difficult, but his reserve service had ensured that he could perform his National Service obligation in the Navy. Some of his contemporaries had left it to potluck and found themselves in the army; some had joined the Territorials or the Air Training Corps in readiness, but it was the Navy that had appealed to George.

He pushed the doorbell marked *RNR* and waited. After a minute or so, a young lad who was a stranger to George opened the door.

'I'm George Barker,' he said. 'I just completed National Service. Is Chief Robinson in tonight?'

'Yeah.' The kid stood aside to let George in.

'Are you new?'

'Yeah.'

'I thought so.' Maybe, when he'd been around for a while, thought George, he might adopt a little self-respect and stop saying 'yeah'.

They took the lift together to the top floor, and George headed for the office.

Lieutenant Commander Brewer, officer-in-charge and a bank manager by day, recognised him immediately.

'Hello, George,' he said, shaking his hand. 'Welcome back. How was National Service?'

'Not bad, sir. I'm glad I did it.'

'Are you coming back to us?'

'I might eventually, sir, when I'm off the Special Reserve List. I just came to see everybody and find out if I could do something useful.'

'Chief Robinson's in the Wireless Room. He'll find you a job, I'm sure. Anyway, it's good to see you again.'

George found Chief Radio Supervisor Robinson, the regular RN instructor, in the Wireless Room, as the officer had said.

'George,' said the Chief, 'how are you?'

'I'm okay, Chief. How are you?'

'Fair to bloody awful, as usual. Do you want a job, or are you just loafing?'

'I thought I'd make myself useful, Chief.'

'Good lad. National Service all right, was it? You're looking well on it.' He beckoned to George to follow him into the classroom, where a number of new recruits, including a girl, as well as the youngster who'd answered the doorbell, sat wearing headphones. They were reading a Morse practice tape. 'Will you take this lot for Voice Procedure? It'll be their first time, so go easy on them.'

'Yes, Chief.'

CRS Robinson stopped the tape machine, thus claiming everyone's attention. 'Listen, everybody,' he said. 'This is George Barker. He's just returned from sailing the seven seas to take you all for Voice. He knows the procedure backwards and he can read Morse at twenty-five words a minute in Russian as well as English

and take it down on a typewriter, so listen to everything he tells
you. Right, square off your desks and get into the bays.'

As the recruits carried out the order, Chief Robinson patted
George on the shoulder. 'It's good to see you again, George,' he
said. 'Don't let 'em get away with anything, will you?'

George picked up the headphones and microphone from his
Radio Telephony bay and addressed the class.

'When you need to transmit,' he told them, 'push down the
pressel switch on the microphone. At any other time, don't touch
it or it'll prevent others from transmitting. Okay?'

Four nodding heads told him that the class understood.

'Right, my callsign is "Delta One".' Pointing to each in turn, he
said, 'You are "Delta Two, Three, Four and Five". The collective
callsign, for when I need to call up all of you, is "Delta Class". Okay,
headsets on and let's get started. Open the book in front of you
and we'll follow the procedure.'

George was patient and sympathetic. Unlike some instructors
he'd known, he saw no point in humiliating his trainees with
wisecracks at their expense. Everyone had to learn, so he guided
them through the first series of exercises, correcting them where
necessary and expressing his approval when they got it right.

At twenty-one-thirty, the class secured, and everyone went to
the bar. It was good for George to see his old friends again, and he
stayed late, catching up on the events of the past two years. Even
so, he knew that his new lifestyle made it difficult for him to carry
on as before.

5

Despite his father's urging, George could find little enthusiasm for his new job. The work was routine and repetitive, and he found himself looking forward more than ever to his evenings at the club. Life at Wilkinson's had its occasional incidents and diversions, however, and one occurred towards the end of George's fourth week.

He returned from the canteen after lunch to find the women in the accounts office fussing over Neville, the junior clerk, who appeared to be shaking and babbling incoherently. He wondered at first if the lad might be having a fit, although the symptoms were different from those he remembered from his first-aid course.

'We found him locked in the stationery cupboard,' Janet Firth, the older of the two women, told George. 'We heard him hammering on the door. He was in an awful state.'

'He still is.' Crouching in front of the lad, he said, 'Neville, you've got to breathe slowly. Come on, try.' He turned to the two women and asked, 'Has anybody got a paper bag?'

'No.' Janet frowned. 'What d' you want a paper bag for?'

'It doesn't matter now. He's beginning to calm down. Neville, slower, mate. Breathe in for five seconds and out for eight. One, two, three, four, five and out.... That's right.'

'What does he have to do that for?' The question came from Denise Threadgold, who had been watching George as a missionary might observe a witch doctor performing a mysterious ceremony.

'He has to get less oxygen and more carbon-dioxide into his blood stream. Too much oxygen raises the blood pressure and... things.'

'I thought oxygen was good for you.'

'Well, it just shows, doesn't it? You can have too much of a good thing.'

Denise appeared to consider the information and then asked, 'How do you know all that?'

'I learned first aid in the Navy.'

'Did you really? Hey, I can imagine you in a sailor suit.'

'Can you? I'll wear it for you if you like.'

'Now then.' Janet intervened on the side of propriety. 'Behave yourself, George, and remember she's spoken for.'

George's sigh of regret wasn't lost on Denise, who gave him a cheeky smile. It was worth remembering, but he hadn't forgotten Neville, who was now looking more settled but far from happy. He asked, 'Who shut you in there, Neville?'

'I don't know.' He was still shaking. 'I just h… heard the door slam sh… shut and somebody t… turning the key.'

'Has this sort of thing happened to you before?'

'Yeah, my brother sh… shut me in the c… coal cellar when I was little. I n… nearly went mad.'

'It seems everybody has it in for you, you poor little bugger.'

'Language, George,' said Janet. 'There are ladies present.'

'Sorry,' said George, 'but I wonder if this is the culprit.' Michael Burchett had just walked into the office.

'Michael,' asked Janet, pointing somewhat unnecessarily at Neville, 'are you responsible for this?'

'No, you've got to blame his parents for that.'

'Don't play the clever dick with me. You're lucky Mr Patchett isn't here today. Did you lock Neville in the stationery cupboard?'

Michael took his place at his desk before answering. 'It was only a bit of fun. Has he been telling tales?'

'No, he hasn't,' said George, 'but the poor kid suffers from claustrophobia.'

'How was I supposed to know?'

'He was in a hell of a state when they found him. What time did you lock him in there?'

'I don't know.' His bravado had given way to sulky defiance.

'If you want to do something useful,' said George, 'go and get him a cup of tea from the canteen. You owe him that at least.'

'He takes two sugars,' said Denise helpfully.

'I don't see why I should.'

'I do.' Seizing Michael's left arm with one hand and holding the elbow straight with the other, George propelled him towards the door, saying, 'Tea with two sugars, and quick about it.'

Denise watched, open-mouthed. 'Did you learn that in the Navy as well?'

'Yes, but not officially. I learned it from a lad on my messdeck, a bit of a roughneck but a good mate. He was from Glasgow.' He added, 'I don't make a habit of it.' He didn't want her to think he was a roughneck as well. He might just have a future there.

<hr/>

'So was anything said after that?' It was Saturday morning at the *Sorrento* coffee bar, and Norma was keen to hear more about the incident.

'Mr Patchett called me into his office yesterday morning. Burchett had made a complaint about me. I told him what he'd done to Neville but he wasn't impressed. Burchett's a trainee accountant after all, and I'm only a cost clerk.'

'That's despicable.'

'I know, and one of the girls told me that Patchett and Burchett's dad are always drinking together at the British Legion, so I suppose that says everything. They're two shits who stick together.'

'I just hope he's going to leave the young lad alone now. An incident like that could lead to all kinds of things.' Distracted for the moment, Norma sniffed the aroma from behind the bar and grimaced. 'I had so much to do this morning,' she said, 'I didn't have time for breakfast.'

'That's no good.' George stood up to speak to the man behind the bar.

Norma waited for him to sit down again and asked, 'What was that about?'

'I just ordered you a toasted teacake.'

'You spoil me, George, but thank you.'

'How are the pantomime rehearsals going?'

'Okay, but we've just had to recast Towzer. The original one's got herself another job.'

'Towzer?'

'The dog, silly. He's a key member of the cast.'

'Played by a girl?'

'No one will know the difference, at least until the curtain call,' she assured him.

'I'm looking forward to it anyway.'

Talk of the pantomime evidently reminded Norma of something that had been on her mind, because she became more serious. 'Look,' she said, 'I know you like Price but you mustn't get too keen on her.'

'Jeanette? I probably don't stand a chance with her anyway, but why not?'

She waited until the assistant had put the toasted teacake down, and thanked him before going on. 'She's very pretty, I know,' she said, 'but she's not a girl to get serious about.'

It was too cryptic for George, who was feeling quite nettled. 'What do you mean exactly?'

Norma opened her mouth and then hesitated before saying, 'I don't want you to get hurt, George. That's all.'

As she seemed unlikely to go beyond that veiled warning, and knowing her as he did, he changed the subject for the time being.

'I went to the Reserve on Monday,' he told her, 'just to see some old mates and catch up.'

'Oh, that must have been nice. Are you going to join again?'

'No, I might think about it later but I wouldn't be able to put the time in just now, with my job at the club. I could manage Tuesday nights, but weekends would be impossible. In any case, I'll be on the Special Reserve List for some time, being ex-National Service.'

'That's a shame. You used to enjoy the drill nights and weekends.'

'Well, I'll leave it for now.' He had enough to do, and that included making sense of Norma's warning about Jeanette. He also needed to call at the newsagent's in Northgate, where they sold jokes and novelties.

————◆◄————

It seemed that Michael Burchett was slow to learn his lesson, because he was still teasing Neville on Monday, even threatening him on one occasion with the stationery cupboard, an act of intimidation that George was quick to notice. He'd also noted that one of Michael's less endearing habits was to help himself, without asking, to the contents of other people's desks. Such items were nothing more than office consumables and other company property, but his high-handed attitude was no less irritating for that, and it annoyed George as much as the others.

He waited for what seemed a long time, and eventually Michael approached him in his usual self-important way.

'Have you any treasury tags, George?' Without waiting for a reply, he opened the side drawer of George's desk and then leapt backward with a cry of horror. His sudden exclamation summoned the attention of everyone in the office. Only George knew the reason for it but he maintained a straight face as Michael yelped, 'There's a snake in his drawer!' His face was white, and George was gratified to notice that he was shaking with fright. He opened his drawer and picked up the offending serpent.

'Do you mean this snake?' It was black and it appeared to be wriggling as he held it up for everyone to see. 'It's made of rubber, you daft bugger.'

'You should be locked up for that!' Whether he was still affected by the original shock, the realisation that he'd made a fool of himself or the embarrassment of being a target for general laughter, his anger was making him almost tearful.

George dropped the snake back into his drawer. 'You were scared, weren't you?'

'What do you think? How was I to know it wasn't real?' The

hapless dupe was still shaking but probably with indignation. 'I can't stand snakes. I never could.'

'So now you know how Neville must have felt when you locked him in the cupboard.'

'Are you never going to forget that?'

'Only when you stop bullying the poor little sod.'

'All right, but it was only a bit of fun.'

'So was the snake. Anyway, now we've both had a bit of fun, so leave the kid alone, right?'

Inevitably, that was not the end of the matter, because Mr Patchett called George again into his office.

'I gather there's been another incident involving you and Michael,' he said. He was bald except for a narrow fringe around the back of his head, but hair sprouted in excess from his ears and nose, and George found him difficult to take seriously.

'It was unfortunate, Mr Patchett. I'd no intention of showing him the snake, and he wouldn't have seen it if he hadn't opened my desk drawer without asking.'

'But what were you doing with a toy snake in your drawer in the first place?'

'I bought it at lunchtime from the paper shop, and I was keeping it in my drawer just until I went home.'

'What I don't understand is why you needed it at all.'

'It's for the garden. My dad's sick to death of cats digging up his vegetable patch, so he asked me to get a rubber snake. You leave one beside your vegetables, you see, and cats won't go near it.' He added, 'I'm surprised you haven't heard of that.'

'I don't do a lot of gardening.'

'Well, it's worth bearing in mind if you ever do start growing things.'

'Aye, well, thanks for the tip.'

'It's no trouble, Mr Patchett. I'm only happy to pass these things on.'

Something seemed to tell the chief clerk that the conversation had gone off-course, because he said, 'The fact remains that there's ill feeling between you and Michael, and I won't have it in my department.'

'There wouldn't have been any ill feeling if Michael hadn't locked little Neville in the stationery cupboard. The bullying's gone too far. I'm not kidding, Mr Patchett, if you'd been here on Thursday you'd have been as furious as the rest of us. At one stage I thought we'd have to send for an ambulance for the poor lad.'

'Did you really?'

'No kidding.'

'All right, I'll speak to Michael about it.'

'Good, although I think he's most likely learned his lesson.'

'Well, let's just remember that I'm in charge of this department, not you.'

'Right enough, Mr Patchett.'

Poetic justice came in the most unexpected form a few days later, when Michael, who had been very quiet throughout most of the morning, came from Mr Patchett's office, looking haunted. George had to ask, 'Is anything the matter, Michael?'

As if coming out of a trance, Michael answered, 'I've got my call-up papers for the army.'

'I thought you'd had it deferred.'

'I did, but I failed Statistics and Economics twice.'

'You kept quiet about that, didn't you? Anyway, what difference does it make?'

'They withdraw deferment after two failures.'

'Oh, bad luck.' George crossed his fingers as he spoke. 'Still, six weeks' square-bashing might break your heart and cover your feet in blisters, but it won't kill you.'

From time to time, George treated Michael to little gems of advice in preparation for his forthcoming military service. One such tip concerned the dreaded square-bashing.

'Soften your boots and keep them soft,' he advised.

Michael roused himself from his normal state of misery to ask, 'And how am I supposed to do that?'

'Pee in them and let it soak in overnight.' Fortunately, squad drill hadn't featured significantly in George's National Service, but he'd learned about the disgusting practice from one of his friends who'd served in the army.

'That's foul.'

'It's the only way.'

'Are you sure?'

'Absolutely.' George watched him assimilate the information. 'Of course,' he said, 'you might not have to do it yourself.'

'What?'

'There's always the likelihood that others will do it for you.'

It was too much for Michael. 'Oh, now you're just being foul.'

'Not at all. One of your hut mates will get up in the night, desperate for relief after a session in the local pub, and your boots will be there at the foot of your bed, waiting for him.'

'You're disgusting.'

'But you'll be able to get your own back another night.'

'I wouldn't dream of it.'

'Maybe not,' agreed George, but you'd shut Neville in the stationery cupboard.'

Michael gave a long-suffering sigh. 'Are you ever going to forget about that?'

'I told you before. Only when you stop bullying him.'

After a while, George stopped teasing him. After all, his departure wasn't far away, and once he was in uniform and at everyone's mercy, he would soon learn all about bullying, but from the victim's perspective.

———▶◀———

The office became a friendlier place after Michael reported to the National Service depot, and the atmosphere at the Club was greatly improved as well. Having accepted that George was more than adequate as an organist and highly popular with the members, Gilbert was more inclined to allow him some space, with only an occasional, half-hearted warning, just to preserve the *status quo*.

George had voluntarily increased his housekeeping

contribution to five pounds a week, and that had afforded him temporary immunity from parental criticism, so home was now a happier place as well. He was looking forward to Christmas and, in particular, to the hospital pantomime, so Norma's phone call was quite unexpected. It came shortly after he reached the office.

'George, can you help us? We're in awful trouble with the pantomime.'

'What's the problem?'

'Dr Beatty, who's been playing the piano for us, has broken his wrist playing rugby, and we've no one to take his place. One of the physios can play but she can't learn the music in the time we have left. Do you think you can help us?'

'When do you have your rehearsals?'

'Evenings, but we'll fit in with you if you'll do it.'

George thought quickly. 'It'll have to be Monday and Tuesday nights and daytime at weekends.'

'We can work around that, I'm sure, but I'll phone you again when I've spoken to everyone.' As an afterthought, she asked, 'Do you need to see the music before the next rehearsal?'

'No, I'll manage all right.'

'I thought you would. Thanks, George.' He could hear the relief in her voice. Then he heard her say to someone, 'He says he'll do it!' There were the sounds of a minor celebration before she put the phone down. It was good to be popular, and he couldn't help feeling pleased, also, that it would bring him into contact with Jeanette, regardless of what Norma might think of that.

—————◆I◆—————

The first rehearsal took place in a large, bare room in the hospital basement, so that the opening number, 'Happy Days are Here Again', seemed a mockery, but no more so than the piano, which had presumably seen happy days long since gone. It was out of tune and some strings were missing, as was one of its castors, so that it rocked at the most inconvenient moments.

George asked, 'This isn't the piano we're going to use for the performance, is it?'

Norma assured him that it was. 'The porters are going to move it up to the ward when we need it,' she told him. 'It's not very good, is it?'

'It's bloody awful.' After some thought, he asked, 'As there are nine music numbers, do you think anyone would mind if I brought an organ in just for the day?'

'I don't think so. It won't be much bigger than a piano, will it?'

'Not much,' he confirmed. 'It'll be quite a small organ.'

It seemed too good to be true, because her next question was, 'Where will you get one?'

'I'll hire one from Gledhill's.'

'But that'll cost a fortune.'

'Not really, and it'll be part of my contribution.'

In the end, he hired a Hammond B3, like the one he played at the club. It would be money well spent.

6

CHRISTMAS DAY

There were only eight children on the ward, but quite a lot of ex-patients had returned just for the pantomime. The porters had moved the beds and chairs to one wall and the backdrop and scenery were arranged opposite, with the organ beside them, stage left.

After the opening number, the chorus parted to reveal the kitchen of Baron Hardup's castle, where the Ugly Sisters were scolding Buttons, the footman. The three, assisted by Towzer, the dog, made an awful mess of the kitchen, to the children's delight, and then there was a knock on the door. The visitor turned out to be a messenger from the King, with invitations to a ball. There was more silliness involving the Ugly Sisters, but now George had to concentrate, because a music number was coming up.

The first act went well; one little boy had laughed so hard at the kitchen scene that his pyjama trousers fell down, but that only added to the entertainment.

Before long, they reached the scene where Cinderella sat heartbroken in front of the hearth because she wasn't allowed to go to the ball. Even in Cinderella's rags, Jeanette looked lovely, as she always did in George's eyes.

The fairy godmother, a student physiotherapist, made her entrance and sang her song particularly well. Singing wasn't actually Jeanette's best thing, George had to admit, but her appeal for him remained undiminished in spite of that.

While the coach was being prepared, Buttons came on stage to tell jokes and lead the children in song, and George had to admire his skill, even though he was the junior houseman who was going out with Jeanette. George owed that piece of information to Norma.

Eventually, the curtains opened on the coach, horses, coachman and footmen, the children and their parents appearing equally enchanted with the spectacle. The scene ended with a chorus of 'When You Wish Upon a Star', and it was time for George and the cast to have a welcome cup of tea backstage.

The first person he met was Jeanette, who asked, 'How do you think it's going, George?'

'Well, I'm enjoying it, and I'm sure the kids are.'

'It's good of you to do this,' she said, kissing him lightly on the cheek.

'It's no trouble, really.' He hoped he didn't look as flustered as he felt.

Norma brought him a cup of tea and examined his face. 'Honestly, Price,' she said to Jeanette, 'you've covered him in lipstick. Have you got a hanky, George?'

He gave her the handkerchief from his top pocket, and she rubbed the lipstick away. Meanwhile Jeanette had drifted off to speak to Buttons, who looked strangely serious.

'You're still a great principal boy,' said George, in an effort to convince his sister that his eyes weren't permanently following Jeanette around the room.

'Even in my old age?'

'You know what I mean.'

'Maybe it's my destiny to play the boy and never the glamorous female,' she said.

'You're pretty enough,' he assured her.

She smiled at the compliment, only half-convinced. 'If my legs are my fortune,' she said, 'thank goodness they go on forever.'

Soon, it was time for George to take his place once more at the organ, to play dance music, and the curtains opened this time on the palace ballroom, where guests were waltzing as well as they could in the limited space available. George was surprised to see Norma, who was a very competent dancer, simply performing a basic box step with Jeanette, but Jeanette looked wonderful, and that was all that mattered to him.

The penultimate scene was as magical as ever, with the Ugly Sisters trying on the glass slipper, and Prince Charming and Dandini about to leave the castle disappointed. Dandini was a student nurse with quite acceptable legs, although they weren't in the same league as Norma's. The difference was academic, however, as George's interest, as ever, was in Cinderella, whom Towzer, the dog towed on-stage in the nick of time.

For the final scene, Cinderella changed into a glamorous costume and looked more enticing than ever, so that George had to make an effort to concentrate on the finale.

———◄►———

He was retrieving his coat from the basement room after receiving the thanks of the cast, when a voice from the doorway said, 'Just a minute, George. We haven't wished each other a merry Christmas.' It was Jeanette, still in her princess costume and no less appealing than when she was on stage.

'Hello, Jeanette. You were great this afternoon.'

'So were you. Are you going to give me a kiss for Christmas?'

'Okay.' He felt like kicking himself for saying that, but she'd caught him completely off his guard. Feeling clumsy and inept, he moved towards her to deliver the obligatory peck on the cheek. As he approached her, he became aware of her scent, something he'd never noticed until then, presumably because she'd always been in uniform and hadn't worn perfume. It was heady, like a drug. Elated and bemused, he bent to kiss her cheek.

'Not like that, George.' It was the gentlest reproof. 'You're not greeting your granny.' She reached up and kissed him slowly and sensuously, so that he felt aroused, but curiously helpless at the same time. Finally, she said, 'Merry Christmas, George.'

'Merry Christmas, Jeanette.' It was almost a croak. He wanted to find his voice and say more, but then she was gone, leaving only a trace of perfume to assure him that his imagination had not been working overtime.

———▶◀———

When he and Norma arrived home, they found that, as well as Elsie and her dreary daughter Carol, their father had invited Sandra and her mother from next door. Norma's boyfriend David was on duty at the hospital until six, but he would join them later. The family Christmas meal, formerly enjoyed at lunchtime, had now become dinner, and Elsie would serve it at seven o'clock.

She was the first to greet them. 'Come and tell us how the pantomime went.'

'It was fine,' Norma told her. 'The kiddies enjoyed it, and that's what really matters.'

'Right enough.' It was a world that meant little to Arthur. He covered his awkwardness by motioning to the sideboard and saying, 'Help yourselves to a drink.'

'Have you two been to a pantomime?' Sandra sounded aggrieved.

'It wasn't a public pantomime.' Norma told her, pouring a light ale for George. 'It was just for the children in hospital.'

'I wish I was in hospital. I could have gone to t' pantomime.'

'No, you don't, Sandra,' her mother told her. 'That's a daft thing to wish for.'

'Well, everybody's been to t' pantomime 'cept me.'

'Only George and I,' said Norma, 'because we were in it.'

Sandra's resentment remained unassuaged until George spoke to her mother.

'If it's all right with you, Mrs Young, I could see if I can get tickets for *Sleeping Beauty* at the Playhouse.'

'Oh George, that's kind of you, but don't be out of pocket, love. I'll pay for Sandra's ticket.' Then, as an afterthought, she said to Sandra, 'Haven't you got something to say to George and Norma?'

'Yeah, when are we going?'

'No, about your present,' she prompted. 'Thank you?'

'Oh yeah. Thank you. It's nice.'

'You're welcome.' George remembered giving Norma the

money to buy Sandra's present, but he couldn't remember what she'd bought.

'Look,' said Sandra, helpfully showing off her jumper.

Norma was happy to lay the matter to rest. 'I'm glad we got the size right,' she said.

'Well,' said Mrs Young, 'it's been lovely, but it's time we were going. Come on, Sandra. Say goodbye to everybody and say thank you to Mr Barker for a lovely time.'

When good manners had been observed, Sandra and her mother departed, leaving Elsie to her preparations.

Eventually she returned to the sitting room and said to Carol, 'Are you going to play something for us, love,' inclining her head unnecessarily towards the piano.

'Okay, Mum.' Carol was a first-year student at a teacher training college, and her reputation was her mother's mission.

'Have you got your music?'

'Yes.' Carol opened her music case and took out a book of piano sonatas by Clementi, which she placed on the music desk of the piano.

George watched her, curious to know which she was going to play, although that was the extent of his interest in her, as he found her quite unremarkable both in appearance and in personality. He watched her find the piece, which turned out to be one he remembered from his Grade Seven exam.

Unfortunately, her playing was flawed to quite an extent, by her over-reliance on the damper pedal, which muddied the harmonies and made listening difficult. There was also another, greater, distraction. The memory of his encounter with Jeanette had seldom been far from his thoughts and it was dominating them now. It had been a complete surprise and a delightful one too, but it had also raised a question. As far as he knew, Jeanette was still going out with the junior houseman who'd played Buttons, so why, George wondered, had she kissed him so intimately and so readily?

Polite applause interrupted his deliberations, and he realised that Carol had finished. For the sake of politeness, he joined in the family ovation.

'Very nice, love,' said Elsie, leading the general expression of kindly approval.

Arthur said, 'Yes, it was very nice, but I'm surprised you didn't play something festive.'

'Yes,' agreed Elsie, always ready to translate, 'something Christmassy.'

'I don't know anything,' said Carol.

'George,' said his father, 'you were playing that "Sleigh Ride" the other day, and "Winter Wonderland", weren't you?'

'Give the poor lad a rest,' said Norma. 'He's been playing the organ all afternoon.'

Elsie asked Carol, 'What do you think of the piano, love?'

'It's nicer than ours, Mum. I wish we had one like it.'

'Ah well, you never know what might happen.'

George had his own ideas about that. The piano had been his mother's, left to him in her will. When he left home, as he intended, the piano would leave with him. He was determined about that

He returned later from a call of nature to find that David had arrived.

'Well done this afternoon, both of you,' he said. 'The pantomime was a big success. The night staff will have a job on their hands settling the kids at bedtime.'

Norma asked him, 'How was Simon when he got back to work?'

'Not at his best, I have to say. I had to tell him twice to keep his mind on the job.'

'I think she might have waited until after Christmas before finishing with him.'

'I agree.'

George could only wonder who might have finished with the Simon chap, but it was none of his business so he dismissed the matter.

It had been an eventful day, and there was more to come. He had still to buy tickets for *Sleeping Beauty*, and then, on Monday he would summon the nerve to phone Jeanette at the nurses' home.

7

George was fortunate enough to get three tickets for the Boxing Day matinee, so he and Norma took Sandra to see *Sleeping Beauty*. It was an excellent production, although in George's estimation, the girl who played the lead came a poor second to Jeanette. For Sandra, however, the pantomime was flawless; in fact, she laughed so hard at the inevitable kitchen scene that, recalling a previous accident, her companions feared for her continence. She held out until the interval, however, and all was well.

George was less successful with the second item on his agenda. As Norma would return to work on the twenty-seventh, he'd imagined Jeanette would do the same. However, when he phoned the nurses' home, the porter told him she was on leave until Tuesday the twenty-ninth. He decided to phone her then, after her shift.

During the morning, distraction intervened in the shape of a rechargeable cost that had to be typed up and on Mr Patchett's desk by lunchtime. Unfortunately and despite George's entreaties, none of the typists was available, so he took the office's only typewriter to his desk and made the best of a trying situation.

Watching him, Janet asked, 'How did you learn to touch-type?'

'I learned it in the Navy.'

Denise asked, 'Is there anything you didn't learn in the Navy?'

'One or two things.' George gave her a slow wink. He could always be smooth when it wasn't important. It was only when he was with Jeanette that he was awkward and tongue-tied.

'Hey, you,' said Janet, 'I've told you before, she's spoken for.'

Denise nodded without enthusiasm, and it seemed to George that opportunities presented themselves at the most inopportune times. He might have been interested in Denise had he not been completely preoccupied with Jeanette.

He continued to type, and was nearing the end of the document, when the external phone rang. A few seconds later, Janet called, 'George it's your sister.'

Intrigued, George picked up the receiver. 'Hello, Norma'

'Oh George, will you do me a big favour? I wouldn't ask, but Christmas has left me skint.' She sounded fraught. 'Will you lend me a couple of quid until pay day?'

'Of course I will. Why didn't you say something on Saturday?'

'I couldn't, not when you'd paid for everything. I didn't like to ask then.'

'Don't be so daft. I'll come over tonight.'

'Oh thanks, George. You're wonderful.'

'I'll see you later.'

He put the phone down, realising he would have to postpone his call to Jeanette.

————— ►◄ —————

It was the first time he'd ridden down Mount Street since it was resurfaced; it had been closed to traffic while the work was in progress, but George could now enjoy the relative luxury of a road free from potholes and unevenness. He freewheeled down the steepest part, only braking as it levelled out before joining Beckworth Road. It was a route he'd taken many times, but the novelty of the new tarmac made him careless, so that he failed to see the loose gravel that other vehicles had scattered, and which encroached on to the carriageway. The first he knew was that his locked wheels were skidding from beneath him, and he'd completely lost control.

He put out his left hand to save himself, but when the impact came, it divided its force equally between his hand and his knee.

He lay in the road for a moment, shaken, winded and still straddling his bicycle, until he recovered his wits and hauled himself to his feet. Thankfully, the road was free of traffic.

Wincing at the pain in his hand and then in his knee, he checked the bicycle for damage, which, as far as he could tell, amounted only to a misaligned front wheel. He remedied that by holding the handlebars from the front and straightening the wheel between his knees. His hand was horribly skinned, and he could only guess at the state of his knee, but he remounted nevertheless and continued painfully on his way.

When he reached the nurses' home, he limped into reception. Herbert, the porter, greeted him and, seeing his torn trouser leg, asked unnecessarily, 'Been in the wars, have you?'

'Fell off my bike. Is my sister around?' He didn't want to go into the details of his accident with Herbert.

'You look as if you need a nurse, but I'm afraid she's not here yet.'

'I'll wait, if that's all right.'

'Sit yourself down.' Herbert nodded in the direction of a wooden utility chair by the wall.

'Thanks.' George lowered himself stiffly into a sitting position and waited until he heard Jeanette's voice.

'Hello, George,' she said. 'She won't be long. We had an emergency at the end of the shift and it put things back a bit.'

'You might have to put him to bed, Nurse Price,' said Herbert. 'He's been practising somersaults over his handlebars.'

Jeanette took a closer look and said, 'You'd better come with me, George.' As she helped him up, she said to the porter, 'It's all right, Herbert. I'll take him into the sitting room.'

George let her help him. He was capable of walking unassisted but he was enjoying the physical contact and, despite the discomfort of his injuries, quick to recognise an opportunity.

'How did you do this?' Jeanette led him to a chair beside the sink.

'I skidded on some gravel. It's only my hand and knee.'

'I'll clean them up and dress them.'

'Thank you.'

She ran warm water into the sink and, taking some cotton wool from the first aid box, began washing his hand gently. 'I don't know how you'll manage to play the organ with this,' she said.

'I'll be okay.'

'What a brave soldier.' Her mockery was good-natured. 'I suppose,' she said, correcting herself, 'I should say "sailor".'

'That's right.' Their heads were almost in contact and George could feel his face glowing. Summoning his nerve, he asked, 'Jeanette?'

'Mm?'

'Are you going out with anybody?' As he asked the question, he felt clumsy.

If she were surprised, she gave no indication but said simply, 'Not just now, George.'

For a second he misunderstood her. 'I'm sorry,' he said. 'I shouldn't ask you when you're working.'

'No,' she laughed, 'I meant I'm not going out with anybody just now.'

'Ah.' Relief and embarrassment made his face burn even more. 'There's a good film coming to the Plaza next week. I know that,' he added lamely, 'because they're showing it at the Picture Palace this week.'

'Are you going to see it twice?' She was smiling again.

'No, I just...'

'What's the film?'

'*Room at the Top*. If it's anything like the book, it'll be good. I wondered if you'd like to go.' He'd said it. The words were out of his mouth. He could only wait.

'You'll have to be brave for a minute, George. This is going to sting.' She dabbed yellow liquid on to the wound and George bit his lip. The stinging, however, was not half as bad as the suspense of waiting for her reply.

Eventually she said, 'Yes, all right. When do you want to go?'

'My nights off are Monday and Tuesday.' His heart was beating so hard he was almost breathless. He hoped she hadn't noticed.

'Tuesday's better for me. Stick your thumb out so I can bandage round it.'

'Okay, Tuesday. I'll pick you up at half-past six, if that's all right.'

'The bus stops outside here at half-past.'

'I don't think we'll need it, Jeanette.' That was something else that had been on his mind during his painful journey to the hospital. 'I've been thinking for a while now about buying a car, and this thing tonight has helped me make up my mind.'

'How exciting.' She fastened off the bandage with a safety pin.

'What's exciting?' Norma's voice came from the doorway, and then she saw what Jeanette was doing. 'What's happened to you, George?'

'I had a spill on the way here. I was just telling Jeanette I'm going to look for a car this week. I reckon it'll be safer.'

Norma shook her head at the wonder of it all. 'There's just no stopping you on your quest for the high life,' she told him.

Jeanette was peering at his bloodied knee. 'Can you pull your trouser leg over it, or are you going to drop 'em in front of all these girls, George?'

His main preoccupation had been such a distraction that he had been unaware of any other off-duty nurses in the room. Now, as he looked behind him, he saw that most of them were watching TV, oblivious of his plight. 'They're relaxing,' he said, gathering up his trouser leg. 'I don't want to distract them.' He was in a triumphant and generous mood.

———◆◄———

The owner of the car, Mr Snowden, looked as old as he had sounded on the phone.

'I don't need a car now,' he said, 'and with the way things are, I don't enjoy driving as much as I used to.'

'It looks very nice,' said George. The Ford Anglia was registered in 1953, the year the new model was launched, but six years later it was still in good condition, with immaculate pale-blue paint, and it had done only a little over 30,000 miles.

'I had the heater put in from new. It was an optional extra, you know.' Mr Snowden motioned towards the driver's door. 'It's insured for any driver,' he said. 'Do you want to take it out and try it?'

'Yes, please.' George took the key from him.

'It'll be cold,' Mr Snowden told him, lowering himself into the passenger seat. 'You'll need to give it full choke.'

'Right.' George pulled out the choke and turned the key. The engine fired immediately, so he pushed the gear lever into what he thought was first.

'No,' said Mr Snowden, 'that's reverse. It's a three-speed box.'

'Sorry.'

'Don't worry. First is left and back.' The old man exuded patience.

Embarrassed, George selected first gear and set off. He soon got used to the three-speed gearbox, and he found the car easy to handle. Naturally, he was careful not to go too far, much as he enjoyed driving it, and the remainder of the trial journey was uneventful. He was very satisfied.

As he drew up in front of Mr Snowden's house, he said, 'It's a lovely car, Mr Snowden. I think the advert said two-sixty.'

'Or near offer.'

George thought hard about the price. The old boy couldn't have been pleasanter or more honest, and he could no sooner bargain him down than steal the car outright, so he said, 'I'm so taken with it, can we say two-fifty, Mr Snowden?'

Not surprisingly, Mr Snowden agreed and, after a trip the next day to the insurance broker in Northgate, George was able to drive his car home. His life was improving all the time.

8

There were worse misfortunes than to fall foul of a jealous parent, or so George imagined, although the concept, not to mention the reality, was unpleasant enough. Predictably, his father had found plenty to say about irresponsible spending and the recklessness of youth, but it was clear to George that his most damning offence was to be the first in the family to own a car.

'I suppose you realise,' he said, 'that there's more to running a car than just buying petrol?'

'Yes, there's the Road Fund Licence, insurance, servicing, tyres, and repairs.' He found it hard to believe that his father imagined he'd not considered those things.

'And you can take that bored look off your face when all I'm doing is trying to make you see sense.' It was a familiar and infuriating situation; Arthur Barker could only ever see his side of an argument, and George's patience had reached its limit.

'That's not all you're doing. When I bought the car, I felt good about it, but you want to take all that good feeling away from me. It's the same with everything I get. I got a good job at the club, and you had to pour shit and derision on that. You just won't let me enjoy anything.' He sensed his father's burgeoning anger but, strangely, he no longer cared.

'I'll thank you to watch your language, young man, and we'll have some respect while you're living under my roof. I don't know what's got into you. That kind of language and behaviour might be all right in the Navy but I won't have it in my house! Do you hear me?' His voice had risen so that the neighbours on both sides must have heard him quite clearly.

'In that case, I'll find somewhere else to live.'

'Don't talk daft. How are you going to run your own place and a car as well?'

'I'll manage.'

'How, when you're not old enough to sign a rent agreement?'

'That's not going to stop me.' He had no idea how he would negotiate that obstacle but he was determined to move out as soon as he could.

———————

The Cullington Herald was of little help; the only properties to let were houses, and they were beyond George's pocket. By the following evening, he was feeling quite despondent until Bernard offered a suggestion.

'Albert Holmes might have something,' he said. 'He's been talking about letting the flat above his shop.'

'Albert Holmes?' George had heard the name but it brought no one readily to mind.

'The greengrocer in Cheapside,' Bernard prompted. 'He's a member here. If he's in tonight, you'll be able to ask him.'

George was hopeful again, but he tried to put it out of his mind while he concentrated on the music.

Bernard left his drum kit at the interval, and returned after a brief absence with a short, grey-haired man, possibly in his fifties, whom he introduced to George as Albert Holmes the greengrocer.

'I hear you're looking for somewhere to live,' said Albert.

'That's right. Bernard says you have a flat over the shop. Is that right?'

Albert nodded. 'It has a bed-sitting room, a bathroom and a scullery with a gas cooker. It has carpets, a table, an armchair and a double bed. The last tenant took the electric fire with him, or there'd have been one of them an' all. Do you think you might be interested?'

'I might be. It depends on the rent. When can I come over and have a look?'

'Come tomorrow if you like. Any time's fine.'

George arranged to look at the flat during his lunch-hour.

———————

The shop was quiet when he arrived, so Albert was able to take him up to the flat.

As he negotiated the narrow, winding staircase, he realised he would never get his piano up there. The same was likely to apply to any flat, but it was still a setback he had to consider.

'Here we are,' said Albert, leading him into a small bed-sitting room. 'It needs cleaning and dusting, but that's because there's been nobody up here for a month or so.'

'That's fine.' George looked around him at the double bed with its bare mattress, the worn table, two dining chairs and the armchair, which looked quite serviceable. 'Where's the bathroom?'

'This way.' Albert opened a door off the sitting room, and George peered in.

The room contained a WC and washbasin, both from an earlier age, and the smallest bathtub he had ever seen. It must have been no more than five feet long.

Albert saw where he was looking, and asked, 'Do you reckon you could manage in a bath that size, George?'

George nodded. 'It wouldn't be easy but I'd manage.' It seemed to him that any bathtub was better than none at all, even if he had to sit with his knees almost under his chin.

'Come and look at the rest of the facilities.' Albert took him to a tiny scullery with an earthenware sink and an elderly gas stove. Again, he was used to better things, but he was learning quickly that quality came at a price. The flat was far from luxurious but it would probably suffice, although he had one reservation.

'It's just a shame I can't move my piano in.'

Albert looked puzzled. 'Why can't you?'

'They'd never get it up that staircase and round the corner at the top.'

'Come this way, lad.' Albert took him to the landing and pointed to a wide doorway that seemed at first to be sealed off, but he slid back two bolts and opened the double doors.

All George could see at first was a sheer drop into a yard behind the shop. 'What are you showing me, Albert?'

'Look over your head.'

George peered upward and saw a huge steel joist with a pulley block.

'This building used to be the Co-op grocery store,' Albert explained, 'and this whole floor was just warehouse space.' Indicating the hoist, he said, 'That thing has a safe working load of half a ton, so it'll lift a piano easily. Do you know Alec Barnes at the club?'

'The removal man? I think so.'

'Alec and his lads could have your piano up here without any bother at all.'

'Get away.'

'He could.' Albert looked at his wristwatch, no doubt anxious not to be missing from the shop much longer. So, now we've sorted that problem, what do you think?'

Piano removal was a mystery to George. He could only accept Albert's word that it wouldn't be a problem. 'What's the rent, Albert?'

'Ah well, I'd better explain that it's got its own electric meter. It's a bob-in-the-slot meter, so you'd pay for that yourself, but the rent takes into account gas and rates. It's only right when all's said and done.'

George prepared himself for an unpleasant surprise.

'What would you say to two quid a week?'

'Two quid?'

'I can't do it for less, lad.'

'No, that's fine, Albert. It really is.' He'd expected it to be quite a lot more. Only one question remained. 'Do you want me to sign a rent agreement? I'm not twenty-one until July, but my sister says she'll stand guarantor for me until then.' Norma's income was a fraction of George's, but she was at least old enough to sign for him.

'Nay, I don't think we need bother with all that, George. You're our regular organist, and that's good enough for me.'

George was naturally delighted. He'd bought a car, he'd found a flat, and before long he would be free from his father's petty unpleasantness.

He returned to the office in a sunny frame of mind. Janet was the first to notice the improvement.

'You're looking pleased with yourself,' she said.

'I've just got myself a flat,' he told her.

'A car and a flat? Have you come into money or something?'

'No, Janet,' he said in a fair impression of Mr Patchett, 'I'm just careful. I look after the pennies, and the pounds take care of themselves.'

'I wish I could afford a flat,' said Denise.

'You and Desmond will get your own place soon enough,' Janet reminded her.

Denise was less than assured. She asked, 'Whereabouts is your flat, George?'

'It's above the greengrocer's in Cheapside.'

Janet frowned. 'It doesn't sound all that nice,' she said.

'It's nice enough, and think of all the fruit and vegetables I'll get on the cheap. You'll be green with envy, Janet.'

'Maybe.' She returned to her work, and Denise became thoughtful, possibly considering the freedom that a flat would afford. Still basking in his happy glow, George attended to the pile of stores issue notes on his desk.

———◂▸◂———

'There'll be no stopping you now,' said Bernard, 'not now you've got yourself a passion pad.'

'It's early days yet,' George reminded him.

'But just a matter of time. Just imagine, young George. Before long, you'll have to take extra vitamins just to stay on your feet.'

'What do you mean?'

'Well, it stands to reason. You'll need to take something to keep both of you upright at the same time, you and your....' He whispered the last word and then sat back with a lascivious grin.

'Are you two going to play some music or talk the night away?'

Gilbert had crept up on them during their conversation and caught them unaware of his approach. 'It's ever since you came, young Barker. You need to watch your step, my lad.'

Another voice said, 'I'd like a word with you, Gilbert.' It was the Club Secretary and he didn't sound very pleased.

George pretended to look through a pile of music. 'What's all that about, I wonder?'

'Hush, I'm trying to listen.' Bernard was tweaking his wire brushes minutely, although they looked to be in perfect condition.

Gilbert and the Secretary parted, and Bernard said, 'I'll tell you later, George, but play something for now.'

'Let's have a foxtrot,' said George. 'Let's dance to 'Love Walked In".' He began playing, the matter of Gilbert and the Club Secretary forgotten for the moment as he concentrated on George Gershwin's memorable number.

At the end, Bernard said, 'We can expect better manners of Gilbert from now on. I heard the Secretary giving it to him good and proper about the way he just spoke to you. He told him that concert secretaries were easier to find than good organists.'

Suddenly, the world was becoming a better place altogether.

9

He parked round the corner from the nurses' home and waited five minutes, not wishing to be conspicuously early. Even so, when he arrived in reception he found that Jeanette wasn't ready.

'She never is,' the porter told him. 'There are three time zones at this place: Greenwich Mean Time, British Summer Time, and Nurse Price's Time. You'll get used to it.' He was one of the younger men on the team, and George was thankful he wasn't going to be embarrassed by Herbert's attempts at wit. He took a seat in the reception area and waited, hoping she wouldn't be very late.

In the event, she took only five minutes, and the result was well worth the wait. Her dark hair, usually pinned so neatly beneath her cap, was down to her shoulders and touching the halter of a dark-green dress with a full, knee-length skirt. It was the first time he'd seen her in high heels, except in the pantomime, and he found she was quite tall, coming to just above his shoulder.

'Jeanette,' he said, 'you look fantastic.'

'Thank you, George. I'm not late, am I?'

'Not really.' He opened the door for her. 'I'm parked not far away.'

'Oh, you got your new car. I can't wait to see it.' She took his arm, and they left the building to cross the car park to where the newly-groomed Anglia stood.

'Oh, is this your car? It's such a lovely colour, and quite new as well.'

He opened the passenger door for her. 'It's nearly seven years old.' He tried not to sound apologetic.

'I don't know all that many people with cars, and none of them are as new as this,' she said, gathering her full skirt so that he could close the door.

'I paid a bit more for it than I'd intended,' he confessed, 'but I think it was worth it.' He pulled out of the car park and into the main road. 'Actually, I felt a bit sorry for the owner. He was an old man and he'd had the car from new, so it meant a lot to him.'

'George, you're a softie. That's really nice.' She patted his knee in a way that felt promising. He kept glancing at her as she told him about an incident on the ward that day and, still marvelling at his good fortune, he only half-heard the story. He would ask her about it later.

The car park across the road from the cinema was half empty, so he parked close to the exit so that they hadn't far to walk.

George always found the foyer particularly engaging, with its old-fashioned *décor* and gilt-framed pictures from forthcoming films, and his excitement and anticipation were naturally heightened on this occasion.

'Two two-bobs, please,' he asked the receptionist. He usually frequented the one-and-ninepennies downstairs, but it would never occur to him to take a girl down there.

Upstairs, the usherette showed them to two seats at the end of a row, and George waited for Jeanette to unbutton her coat and drape it over her seat, before joining her.

The supporting film had only fifteen minutes to run. It was an American slapstick comedy, and George vainly tried to recall the name of the star. Eventually, it came to him. It was Jerry Lewis, but the film was almost over, so it didn't matter. Besides, he was thinking about other things. He had to decide where to take Jeanette on their next date. It seemed important to offer variety. She was a popular girl and she must have been to some spectacular places.

The house lights came up and the ice cream seller appeared with her tray.

George asked, 'Would you like anything?'

'No thanks.' Jeanette's thoughts were elsewhere. 'That girl,' she said, indicating the ice cream seller, 'had her appendix out last year. It was when I was on Women's Surgical.'

'She's looking well on it.' George was glad it was only her appendix and not something embarrassing. Nurses seemed to talk freely about the most personal body parts and functions. He recalled Norma's spell on Obstetrics and Gynaecology with unnerving clarity.

The advertisements came up, and the audience was assured that Ford's latest models could be test-driven at Cullington Motors, that delicious fish and chips could be found at Moorside Fisheries, that weaving operatives were required at good rates of pay at Amalgamated Weavers, and that there was a future in coal in Yorkshire. A group of youngsters with grinning, coal-blackened faces bore testimony to that claim. Its appeal was somehow unconvincing, but it was swept out of mind when the lights went down for the trailers.

Eventually the main film began. George had read and enjoyed the book on his first leave; in fact, he'd been the first to borrow it from the public library, so quite apart from other considerations, he'd been looking forward to seeing the film. It struck him as odd, though, that some of the main characters were struggling with the Yorkshire accent, and he wondered why the film makers had cast them in particular. He looked across at Jeanette and she grimaced too. It seemed a good moment to reach for her hand, which was resting on her thigh. She smiled affably and squeezed his in return.

Accents apart, it was a very good film, and performances by Donald Wolfit and Simone Signoret were more than adequate compensation. Both George and Jeanette agreed that Laurence Harvey had acted the part of Joe remarkably well, although Jeanette had never read the novel and was unable to make a comparison.

As they took the stairs down to the foyer, George asked, 'Have we time for a drink before I take you home?' He knew about the stringent rules in force at the nurses' home and had no wish to get her into trouble.

'Yes, I've got an extension.'

'Great, we'll go round the corner to the Fox and Hounds if that's all right.'

'It sounds good to me.'

The lounge bar at the Fox and Hounds was fairly quiet. Tuesday was never a busy night, and George was pleased about that. He didn't particularly want to bump into anyone he knew.

Escorting her into the bar lounge, he asked, 'What would you like to drink?'

'A dry martini, please.'

'If you like to find a table, I'll bring them over.' He caught the barmaid's attention. 'A dry martini and… a gin and tonic, please.' He'd never had a gin and tonic; he usually drank beer, but he felt somehow confident that gin wouldn't hang on his breath. He paid for the drinks and took them to the table where Jeanette sat.

'After this week, I'll be able to invite you back to my place for coffee,' he said, 'but I have a lot of work to do on it before it's fit to be seen.'

'Your place? Have you got a new flat as well as a car?'

'It's actually the floor above the greengrocer's in Cheapside,' he told her modestly.

'Even so, I'm impressed.'

He was glad she was impressed. He took a sip from his glass and was surprised and somewhat alarmed by the aroma of juniper berries. His association with gin and tonic was likely to be short-lived.

'What made you move out?'

He wondered how best to explain the situation. Eventually, he said simply, 'I had an argument with my dad. He told me that as long as I was under his roof I had to live by his rules, so I found a flat.' Shaking his head at the memory, he said, 'He's impossible to please.'

'That's what your sister said when she moved out.'

'That wasn't quite the same thing. It was more to do with him taking up with a new girlfriend so soon after our mum died. Norma found it difficult to adjust to that.'

'I imagine it wasn't easy for you either.'

'I was lucky. I was away in the Navy when all that happened. I was only frustrated because I couldn't be with Norma when she was so upset.'

'It must have been a rotten time for you both.' She took his hand between hers.

To change the subject to a happier one, he said, 'I've wondered, sometimes, why you nurses only ever have surnames. It's very odd.'

'Oh, that.' She smiled. 'I really don't know. It's just tradition, I suppose.'

'I think it sounds unfriendly.'

'Oh, we're friendly enough, at least to each other's faces. The bitchiness goes on behind our backs.'

After a while, she asked, 'Do you mind if we leave now. I don't want to cut it too fine.'

'Of course I don't mind.' He saw off the last of his gin and tonic, resolved to find an alternative drink for a future occasion, and helped her on with her coat.

As they approached the nurses' home, George asked, 'Would it be better if I parked round the corner?'

'There's no need for that. Anyway, no one can see anything at this time of night. All the curtains are drawn.' Smiling at his sensitivity, she said, 'Behind the coke bunkers is a good place to park.'

He drove into the place she suggested and switched off the engine.

'It's been a lovely evening,' she said. 'I've really enjoyed it.'

'I'm glad. So have I.' He leaned forward, feeling clumsy, just as he had after the pantomime, but she joined him naturally. He touched her parted lips with his, tentatively at first, and then, as desire overcame diffidence, their kisses became increasingly sensuous. George could scarcely believe it was happening.

After a while, the sound of a car engine distracted Jeanette, and she turned to look out of the window. It was a Morris Eight Series E, and it was coming from the main hospital entrance. She watched it pass, and it was clear that its driver had noticed her.

George was curious. 'Was that someone you know?'

'Only vaguely. I think he's one of the house surgeons.' She settled again and smiled apologetically. 'I'll have to go inside soon,' she said.

'Of course.' He kissed her again and slipped his hand inside her coat to feel her warmth through the fabric of her dress. 'I've been thinking,' he said after a while.

'Mm?'

'Do you like dancing?'

'Yes. What do you have in mind?'

'The Oak Tree Restaurant has a band that's quite good. I'm pretty sure they do Mondays or Tuesdays as well as weekends. Do you fancy it?'

'The Oak Tree, you say? That's quite posh.'

'Not too posh for you and me. I'll let you know which day it is, shall I?'

'Fine, if you're happy with it.' She sat upright again. 'I really must go, George. Thanks ever so much for a lovely evening.' She kissed him again and opened the car door. 'There's no need to see me in. I'll be all right.'

George watched her go, pleased that the evening had gone so well, but reluctant to let her go. The memory of her, warm and amenable, was compelling. He decided that next Monday or Tuesday, whichever it was, couldn't arrive soon enough. Norma had often accused him of living in his own, ideal world, and that was just how things felt.

10

On his way to the club, George called at his father's house – he no longer thought of it as 'home' – to pick up some sheet music. He'd moved most of his property out, the record player and his mother's records, and now the piano was gone, as Alec had promised. Just a few items remained.

He found his father in the sitting room, glowering at the space the piano had occupied.

'What's the meaning of this?' He pointed quite unnecessarily to the bare wall.

'It means my piano's gone. It's at my flat.'

'*Your* piano?'

'Yes, my property.'

'Anything that's in this house is *my* property.' It was a ridiculous assertion but he was no less emphatic, and George was all the angrier because of it.

'But it's not in this house, it's in my flat.'

'Do you realise,' said his father, 'that Carol's been looking forward to practising on that piano when she comes home from college?'

'I'm not surprised. She needs all the practice she can get.'

'And what's that supposed to mean?' His father looked ready to explode, and George remembered being afraid of his temper in years gone by. All that was past, and he was simply angry at the dishonest stance his father was taking.

'It means she's not very good.'

'She's a student at a teacher training college. You could have done that if you'd worked harder and passed your scholarship.'

'As well as training to be an accountant?'

'Don't get sarcastic with me! You're not too big to feel the flat of my hand.'

George looked at his watch. He had to be at the club in twenty minutes. 'Maybe not,' he said, controlling his anger with difficulty, 'but, for your sake, I wouldn't advise it.' He picked up the pile of music. 'My mum left me the piano in her will, as you well know, so you'd better make other arrangements. Anyway, how's Carol going to spend so much time round here?'

'Elsie and I are getting married, and she's moving in with me.' His announcement might have been intended as a bombshell, but George simply continued to the door. He'd been expecting it for some time. As he stepped outside, he said, 'In that case, it's just as well I don't live here any longer.'

Although he'd managed to appear calm throughout the exchange, he realised, when he got into the car, that his hands were shaking, and he sat for a few minutes before driving off.

When he reached the club, he felt a good deal more settled, but it was a difficult experience to dismiss from his mind, and he was happier when he had something to do. It was a free-and-easy night, which was straightforward enough, and he even began to relax after the first number.

Bernard spoke to him when they took their break. 'What's bothering you, George? You look as if you've lost a quid and found a tanner.'

'I had a row with my dad on the way here.'

'I thought you'd moved out.'

'I have, but I called in to pick up some dots.'

'It was the same with me and my dad,' said Bernard. 'We had one row after another, usually about money, right up to when I got wed and moved out.' His face brightened as he found a more cheerful topic. 'Anyway, how was the date?'

'Brilliant. I'm seeing her again on Monday.'

'Oh George, be careful. You have the look of a love-sick poet.' He laughed easily and picked up his brushes. 'What are we going to play next?'

'A tango, I think.'

'Why not? Let's get the buggers moving.'

George switched on the microphone to announce the next dance. 'Take your partners for a tango,' he said. 'It's "Softly, as in a Morning Sunrise".'

Oddly, he felt better for his conversation with Bernard. It was no more than a meaningless exchange with a friend, but that was all he'd needed. He got through the rest of the evening in an improved frame of mind.

———◆◄———

He spent the weekend cleaning his flat, and Norma came over to lend a hand.

'I gather you had a good time on Tuesday,' she said in the loaded way that women sometimes adopted.

'Yes, it's a good film.'

'Price has been telling everybody about it, and about this new fella she's found.' She dipped a sponge into a bucket of soapy water and began washing paintwork. 'Mind you, I'm surprised she's not here now, helping with this.'

'She had to visit her mum and dad this weekend.'

He half-expected Norma to criticize Jeanette for her absence, but she said simply, 'That's one job we don't have to do, eh, George?'

'It'll be a while before I'll go round there again. I suppose we'll have to go to the wedding, but that's as much as I'm prepared to do.'

'I'm not surprised. I can't believe he was going to let Carol have your piano.'

'You know what he's like.' He filled the kettle and put it on the gas stove. 'Mind you, I won't be very popular with Elsie now. I think she was behind it. She was certainly dropping hints to Carol about it at Christmas.'

'Yes, I remember.' She paused from her work to ask, 'What's more important to you, the piano itself or that it was Mum's?'

He hesitated, trying to put his thoughts into words. 'It's a nice

66

piano,' he told her eventually, 'but the important thing is that it meant a lot to her, so it's a part of her that's still here.'

She nodded understandingly.

'I wonder, sometimes,' he said, 'if she knows what's going on down here. If she does, she won't be too pleased about yesterday's row.'

'She had many a battle royal with him, George. I think you'd have her sympathy in that little debate, especially as it was about the piano.'

'Mm.' His thoughts took a minor turning, and he said, 'I can't help feeling a little bit selfish. I mean, Carol really liked the piano, and she's going to be doing it for a living, after all.'

'Stop there, George.' Norma dropped her sponge and stood up to rest from her crouching position. 'You haven't seen the worst of Elsie, not by a long way.'

'What do you mean?'

'Only that if she wants something, she takes it, and she doesn't care whether it suits, pleases or grieves. You should have seen her going through Mum's clothes and jewellery. That was the final straw for me.'

'I was away in Petersfield when he took up with her. You wrote to me about it.'

'Be thankful you weren't there, George. It was a horrible time.'

The whistling kettle provided a merciful interruption, and George left her to make tea. When he returned, Norma said, 'I told David you were short of china, so we're going to get you some.'

'That's very kind of you, but you shouldn't spend your money on me. You've little enough as it is.'

She accepted a mug of tea, taking care to drink from the side that wasn't chipped. 'David's paying for it, not me.'

'In that case I'm grateful to him.' The thought of them shopping together prompted a question that had been on his mind for a while, and he asked, 'When is he going to make an honest woman of you?'

'Just as soon as he gets a registrar's job. It could happen in a year or so.'

'And that could mean going to live anywhere, I suppose?'

'Yes, but I'll still want to see my little brother.' Suddenly, she beamed and said, 'Just imagine, one day I'll be married to a consultant immunologist. What do you think about that?'

'I don't think it'll go to your head, any more than it'll go to David's.'

'No, I don't think it will.' She finished her tea and stood up. 'Let's get on with it,' she said, 'if you want it to be spick and span when you bring your conquests back here.'

The rest was fairly straightforward. He bought an electric fire, some towels and bed linen, and the flat began to feel lived in. Just one thing remained to be done, and it was unfortunate that it necessitated a call to his father at the office.

'Dad, it's me.'

'What do you want?' It wasn't the most promising start.

'I want to make arrangements for Fred and Ginger. If you like, I can call round and feed them, then you don't need to worry about it anymore.'

'There's no need for you to bother.'

'It's no bother. I don't mind.'

'I mean there's no need.'

George took a deep breath and said, 'You're not making sense, Dad.'

'Well, maybe this makes sense. The cats have gone. Elsie took them round to Schofield's.'

An icy shock ran through his veins. 'Schofield's Chemists? What for?'

'To have them destroyed. It's cheaper there than having it done by a vet.'

'What?'

'In the end, somebody in the queue said she'd take them home rather than see them destroyed – you're not the only soft article in this town – so Elsie let her have them. It saved us a few bob.'

For a moment, George thought it must be his father's idea of a sick joke, but then the horrible truth came home to him. 'You're bloody evil,' he said, 'both of you. Do you know that? You and Elsie are too horrible for words.'

'That's enough of that kind of talk. If I had you here, I'c take the side of your face off for that remark.'

'No, you wouldn't. You're too old and too slow, and in any case, I'm so furious, I wouldn't trust myself to keep my hands off you.' He put the phone down with a shaking hand.

Alerted by George's raised voice, Denise asked, 'What's the matter, George?'

For a minute, George was unable to speak. When he did, it came out as an irate whisper. 'My dad and the woman he's going to marry have got rid of my cats. They took them to the chemist's to be destroyed. Fortunately, somebody rescued them in the nick of time, but it was still a horrible, cruel thing to do.'

'Oh, George.' Denise's face said the rest.

'Well, I have to say, I'm not keen on cats,' said Janet. 'They bring all sorts of things into the house. I mean, you can see their point of....' Her voice tailed off. She asked, 'What are you looking at me like that for, George?'

———◆I◆———

By the day's end, George had calmed down sufficiently to accept Janet's apology. It had taken some straight talking from Denise to persuade her to put things right with him, and he was gratefully aware of that.

'She just opens her mouth,' said Denise later, when Janet was out of the office, 'and out it comes whether you like it or not.'

'Aye.' He gave her a tired smile. 'Thanks for taking my side, Denise.'

'It was a rotten thing to happen to you, George, and I can't abide cruelty to animals.'

———◆I◆———

He called at the nurses' home on his way to the Club, and told Norma about the cats.

'Oh, that's just bloody typical,' she said. 'George, I'm so sorry.' Norma had never been as close to Fred and Ginger as George was, but she liked them and she knew what they meant to him.

'Sometimes,' he said, 'I don't know how he could be our dad; in fact, I wish....' He was almost ashamed of what he'd been about to say, but the circumstances were extreme.

'Sometimes wishes come true, George, only this one was true all along.' She had the look of someone about to impart important information.

'What do you mean?'

'He's not really our dad.'

It was a strange thing for her to say. 'I'd like to believe that,' he said, 'but I can't see how it can be true.'

'Well, it *is* true, so now you can believe it. In view of everything that's happened lately, I reckon it's all right for me to tell you. In fact, it's probably as good a time as any.'

'Tell me what, Norma? You're talking in riddles.'

'Mum only told me this because I had a similar experience to yours, and she asked me not to tell you in case it upset you. That's why she'd kept it from both of us for so long.'

'The suspense is killing, Norma.' Had she been anyone else, he would have put it more strongly.

'Our real dad was killed early in the war. You'd only just been born, and I was one year old, so I don't remember him at all, but Mum told me he couldn't have been more different from the one we know.'

It made no sense at all to George. 'But everyone says I'm the image of....' He hesitated to use the word. He had to refer to him by some title, but he was unable to think of a suitable one.

'He's our uncle, our dad's brother. Mum was left with two children to bring up on a war widow's pension, so Uncle Arthur, as he was, stepped in. He'd always fancied Mum, anyway, even when she was married to his brother, and it seemed the only solution for her.'

'And she never said a word.'

'She didn't see the point. We were a family, and that was all that mattered.'

It was an awful lot for George to digest, but he managed, eventually, to come to terms with the news, and he was left with two conflicting realisations. On the one hand, he was relieved that the man he'd come to dislike and resent wasn't his father after all, but he was saddened by the thought of those seventeen difficult years his mother had been obliged to endure as his wife.

11

The Oak Tree Restaurant was closed on Mondays, but the band played there on Saturdays, Tuesdays and for special functions, so George was happy to reserve a table for the following Tuesday.

Bernard might have been closer to the truth than he realised, with his 'love-sick poet' reference; in spite of Norma's recent revelation, which had occupied his mind for the past few days, George could only think, that Tuesday, of his forthcoming date, so it was fortunate that costing was a routine and repetitive task. In fact, Denise had to repeat herself twice before he realised she was speaking to him.

'You were miles away, weren't you? Would you mind moving the typewriter on to my desk, please?'

'Okay.' The electric typewriter, the only one in the office, was particularly heavy, so George was happy to move it for her.

As he put it down, she asked, 'Where are you taking your new girlfriend, George? Somewhere nice, I'll bet.'

'Yes, we're going to the Oak Tree.'

'The Oak Tree?' Her blue eyes were opened wide. 'She's a lucky girl. I never get taken anywhere like that.'

'That's because your Desmond's saving up for when you get married.' In her self-appointed capacity as human chastity belt, Janet was ready as ever to remind Denise of her affianced status.

'Maybe he'll take you there after you're married,' suggested George. 'All kinds of nice things start happening then, they tell me.'

'That's enough of that sort of talk from you, George,' said Janet. 'She asked you to move the typewriter, not give her ideas.'

'Ideas is all they are,' said Denise wistfully.

'Aye well, see that you keep it that way.'

George thought he should show some interest in Denise's nuptials, so he asked, 'When are you going to get spliced, Denise?' As an aside to Janet, he added, 'That's a naval expression, by the way.'

'It'll be something rude, knowing you.'

'I was just asking when Denise is getting married.'

Denise looked glum. 'We haven't decided yet. We can't agree.'

'You'll work it out between you,' Janet assured her. 'Couples usually do.'

As he returned to his desk, George wondered how Janet was going to cope after the wedding, unless Wilkinson's employed another virgin for her to watch over. He imagined she must have a very empty life.

After a little thought, he returned his attention to the work on his desk, feeling that he should make an effort for the last forty-five minutes of the day.

The Oak Tree was an opulent hotel in what had been a rather grand house set in spacious grounds. George had naturally reconnoitred the place to establish the whereabouts of the restaurant and the best place to park. It was better than looking a fool when the time came.

On their arrival, a waiter asked if they would like a drink or to go straight to their table. Strains of 'Autumn Leaves' were coming from the restaurant, so George suggested they went to their table, and the waiter led them into the oak-panelled restaurant, where a four-piece combo was coming to the end of the number.

The waiter left them with the menu and wine list, and George was now able to see Jeanette properly. She was wearing a dark-red dress with a cross-over front. He'd already noticed the full skirt, and the whole effect was wonderful to his eyes.

'You look terrific,' he told her genuinely.

'Thank you. This is the limit of my wardrobe, you understand. Nurses aren't spoiled with pay, as you know.'

'No, but I admire your taste.' He picked up the menu. 'Shall we decide what we're going to eat? Then we can choose the wine.'

'You're so urbane, George. That's the word, isn't it? You're completely at home in these surroundings.'

'Oh, I don't know.' With his careful upbringing on a limited budget, he'd always regarded restaurants such as the Oak Tree as something from another planet, and he'd been clueless about menus and wine lists until one Trafalgar Night on board ship, when the Chief Steward had borrowed a number of ratings, including George, to help out at the Wardroom dinner. Their preparation had amounted to a crash course in stewardship that had opened George's eyes to another world. He would naturally continue to learn, but the experience had been an invaluable introduction to fine dining, and he'd taken full advantage of it.

They both opted for the sirloin steak and chose starters accordingly, but when the waiter arrived to take their order and asked how they would like their steaks done, George saw the uncertainty in Jeanette's eyes.

'Medium-rare for me, please,' he said, throwing her a line.

'Yes, for me too,' she said.

'Would you like me to send the wine waiter to your table, sir?'

'Yes, please.'

George opened the wine list and asked, 'Shall I choose?'

'Oh yes, I haven't a clue about wine.' Her relief was apparent.

The wine waiter arrived, and George made his choice.

'The number forty, please.'

'The Mouton Cadet? Certainly, sir.'

George had deliberately not asked for it by name, being unsure of the pronunciation. All he knew was that it was a reasonably-priced red Bordeaux, and that was sufficient, except that he now knew how to pronounce it, another piece of information he would file mentally for future use.

The band began to play 'La Ronde', a popular waltz, and George asked, 'Would you like to dance?'

'All right.' Jeanette let him lead her on to the floor, where only two other couples were dancing.

She asked, 'What's this one called?'

' "La Ronde," ' he told her. 'Sometimes it's called "Love's Roundabout".'

'I like it.'

They joined the dance, and George was aware from the start that it was not what Jeanette did best, but the pleasure of holding her and dancing close outweighed any weakness on her part.

At the end of the number, they returned to their table. A minute later, the wine waiter brought the wine, opened it and asked George if he would care to taste it.

'Yes, please.' George held the glass beneath his nose and inhaled before taking a sip. 'That's good,' he said, happily aware of Jeanette's admiring gaze. He had seen people do some strange and arcane things when they were tasting wine, but he had no intention of overdoing it.

'Very good, sir.' The wine waiter poured the wine and left them to enjoy it.

'There's something I've been wondering,' said George. 'Yours is quite an unusual name, isn't it?'

'Yes, my mother told me she named me after some film star from way back.'

'Jeanette MacDonald?'

'I think so. I don't think I've ever seen her. I'm not all that keen on old films. Are you?'

'Oh yes, I am. Jeanette MacDonald was a wonderful actress and singer, and a great beauty as well. She had everything.'

Jeanette looked agreeably surprised. 'You know,' she said, 'I'm beginning to feel better about my name already. You're welcome to the old films, though. I like a bit of modern life, myself.'

The starters arrived. George had tasted chicken liver *pâté* only once, when one of the chefs on board ship had let him sample some that was destined for the wardroom table, but he decided immediately that he liked it, and had ordered it on this occasion without hesitation. He suspected Jeanette had followed his example, being somewhat out of her depth. Not that it mattered at all; he would enjoy introducing her to new experiences, at least as far as his slender knowledge allowed.

She watched him butter a piece of toast and spread *pâté* on it, before helping herself. 'This is really nice,' she said. 'You know, this is all terribly new for me.'

'I don't do it every day,' he said truthfully.

'But how is it you're so clued up about these things?'

He decided to be honest. 'I learned a lot, helping out when the chefs and stewards had an important function on their hands.'

'When you were in the Navy?'

'Yes.'

She seemed confused. 'Well,' she asked, 'what was your job, if you weren't a chef or a steward?'

'I was a radio operator.'

'Was it exciting?'

'Not usually. It was very routine, mainly monitoring Soviet transmissions.' He added, 'Waiting at table made a welcome change.'

'You know, George,' she said, as if the thought had just occurred to her, 'one of the things I like about you is that you're so honest.'

'What makes you say that?'

'You don't pretend to be anything you're not.'

'There's no point in pretending, is there?'

'You'd be surprised how many men do.' She spread another piece of toast thickly with *pâté*, evidently enjoying it. 'Actually,' she said, 'you're maybe too honest and obliging for your own good.'

'I didn't know that was possible.'

'It is, George, believe me.'

The band began 'Bewitched.' George asked, 'Would you like to dance again?'

'What is it?'

'It's a foxtrot.'

She looked at him awkwardly. 'Could we wait for a waltz?'

'Of course we could, but what's the problem?'

'It's my turn to be honest,' she said. 'I can't really do the foxtrot. I'm okay at the waltz, the cha-cha-cha and the jive, but that's about my limit.'

'All right, let's just shuffle. We won't be the only ones.'

'Okay.' She let him lead her on to the floor again and take her in hold, before asking, 'How did you get to learn all these dances?' She grinned. 'Don't tell me you learned them in the Navy as well.'

'No, I didn't.' He tried to think quickly of a story, but opted as usual for the truth. 'Promise you won't laugh?'

'I promise.'

'My mum taught both of us, Norma and me. She said it would be useful socially.'

'It could be useful,' she agreed, mercifully not laughing, but sounding thoughtful.

'What do you mean?'

'You could teach me the foxtrot.' She added quickly, 'Not right now, but some other time.'

'What are you doing at the weekend?'

'Not much. I've got Saturday off.'

'I have to work evenings, but we could have a session on Saturday.'

The idea seemed to appeal to her. 'Where?'

'My place. If we shove everything back we should have room for you to learn the box-step.'

'What's that?'

'The basic step, the way you danced the waltz in the pantomime when you were short of space. Once you've mastered that you'll have no trouble learning the rest.'

'You're amazing.' She rested her head on his chest and moved happily through the remainder of the number.

Eventually, George drove her back to the nurses' home and parked behind the coke bunkers, as he had earlier. 'I was going to suggest going back to my place for coffee,' he said.

'That would have been nice, but it's nearly pumpkin time.' She leaned towards him to say, 'Thank you for a brilliant evening. I've really enjoyed it.'

'Me too. What time do you want me to pick you up on Saturday?'

She thought for a moment. 'About one-thirty? Is that all right?'

'Fine.' Gently, he unfastened the top three buttons of her coat.

'George,' she asked with mock coyness, 'what are you doing?'

'Warming my hands.' He slipped his right hand inside her coat and drew her close until his lips touched hers, and they kissed as deeply as before. Inside her coat, she was delightfully warm. He explored further, enjoying that warmth and softness, until his hand cradled her breast.

'Don't get carried away, George.' It was the gentlest reproach, but he abandoned his quest all the same.

'Sorry.'

'It's just a bit public here.'

'Yes, I suppose it is.' His tone was contrite, but her remark had sparked a degree of optimism.

'I have to go in, George,' she said, reaching for the door handle. 'Thank you again for a lovely evening.' They kissed once more, and she got out of the car.

12

Bernard arrived at the club on Wednesday with little time to spare, so social chat had to wait until their first break.

'How's love's young dream, George? Still going strong?'

'Stronger by the day, Bernard. She's coming over to my place at the weekend. I'm teaching her the foxtrot.'

'Teaching her the foxtrot, eh? If that's a euphemism, it's a new one on me.'

'A what?'

'A euphemism. It's a nice way of saying something naughty.'

'Leave it out, Bernard. I really am teaching her the foxtrot. You know – slow, quick, quick, slow.'

Bernard pursed his lips in mock disapproval. 'It's a slippery slope, George. You know what George Bernard Shaw said about ballroom dancing, don't you?'

George knew that Shaw was a playwright, but that was the extent of his knowledge. He knew there would be a silly answer, but he had to ask. 'What did he say?'

'He said it was a perpendicular expression of horizontal desire.'

George considered the information. 'Well,' he said, 'you never know your luck, do you?'

'Let's play some romantic music to put you in the mood.'

'Yes, let's.' It was good to concentrate on something wholesome and enjoyable, because that was how life should be.

———————

Jeanette was wearing a plaid shirt and capri pants, not as George had seen her or ever imagined her, but she was no less appealing for that.

'This is really good of you, George.'

'Teaching you the foxtrot? It's a pleasure, and next time we go somewhere to dance it'll be another one for your repertoire.' It was a new word for George, like 'euphemism', and he looked forward to using that one as well, should the opportunity arise.

He parked outside the shop, waved to Albert, who was behind the counter, and took Jeanette upstairs to the flat.

'Oh,' she said, looking around her, 'this is nice, and you've even got a piano.'

'Yes,' he said, still feeling bruised after the argument with his step-father about that and various other matters. 'What would you like? Tea or coffee?'

'Coffee, please, if you're making it.'

One of George's recent investments was an electric kettle, and he filled it while Jeanette looked around the flat.

'What are all these books for, George? There's ever such a lot.'

It seemed an odd question. 'I like reading,' he told her. 'Don't you?'

'No, I don't. Having to read books to pass nursing exams is bad enough. I'd never do it for pleasure.'

'What do you do for pleasure?' It would be interesting to find out.

'I go to the pictures, watch the telly, listen to music.... Same as most people, really.'

'There you are,' he said, handing her a mug of coffee, 'milk, no sugar.'

'That's right.'

'Come and sit down.' He indicated the sofa, and she joined him.

'This is really nice,' she said again. 'These are, too.' She was pointing to the new coffee mugs.

'Ah, they're new. Norma and David bought me a whole set of china when I moved in.'

'Your sister did well to take up with Dr Wainwright. She wasn't the only one after him.'

'I don't know that she ever set her cap at him,' he said. 'It came as a surprise when he asked her out, but they're happy together, and that's all that matters. David's a decent bloke, and I'll be pleased to have him as my brother-in-law.'

The subject seemed to excite Jeanette's curiosity, because she asked, 'Are they really thinking of getting married?'

'Yes, just as soon as he can get a registrar's job.'

'Well, I never.'

George put his mug down. 'Right,' he said, 'shall we make a start?'

'Okay.' She stood up and put her mug on the table.

George pushed the sofa back to make a little more room and then beckoned to her to join him. 'Just stand beside me for now,' he said, 'and I'll show you the steps. Take your right foot back then your left, bring your right to join it, and then your left forward. Let's try that.'

She wasn't a natural mover, but he knew that already. She would need practice, and he was happy to provide that.

'Okay, hold my hands and we'll go through it together. Slow, quick, quick, slow. That's right.' They practised it for a while, and then he said, 'Let's do it in hold. Not face to face. Instead, we have to be offset, with you looking over my shoulder and me looking over yours. Ready? Slow, quick, quick, slow....'

'This is fun.'

'Good. I'll put some music on now.' He hadn't yet found time to arrange the records properly, so he searched through the stack until he found 'Just the Way You Look Tonight.' In choosing accomplices, he could do worse than Jerome Kern and Fred Astaire.

Gently, he led her through the basic box step to the music until it came to the middle eight bars. 'That's where we stop for now, because the tempo changes and makes it more difficult,' he explained.

'I enjoyed that.'

'We haven't finished yet,' he told her.

He spent the next twenty minutes or so taking her through the left turning box step, and he did some work on the subtle rise and fall of the foxtrot, until she seemed sufficiently confident to take the floor. The rest could come later.

When the time came for her to leave, he drove her to the nurses' home. 'I'll give you a ring tomorrow,' he said, 'and we can arrange to meet again.' He had in mind a visit to the cinema but he needed to check the programme.

'Yes. Thank you for this afternoon.'

'I enjoyed it.'

'Good.'

Because they were in broad daylight, she kissed him quickly before disappearing into her quarters.

After the turmoil of recent weeks, he felt a new optimism. Everything, he felt, was now going his way.

————◆◀————

The Club had booked a husband and wife act. They sang together, he doubled as a comedian, and they were a very good act. As a bonus, they brought with them copies of their music in usable condition and sang their songs without the need for cuts or transposition.

'It makes a pleasant change when we get an act like that,' said Bernard at the end of the evening.

'It's a pleasure to work with them,' agreed George.

Bernard picked up his sticks and brushes to leave. 'I'll be away, then,' he said, adding with a wink, 'I reckon I'm in line for seconds tonight.' As he left, he turned to say, 'Your turn can't be far away, young George. Keep playing your cards right and you never know what might happen.'

George's thoughts were on a higher plane. He was still revelling in the heady realisation that things were going well with Jeanette. True romance, after all, was a matter of innocence, to be enjoyed all the time, and not as a weekly event with the tantalising possibility of seconds on Saturday.

————◆◀————

That night, he slept better than he had for some time, one of the benefits, he imagined, of a contented mind, so that, when he eventually emerged, he enjoyed a leisurely breakfast, having laid in bacon, eggs and sausages in shameless self-indulgence. In view of recent developments, he felt that he was due for a treat.

It was shortly after eleven when he walked down Cheapside to the phone box. When he arrived, he found that someone was making a call, but he didn't mind waiting. The day was mild and sunny, and he was happy to stand for a while, idly looking around him.

The call box became free, and George stepped inside to dial the number of the hospital.

'Beckworth General Hospital.'

'Will you put me through to the nurses' home, please?'

In a short time, he heard the voice of the woman with the wrinkles of disapproval.

'Nurses' home.'

'I'd like to speak to Nurse Price, please.'

'Nurse Price,' she confirmed. 'Who's calling?'

'George Barker.'

'Hold the line.' There was the usual thump as the receiver hit the desk. A few seconds later, she said, 'Nurse Price is on the night shift.'

'She can't be. I saw her yesterday afternoon.'

'It says here in black and white that she's on the night shift.'

There must have been a mistake. 'In that case,' he said, 'I'd like to speak to Staff Nurse Barker.'

'Who did you say was calling?'

'I'm still George Barker.'

'There's no need to be sarcastic.' The phone went down again very briefly, and then the woman said, 'Staff Nurse Barker signed out this morning. You could try her this evening.'

'Thank you.'

He walked back to the flat, turning the question over in his mind. He could only imagine that Jeanette's name had appeared on the list of those on the night shift because of a clerical error. He'd worked in offices long enough to know they were always possible. Even so, he brooded about it for the rest of the day.

By twenty-past-six, he made the decision to drive to the nurses' home, where he might catch sight of Jeanette or maybe Norma if she was back.

He parked in his usual place and saw two cars leave. Happily, Jeanette wasn't in either of them, so he walked into reception. It was a day for familiar faces, because Herbert was on duty.

'Good evening,' said George. 'I wonder if it's possible for me to speak to Nurse Price.'

'Bear with me.' Herbert consulted the document on his desk and said, 'Not unless you fall off your bike again and get brought in an ambulance. Nurse Price is in Men's Surgical, on the night shift.'

'That's ridiculous. She was with me yesterday afternoon.'

'It happens.'

'Look, can I see Staff Nurse Barker, please?'

Herbert consulted the document again and said, 'I'll see if she's in the sitting room.'

He disappeared, leaving George bewildered. Then, to his relief, Herbert returned with Norma, who said, 'George, what brings you here?'

'Can we talk?'

'Of course. Come through.' She led him into the familiar sitting room. 'Would you like a cup of tea?'

'No thanks. I had to come over.' He scanned the room but saw no sign of Jeanette.

Norma asked, 'Is this about Price?'

'Yes. I said I'd phone her today, but they told me she was on the night shift.'

'She is. She transferred to Men's Surgical yesterday, and the shift she's joined is on nights.'

Nothing made sense. 'She didn't mention it when I saw her yesterday, and she knew I was going to phone her today.'

Norma felt inside her apron and took out an envelope. 'She asked me to give you this,' she said, handing it to him. 'I tried to warn you, George.'

With a feeling of inevitability, George opened the envelope and took out the note. It read:

Dear George,

I'm afraid I have to disappoint you. It's been lovely, going out with you and doing unusual things, but it has to end. It's not because of anything you've done. You're a lovely chap and you deserve better than this. It's just that I've found someone else.

I hope you find someone you like, too.

Take care.

Love,

Jeanette.

He folded the note and put it in his pocket. 'I think I'd like that cup of tea,' he said, 'if it's not too much trouble.'

'Of course not.'

While Norma poured the tea, he looked around the room again, remembering the excitement of meeting Jeanette and then the time he had the accident and she patched him up. That was when he made the first date with her, and now it was all over. It was as if a trapdoor had opened beneath his feet.

'There you are, George,' said Norma, handing him a cup of tea. 'The reason she asked for the transfer to Men's Surgical was so that she wouldn't have to face me every day.' She let him digest that and then said, 'Also, the new man of the moment is a junior house surgeon.'

13

George told Bernard about Jeanette's note, but only in response to his usual friendly enquiry. Otherwise, he told no one, basically because he didn't want to talk about it. He got on quietly with his work at the office, and even managed to avoid clashing with Janet, if only for a few days. The inevitable confrontation came about when Denise, who had been observing George closely, came to his desk to speak to him.

'What's the matter, George? You've not been your cheerful self lately.'

There was no harm in telling her. 'There's been a parting of the ways, Denise. I got my marching orders on Sunday.'

'Oh, that's awful. Can't you patch things up between you?'

'No, she's found another bloke, a doctor at the hospital.'

Denise was about to say something, but Janet weighed in with her customary offensive.

'Leave her alone, George. You've a girlfriend of your own, remember.'

It was too much for George in his current mood. He walked over to Janet's desk and leaned over it to speak to her.

'We were talking about something that has nothing at all to do with you, Janet. Don't you think it's time you found a new hobby?'

Uncertain but defiant, Janet asked, 'What do you mean by that?'

'Just for the novelty, you could try minding your own business.' He couldn't trust himself to say more, so he walked down to the shop floor. As he reached the bottom of the stairs, Harry Wright, the chargehand storekeeper saw him.

Ray Hobbs

'All right, George?'

'Well enough, Harry.'

They had a friendly conversation about matters of mutual interest, including Yorkshire County Cricket Club's squad for the new season, and then George went back up to the office. If he were away too long, the likelihood was that Patchett would ask questions on his return, and George really didn't want to be bothered with that.

It seemed that he'd misjudged his timing, because Patchett was waiting for him when he returned.

'Where've you been?'

'Stores, Mr Patchett. I went to see if there were any issue or return notes waiting.'

'Harry Wright brought the last lot up half an hour ago. You knew that. You'd best come into my office,' he said in the tone that was usually the prelude to a reprimand.

George followed him into the glass-fronted office and waited.

'I've had another complaint about you, George.'

'How many's that this week, Mr Patchett?'

'Don't get clever with me, young man. You've been disrespectful to an older member of staff. I'm talking about Mrs Firth.'

'Who?'

'You know who I mean. You told her to mind her own business.'

'Oh, Janet.' Now it clicked into place. He'd probably heard Janet's surname once since his arrival. It wasn't the kind of thing he filed away for future reference. As for being older, she was thirty-six. She'd told everybody at her last birthday.

'Her name is Mrs Firth. I think we'll have some respect shown in this department. In any case, this is the third time I've had to speak to you about your attitude.'

'And it's always my fault, I suppose?'

'I don't see who else could have been at fault.'

'Well, no, you wouldn't, would you?'

Patchett slammed his fist down on the desk. 'I've had just about enough of your insolence. I'm referring you to Mr Wilkinson. Until he sends for you, you'd better get on with your work.'

——▶◀——

Ernest Wilkinson, Managing Director, was not immediately available, so George had to wait until shortly after four, when the phone call came demanding his attendance. Accordingly, he took the stairs to the seat of power and reported to Mr Wilkinson's secretary, a grim-looking matron, whose desk was laid out as if it were a barrack square.

'Mr Wilkinson sent for me,' he said. 'I'm George Barker.'

She nodded curtly and spoke into the intercom. 'George Barker is here, Mr Wilkinson.'

A voice that sounded distinctly unfriendly said, 'Send him in.'

'You're to go in,' said the matron unnecessarily.

George knocked and entered. He'd never seen Mr Wilkinson, but he'd thought of him as tall, lean and dynamic. The reality came as a surprise, because the man behind the desk was possibly nearing sixty, extremely overweight and with a large, untidy moustache that gave him the appearance of someone peering angrily over a badly-maintained hedge.

He said, 'You've been making yourself unpopular in the accounts office, I hear.'

'If that's what Mr Patchett told you.'

The moustache quivered. 'It's exactly what he told me.'

'Do you want to hear what I've got to say, Mr Wilkinson?'

'Why would I be interested in what you've got to say, Barker? I've heard all I need to know from Mr Patchett.'

'I only took this job to please my fath... my stepfather, and I've been bored mindless ever since I arrived. I've only upset Michael Burchett, Janet Firth and Mr Patchett, and I had a good reason every time.'

Mr Wilkinson seemed about to explode. 'I'll thank you to keep your opinions to yourself, Barker—'

'Let me finish. I'm resigning. I'll put it in writing and work my notice if you want me to, or I'll leave now. It's up to you.'

'Get out of my office, Barker!'

'I'll wait downstairs until I hear from you.'

'Get out!'

George let himself out, satisfied that he'd made his feelings known, and with the lowest possible opinion of his employer.

Returning to the accounts office, he opened his desk drawer and looked through the various bits and pieces. Very few of them were his; there was a bottle of ink, a rubber, a pencil sharpener and the rubber snake. Everything else belonged to the company, and they were welcome to it. As he removed his belongings, he was aware that he was under scrutiny. Denise and Janet were watching him, and so was Mr Patchett from inside his aquarium. It seemed that Patchett could contain himself no longer, because he opened his door and beckoned George inside.

'Well? What did Mr Wilkinson say to you?'

'Not much. He splutters a lot, doesn't he?'

'Don't be impertinent. Tell me what he said.'

'I've told you, Mr Patchett. He didn't say much. When I left him, he hadn't decided whether to let me work my notice or to pay me up in lieu. I told him I'd wait to hear from him.' George was beginning to enjoy the situation. It was the first fun he'd had since Saturday, and the memory of that was tainted. He looked up at the big wall clock and said, 'It's taking him a long time, isn't it?'

'Wait at your desk. I'll send for you when I hear from him.'

George obliged. Then, taking a sheet of paper, he went to the office typewriter and typed:

25th January, 1960.
For the attention of Mr E. Wilkinson, Managing Director.
Dear Mr Wilkinson,
I wish to confirm my resignation from the post of Cost Clerk, giving one month's notice from the date of this letter.
Yours sincerely,
George T. Barker.

He was confident of the wording of the letter because he'd often imagined himself writing it.

Janet and Denise were still watching him, but before he could say anything to them, Mr Patchett called him again into his office.

'Come in, George.'

George picked up his resignation and handed it to him. Patchett only looked at it briefly.

'Mr Wilkinson has asked me to pay you up in lieu of notice. I'm just waiting for Payroll to do you a payslip and bring the money, and then he wants you to leave the premises.'

'He's not the only one.'

'What do you mean by that?'

'I'm not keen to hang around, Mr Patchett. This is a bloody awful firm to work for, and I'm not sorry to leave.'

The chief clerk shook his head in disbelief. 'Hasn't it occurred to you,' he said, 'that you'll need a reference from Wilkinson's if you're going to get another job? Let me tell you, you're not going the right way about it.'

There was a knock on the outer door, and Barry Normanton, the Chief Payroll Clerk, came in. He gave Patchett a nod and then handed a sealed envelope to George.

'I'm sorry you have to leave, George,' he said, shaking his hand. 'Good luck, mate. Your insurance cards are in there, by the way.'

'Thanks, Barry. I'll be all right.'

'Right,' said Patchett, opening the glass door, 'pick up your belongings and go.'

'Goodbye, Mr Patchett.' George offered his hand and waited, but Patchett showed no inclination to take it.

As George went to his desk, he saw Neville, who had just returned from technical college. He looked embarrassed. 'So long, Neville,' he said. 'Don't let the buggers get you down, because they'll bloody-well try.'

Neville mumbled, 'So long, George.'

George lifted his hand to wave to Denise and Janet. Denise was in tears, and Janet wasn't far off when she got up to speak to him.

'I never meant you to get the sack,' she said.

Denise caught Patchett's eye and asked, 'Can I see George off, Mr Patchett?'

'All right, but don't take all day. Remember that there's work waiting to be done.'

Tearfully, Denise followed George into the corridor. She said, 'I think it was rotten of them to sack you just for putting that old boot in her place.'

'They didn't sack me, Denise. I resigned. Old Wilkinson wouldn't listen to me, so I told him where to park his job.' He was being creative, but he didn't care. He was more concerned about Denise, who was in tears on his account. She was also the only person he would miss.

'It amounts to the same thing, really,' she sniffed. 'It wouldn't have happened if Janet hadn't interfered.'

He held out his arms to her, and she joined him in a hug. 'Don't worry about me, Denise,' he told her, holding her tight. 'I've still got my job at the club, and it pays nearly three times what I've been getting here.'

'I'm going to miss you, though.'

'I'll miss you, too.' He looked down into her blue eyes, now red-rimmed with crying, and kissed her on the cheek. 'We'll see each other around town,' he said, wanting to console her, but not really knowing how.

'I hope so.' She sounded unconvinced, so he bent again and kissed her slowly and full on the lips. It hadn't been his intention, but he sensed somehow that it was what she wanted.

'Oh, George,' she said with a kind of longing that he would have welcomed in normal times. Unfortunately, Jeanette had left an open wound that would take time to heal. In any case, Denise was engaged to Desmond, as Janet had been so fond of reminding them both.

'I bet you won't tell Janet about that,' he said.

'I won't tell anybody. It's our secret. Take care, George.'

'And you.'

Reluctantly, she broke away from him and returned to the accounts office.

When he arrived at the shop, Albert surprised him by handing him a note.

'A young chap left it for you this afternoon,' he said.

'Thanks, Albert.'

'You're home early, aren't you, George?'

'Yes, I don't work at Wilkinson's now.' He went upstairs to the flat, leaving Albert to wonder.

Once inside, he opened the note and saw it was from David, Norma's boyfriend.

I tried phoning you at the office, but they said you'd left. I hope you're OK. If you fancy going for a pint or three this evening, give me a ring on 2490.

David.

———————•►◄•———————

David put two pints down on the table and pulled out a stool. 'I wondered if you'd gone home sick when they said you'd left,' he said. 'It never occurred to me that you might have left for good.'

'I couldn't stand it any longer, David. That Wilkinson bloke's not even human.'

'There must be a lot like him.'

George drank deeply. A night at the pub was just what he needed, and he liked Whitaker's bitter. 'You know, David,' he said, 'one day, I might employ people. When I do, I hope I never treat them the way old Wilkinson treated me this afternoon.'

'I couldn't imagine you doing that, George. You haven't an ounce of malice in you. You conform to the highest standards of behaviour, and it's just unfortunate that you expect others to do the same.'

George finished his beer and said, 'I'm interested in what you're saying, but just let me get these in first.' He picked up their glasses and put them on the bar. When the barmaid came to him, he said, 'Two pints of Four X, please.'

She pulled on the pump in a practised manner and asked, 'Didn't I see you playing the organ at the Gladstone Club?'

'Very likely. This one of my nights off.'

'I go there sometimes with my mum and dad when I'm not working. That's a rare talent you've got.'

'Thank you.'

'That's three and fourpence, please.'

He paid her, reflecting that beer was quite a lot cheaper at the club.

'Yes, we really enjoyed listening to you.'

'Maybe I'll see you down there.'

'I imagine so.'

As George put the drinks on the table, David said, 'The barmaid seems friendly.'

'Yes, she said she'd seen me at the club. She said she liked my playing.' With a rueful smile, he said, 'I'm popular with somebody, at least.'

'And with many others, I'm sure.'

'I don't know. What were you saying when I went to get the drinks, David?'

'Only that you always expect the best from people, and they don't always live up to that expectation.'

'Norma says I live in an ideal world.'

David nodded understandingly. 'She's been very concerned about you. That's why I suggested coming out for a pint.'

'Because of Jeanette?'

'Yes.' He looked like someone wondering about the best way of approaching a sensitive subject. Eventually, he asked, 'What did you and Jeanette have in common, George?'

'We went to the pictures, and she liked that. She's not very good at dancing, but she enjoyed it when we went to the Oak Tree.' He recalled their conversation about reading, and that reminded him of other conversations. He was beginning to realise something he'd known for some time but been reluctant to admit. 'We didn't have a lot in common,' he concluded.

'I thought not.'

'Why did she go out with me, then?'

'On Christmas Day,' said David, 'she finished with Simon Thornton. He was the junior houseman she'd been seeing. It was quite a shock to him. What he didn't know was that she'd really set her sights on Bruce Stephenson, a junior house surgeon with a future, or so he keeps telling everyone. Unfortunately for her, she found out on Christmas Day that Bruce had started a new relationship with a junior doctor in his firm.' He stopped to ask, 'Are you with me so far?'

'Yes, but what do you mean by a firm? You all work for the NHS, don't you?'

'It's not a firm in the business sense,' he explained. 'Each consultant has his own team of doctors, housemen and a registrar. It's quite a hierarchy, and they're called a "firm". Bruce Stephenson is in Mr Horsley's firm. He's an orthopaedic surgeon.'

'Right.' It was a different world from the one George knew, but he was always ready to learn. He'd learned already, rather to his surprise, that surgeons were addressed and referred to as 'Mr'.

'Jeanette knew you were keen on her, so she went out with you for a while as a stop-gap. As soon as she heard that Bruce was on the loose again, she let him know she was available. That was on Saturday evening.'

It had happened within a few hours of their foxtrot lesson. George bowed his head in abject embarrassment. 'I feel completely stupid,' he said.

'There's nothing stupid about innocence or inexperience, George, and I know what I've told you wasn't what you wanted to hear, but you needed to hear it all the same.'

George stared into his pint glass and said, 'I should have known a girl like Jeanette was beyond me.'

David let that pass for the moment. Instead, he said, 'Looking back, George, what was it that attracted you to her?'

'I suppose it was her looks at first.'

'Exactly. She has all the physical attributes men find appealing, but look beyond that and what do you see?'

'I don't know.'

'That's because there's very little to see. She's vacuous, not particularly able, and she's hell-bent on marrying a physician or a surgeon with a bright future.' David picked up the glasses and said, 'When you've had time to think about it, you'll realise that

Jeanette Price is a pretty girl with not much else going for her. What she has really is skin-deep, George, and you deserve better than that.'

————◆I◆————

Within a mercifully short time, George came to see the wisdom of David's words. His dalliance with Jeanette had never been a good idea, and whilst he still felt the loss to some extent, it was a declining ache that must surely disappear before long.

He'd heard people say that there is often a defining moment when the hurt of a broken relationship is mercifully assuaged, and such a moment came three weeks later, when he decided to spend Sunday afternoon at the club. George was a gregarious soul, and the companionship of the club's members appealed to him.

When he arrived, he was disappointed to find an all-male enclave watching a telerecording of a football match on one of the club's new TV sets. George's game was cricket, and football held no appeal for him, so he joined the small group of women in the other television room. They were watching a film that appeared to be about an aircraft carrier and a silly officer, who rejected a particularly attractive, talented and pleasant girl for the frivolous daughter of his admiral. George picked up the Radio Times and saw that the film was called *Ships With Wings*, and that the main character was played by John Clements. As he watched, he lost interest in the awful, contrived plot until John Clements sat at the wardroom piano and sang a song that was loaded with meaning for George, because it was called 'I Learned About Women From Her'. In some strange, inexplicable chemistry, the corny plot and the song left him feeling, quite suddenly, that his feelings of regret, loss and embarrassment had been swept away in a glorious, spring-cleaning of his emotions. He was once again his old self.

14

Another development that made life pleasanter was that Gilbert Finch's term of office as Concert Secretary came to its end, and he was not re-elected. His successor was a younger, much pleasanter man called Alf Harris. Gilbert introduced him to George and Bernard.

'You'll answer to Alf now,' he said. 'I hope you'll behave yourselves for him.'

'We've had you to train us,' said Bernard, once he'd shaken hands with Alf. 'I have to say, Gilbert, that it's been quite an experience, working here with you as Concert Secretary. What do you say, George?'

'Yes.' George allowed himself a friendly smile. 'It's been an experience all right.'

'Oh, has it? Well, thank you.' Gilbert was almost glowing. 'Right,' he said, 'I'll leave you with Arnold.' He went on his way, leaving them to speak freely.

'I shan't interfere as much as Gilbert has,' said Alf. 'You both know what you're doing, and I'm happy with the way you've been doing it.'

'You're singing our song, Alf,' Bernard told him.

'It's music to our ears,' agreed George.

As he had promised, Alf left them to get on with the job. It was a free and easy night, so they played some of their usual repertoire and mixed in more recent numbers, including the Shirley Bassey hit 'Kiss Me, Honey, Honey, Kiss Me' as well as 'Lipstick on Your Collar' and 'Seven Little Girls'. Suddenly, the job was much pleasanter.

———◆┆◆———

George was shopping at the grocer's, when his eye fell on a shelf containing bottles of sweets, and he remembered that Sandra, until recently his next-door neighbour, was particularly fond of dolly mixtures, so he bought a quarter and took them to her on his way back to the flat.

It was a strange feeling as he parked almost outside his old home, and he wasn't surprised when his stepfather, as he now thought of him, appeared outside his front door. His manner was as truculent as ever.

'What do you want?'

'Nothing you've got.'

'Cheeky sod.' He turned towards the open door and said, 'It's George, Elsie.'

'He's got a cheek, comin' round here.' She stood in the doorway to reinforce her *fiancé*'s insults. 'My Carol has to practise on the clapped-out piano we've had for years because of you.'

George wasn't prepared to stand there facing accusations any longer. He'd come to see Sandra, and that was where he was heading. 'Tell her to keep practising,' he advised as he walked towards next door's gate.

'You should be ashamed of yourself, taking that piano the way you did. You're just selfish. You know Carol could make better use of it than you.'

'One day, maybe, when she's learned how to take her foot off the pedal.' He knocked on the Young's door, ignoring the insults Elsie hurled at him.

Mrs Young opened the door. 'Hello, George,' she said, 'I heard the commotion. Come inside, love.' She called upstairs, 'George is here, Sandra. Mind those stairs when you come down.' Turning to George, she said, 'She fell downstairs last week. It took me ages to calm her down. Mind you, it must have hurt.'

'I bet it did.' Recalling more than one childhood accident, George could only sympathise with Sandra.

'Cuppa tea, George? The kettle's boiling.'

'Yes, please.'

'George!' Sandra had made it downstairs safely and now wrapped her arms round him. 'You're too high up for me to reach,' she complained.

Obligingly, he bent his knees, and she gave him a wet kiss on his chin, the only part of his face she could reach.

'Your chin's all prickly with whiskers.'

'That's what I keep telling the big bad wolf that wants to huff and puff and blow my house in.'

'You're daft, George.' Even so, she couldn't help laughing.

'I've brought you something, Sandra.' He put his hand in his pocket and took out the bag of sweets. 'Happy birthday.'

'It isn't my birthday 'til September.'

'In that case, I'd better take these back to the shop.'

'No, don't. You can give me some more when it's my birthday.'

'All right, but what do you say?'

She thought briefly. 'Please.'

'No, you say that when you want something.'

'I want them dolly mixtures.'

He tried a different approach. 'Fine, but what will you say if I let you have them?'

'Thank you.'

'That's better. Here you are.' He gave her the sweets.

'You're spoiling her again,' said Mrs Young.

'I haven't seen her since Christmas.'

'I haven't seen you and Norma since Christmas,' said Sandra.

'Well, you see, we don't live next door now.'

Mrs Young inclined her head towards next door and said, 'That Elsie's just about moved in with him now.'

George nodded.

'What was all that noise about before you came to the door?'

'Elsie was telling me I was a rotten sod for taking my piano with me when I moved out.'

'It was your property, though, wasn't it?'

'Yes, my mum left it to me in her will.'

'She's got a nerve, wanting it for Little Miss Nobody.'

George laughed. It was a good name. 'Norma reckons she should wear a fluorescent jacket permanently, just so that people know she's there.'

'It's not a bad idea. I can't see her as a teacher. Can you?'

'Who's a teacher?' Frustrated at being left out of the conversation, Sandra almost shouted the question.

'No one, and keep your voice down,' her mother warned her. 'How's Norma these days, George?'

'She's fine. They're just waiting for David to get a better job, and then they'll get married.'

'I am glad. She's a lovely lass. It was such a shame when she had to move out.' Remembering, she said, 'First Norma and then you. Have you got a nice place?'

'It's okay. It beats living next door, anyway. You should have heard him when he saw the piano was gone. What a pantomime that was.'

'What pantomime? When was that? Why didn't nobody tell me about it?' Sandra's volume increased with each demand.

'We took you to the pantomime at Christmas,' George reminded her.

'Oh, yeah. When's it coming again?'

'Not until next Christmas.'

'Why?'

'A pantomime is a Christmas thing,' George explained patiently. 'If you want it more often than that, it's like wanting Father Christmas to come at Easter.'

It was too much for Sandra, who laughed uncontrollably. 'You're daft, you are, George,' she said eventually. 'You're as daft as a brush.'

'She's missed you since you moved out, George,' said Mrs Young.

'That's a shame, but it was the best thing I ever did.' The reception his stepfather and Elsie had given him earlier demonstrated that very clearly.

———◆�►———

He was returning from a trip to Bradford a few days later, to buy sheet music, when he turned into Albert Street and, through the rain, which had been around for most of the day, he saw a stream of people coming out of Wilkinson's. Looking at his watch, he realised that it was just gone five-thirty. Thankful that he didn't have to work there any longer, he continued along the street until he noticed Denise at the bus stop. She was instantly recognisable by her lovely, chestnut hair. He pulled into the kerb edge and lowered the passenger window.

'D' you want a lift, Denise?'

'Hello, George. Oh, please.' She folded her umbrella and opened the door. 'My brolly's wet, I'm afraid.'

'Don't worry about that.' He waited for her to settle in her seat and then drove off.

'It's lovely to see you again, George. How are you keeping?'

'Nicely, thanks. How about you?'

'Oh, all right, I suppose.' She sounded unenthusiastic. 'Life, if you can call it that, at Wilkinson's is as boring as ever.'

'I'm not too sure where you live, Denise. You'll have to tell me.'

'Highfield Road, up past the fire station.'

'Right. So, nothing exciting's been happening then?'

'No, except....'

'Except what?'

'Desmond and I have split up.'

'Have you?' He sneaked a look at her left hand and saw that it was no longer adorned with her engagement ring. 'Did that happen suddenly?'

'No, it had been coming for a while. It would never have worked, anyway.'

He drew up at the lights where Bradford Road met Southgate. 'How do you feel about it now?'

'More than anything, I feel relieved. He was getting to be a pain about all kinds of things.'

'Janet must be upset. I think your engagement meant more to her than it did to either of you.'

'Oh, Janet.' Her tone suggested that the subject wasn't up for discussion.

The lights turned green, and George moved off again. 'It's none of my business, but what made you break it off with Desmond in the end?'

'Oh, all he ever wanted to do was live his own life. Rather than be with me, he preferred playing football and getting into the bath afterwards with his mates. I just couldn't see a future for us.'

'If he preferred to be in the bath with his mates, I'm not surprised you couldn't see a future with him.'

She smiled at his response and said, 'I don't know whether he is that way or not, but I wasn't going to hang around and find out.'

'No one can blame you for that.'

'What about you, George? Last time I saw you, that nurse had just finished with you.'

'Oh, I'm over that, Denise.'

'Good, because it was a horrible day apart from just one thing.'

George turned into Highfield Road.

'Halfway up,' she prompted, 'number ninety-four.'

'What was the one thing that wasn't horrible?'

'It was when we were in the corridor.' She hesitated. 'You don't mind me mentioning it, do you?'

'No, go ahead.'

'Well, I was upset and crying because I thought I wouldn't see you again. That was as well as being upset because I thought they'd sacked you. Anyway, I really wanted you to kiss me. I didn't think you would – I mean, why should you? – but then you did. You know, George, I'd never been kissed like that.' Collecting herself, she said, 'I've embarrassed myself now.'

'There's no need to feel embarrassed.' He pulled up outside her house. 'Will there be anyone at home?'

'Not yet. I'm always the first in. Why?'

'You *are* going to kiss me goodbye, aren't you?' He pulled the handbrake on and stopped the engine.

Her eyes were open wide. 'Of course,' she said, leaning towards him.

George lowered his head and brushed her lips with his, breaking off to ask, 'You're not going out with anybody, are you?'

'No, are you?'

'No.' he bent again. 'I thought I'd better check.'

'George, will you get on with it? My mum will be home soon.' She smiled, realising he was teasing her.

He kissed her slowly and gently, until she looked at her watch and said, 'My mum will be here any minute now.'

'Okay. Are you doing anything on Monday or Tuesday?'

'Not a thing.'

'So, can I pick you up here at half-past six on Monday? We can go to the pictures if you like.'

'Okay, what's on?'

'I don't know. It'll be a surprise.'

'I've already had one surprise today. Maybe it's going to be a habit.' She leaned forward to kiss him quickly and then let herself out of the car just as a bus stopped on the other side of the road. 'My mum's here,' she said. 'See you on Monday.'

15

They saw Kenneth More in *The Thirty-Nine Steps* at the Regal Cinema, and both agreed that it was an excellent film, but that they preferred the older, black-and-white version they'd seen on television in the New Year.

'The women in both films made a big thing of taking their stockings off,' said Denise as they left the cinema. 'I don't know why.'

George knew why, but he was reluctant to say so.

'I mean to say, what's this thing that men have about stockings and suspenders?'

'Search me.'

'Mind you, I could have worn a suit of armour for all the interest Desmond used to take.'

George made himself concentrate on remembering where he'd left his car. Deliberately changing the subject, he asked, 'Would you like to go for a drink or come back to my place for coffee?'

'I'd better not. Just until they've got used to the fact that I'm vacant again, I'd better not be too late.'

He found his car and unlocked it. When they were both inside, he said, 'It sounds funny when you call yourself "vacant".'

'Why? It's the opposite of "engaged", isn't it?'

'Only if you're a public convenience.'

'Don't be horrible, George.'

'I'm not. Anyway, if somebody's vacant, it means they're... you know, not very bright, and you're bright enough, a grammar school girl with O levels and that sort of thing.'

She considered his argument and said, 'All right, what should I call myself now that I'm not engaged?'

' "Unattached", I suppose.' He started the engine.

'You might as well say "loose" as "unattached".'

'No, I'd never call you that, Denise.' A saturnine man and a severe-looking woman walking past the car gave him an idea. 'You could ask Janet in the morning,' he said. 'She'll know what to call you. She's an expert on being engaged, so she must know something about not being engaged.'

'Janet's still trying to persuade me to make it up with Desmond,' she said. 'You don't know what it's like in that office nowadays.'

'I can guess.' A mischievous idea came to him, and he said, 'You could tell her that Desmond's the one that needs persuading. All she has to do is go to one of his football matches and get in the bath with him and the rest of the team afterwards. Then he'll talk to her as if she's a mate.'

They drove off, both enjoying the mental image of Janet in the communal bath.

When they reached the end of Southgate, Denise asked, 'We're not going down Donkey Hill, are we?' Donkey Hill was the local lovers' lane, and it was usually well-populated by ten-thirty.

'No.' George had once driven down Donkey Hill late at night, past a seemingly endless row of stationary cars, all with steamed-up windows, and all of them rocking and swaying as their occupants brought the evening to a lively end. 'No,' he said again, 'not Donkey Hill.'

'Where are we going, then?'

'I'm taking you home.'

'Oh.' She sounded disappointed.

She said nothing when he turned into Highfield Road, but when he signalled left before the old joinery, she asked, 'Where are we going, George?'

'Wait and see.' He drove to the end of the building, which was now a mere skeleton after the fire that had taken hold a few years earlier. Finally, he parked round the back.

'You've been here before, haven't you, George?'

'No, I just thought it might be a good place to say goodnight without setting the neighbours off talking,' he said, switching off the engine.

'This is all new for me, you know,' said Denise.

'What, saying goodnight?'

'No, I mean having a boyfriend with a car.'

'It's quite new for me,' he admitted. 'I mean, having a car, not having a boyfriend with a car.'

'I know what you mean,' she said, leaning forward so that he could put his left arm round her. 'It's a bit awkward in these seats, isn't it?'

'I'll change cars,' he offered.

'Don't be silly.'

'Okay.' He joined her in a lingering kiss.

'Oh, George,' she said as they broke off, 'I haven't been kissed like that since....'

'Last Friday.'

'That's right, and then since the day you left Wilkinson's'

'You've got some catching up to do.' They kissed again at length, until she broke away to look at her watch. 'I must go,' she said.

'You're right. We've got to get you home before this car turns into a pumpkin.' He switched on the engine and released the handbrake.

'You're daft, George.'

'As daft as a brush,' he agreed.

'But you're nice. I've had a lovely time.'

'Good. Would you like to go for a drink tomorrow night?'

She hesitated, and then said, 'It's the only time you've got, isn't it?'

'Until the weekend, and then I have to work evenings.'

'All right. Can you make it seven o' clock this time?'

'I think so.' He drew up outside her house, causing a curtain to twitch. 'Goodnight, Cinders. See you tomorrow night.'

'Goodnight.' As she kissed him and got out, a light came on in the hallway. No doubt Denise's parents were curious about the new bloke in their daughter's life. How old was he? How did he manage to run a car? What were his intentions? He wished her well, because he imagined they were quite strict. Finally, he drove home, still smiling at the image of Janet and Cullington Athletic Football Club enjoying a soak in the suds.

———◆I◆———

He spent Tuesday morning and part of the afternoon cleaning the flat, taking his washing to the laundrette and ironing his shirts. His mother had spoilt him, doing all those things for him, but National Service had made him much more independent. The only job he struggled with was cooking, and he suspected that might fall into place before long. People learned from their mistakes, and he made lots of mistakes, so that surely meant he would learn quickly.

Albert the greengrocer had handed him a note on his return from the laundrette, and he picked it up to read it again.

We've got two boxes of your books and we need the space. If you don't come for them before the weekend, we'll give them to Oxfam.

George noticed that the miserable bugger hadn't even bothered to sign it. He screwed it up and dropped it into the rubbish bin. He would call for the books on his way to Denise's house. Before that, however, he meant to call on Mr Handley, his old piano teacher. To save time, he had an early bath and changed into what had been his interview suit, now promoted to going on dates.

———◆I◆———

Before retiring two years earlier, Mr Handley had taught music at Albion Street Secondary School, where the pupils knew him as 'Tommy', after the *ITMA* comedian. For George, however, he was much more than a popular teacher; he'd been an example and a mentor during a difficult adolescence, and his influence continued to shape George's values.

He rang the doorbell, wondering somewhat belatedly if he should have given some warning of his visit. It was too late to worry about that, however, when he heard the inner door being opened and closed, and then Mr Handley, greyer and more lined than George remembered him, opened the outer door, surprised at first, but clearly delighted to see his former pupil.

'George,' he said, shaking his hand, 'come in.'

They exchanged the usual pleasantries while Mr Handley made tea, and then sat down to catch up properly.

'What have you been doing with yourself, George? You were called up for National Service, I believe.'

'Yes, I did two years in the Navy.'

'You were always keen, I seem to remember.' He poured the tea and handed George's to him. He asked, 'What are you doing now?'

'I'm playing the organ at the Gladstone Club. I gave up my day job last month.'

'The organ.' Mr Handley was intrigued. 'That must be a new skill for you.'

'Needs must, really. I enjoy it, but not as much as the piano'

'Do you still play the piano?'

'Yes, I rescued mine in the nick of time.' He went on to tell the story of his move and the disputed ownership of the piano. 'I'm going round there later on, to pick up some books, the last of my belongings,' he said. 'I really don't know what to do then, about the wedding, I mean, when there's so much ill-feeling between us over the piano.'

'Surely, they will decide.'

George looked at him blankly. 'What do you mean, Mr Handley?'

'Simply that if they don't invite you to their wedding, it will be they who are at fault, and you can live with a clear conscience. However, if they do, you should go. If you don't, you could regret it for the rest of your life.'

It was as it had always been, with Mr Handley dispensing common-sense advice, and always in the kindest way. 'Thank you, Mr Handley,' said George. 'That's good advice. I don't know why I didn't think of it.'

'Put it down to experience, George. I've been around much longer than you.'

George had to agree, and while he was thinking about that, his eye fell on the grand piano. He asked, 'Are you still teaching piano, Mr Handley?'

'Yes. In fact, I have more pupils than ever. Have you given any thought to coming back to the fold?'

'To be honest, I've been so busy with other things, it hasn't crossed my mind until now.'

'I could tutor you for a diploma. Think about it, George. You can't have too many strings to your bow, or maybe I should say, "to your piano", now you're self-employed.'

For a minute, George was bemused. 'Do you mean a teaching diploma, Mr Handley?'

'A diploma in piano teaching, yes. It's something you could always fall back on.'

'What would I have to do?'

'You'd play three pieces from the syllabus, all the scales and so on that you practised for Grade Eight and a few more, there'd be some sight reading, you'd work a paper in theory, analysis and history of music, a paper on piano teaching and a *viva voce* test.'

'A what test?'

'*Viva voce*, a live, spoken exam. I'd take you through everything.' He thought quickly. 'In fact, if you took the Guildhall diploma, the LGSM, you wouldn't do a written teaching paper. They do it all by *viva voce*, and you could take it locally, rather than travelling to London and having to stay overnight.'

It was very tempting, and he had ample time during the day for practice. 'All right, Mr Handley,' he said, 'I'll do it.'

———◆►◄———

When he arrived at his old home, the books were already in the hallway.

'There were just a few that Carol took a fancy to,' said Mr Barker, 'some music books.'

'That's funny. She doesn't look like a magpie.'

'What's that supposed to mean? You left them here, so they can't have meant all that much to you.'

'What music books, anyway?' He was thinking about his conversation, that afternoon, with Mr Handley. He might yet need those books.

'There was a small, buff-coloured book by somebody called Williams, I think she said, and a paperback about theory.'

'*Associated Board Theory*? A red paperback?'

'I believe so.'

'Oh, that's all right.' It was quite a relief. 'I got past them some time ago.'

'You'd better take your piano certificates with you an' all,' said Mr Barker, handing him a pile of board-backed envelopes. 'Elsie doesn't want Carol to see them.'

'Why should she? They're all addressed to Mr Handley.'

'What are?' The enquiry came from the kitchen doorway. Elsie had evidently overheard part of their conversation.

'My grade exam certificates.'

'Aye, well, you might think you're clever, passing Grade Eight with Distinction when you were fourteen, but I don't want Carol to know that. We can't all be gifted. There's some as have to work at it, and she worked as hard as ever she could and she only scraped through.'

George was about to ask how Elsie had managed to see the contents of the envelope, but he opted instead for diplomacy. 'Look,' he said, 'why do we have to be at war just because I took something that was legally mine? I'm prepared to be civil if you are.'

Mr Barker appeared to consider the question, looking at Elsie and then back to George. Elsie shifted uneasily. Eventually, Mr Barker said, 'All right, we'll declare a truce. I've been feeling a bit awkward about the list of wedding guests, and maybe now's the time to do something about it. What do you think, Elsie?'

'Why not? It would only look bad if we didn't invite them.'

'Right, we'll send invitations to you and our Norma.'

'Thank you. When is it?'

'The second of April, a fortnight before Easter.'

'Okay, I'll explain things to Norma.' He picked up the nearer of the two cardboard boxes to take it out to his car, and Elsie pushed the certificate envelopes firmly down the side of the box.

'I'm just making sure they're not going to fall out,' she told him.

He decided against telling her his latest news. She would only expect him to do it by magic, as the talented few did in her world, whereas he anticipated a lot of hard work. Meanwhile, however, he had a date with Denise.

16

When George arrived at Denise's house, instead of hurrying out to the car, as before, she stood in the window, inside the curtains, beckoning him to come to the door. She seemed anxious.

She opened the door to him, whispering urgently, 'My dad wants to meet you.'

'That's all right,' he said, following her into the thickly-carpeted hall and then into a well-furnished, comfortable sitting room, where her parents sat, looking like the interview panel he suspected they would turn out to be.

'This is George,' announced Denise, sounding embarrassed to the point of despair.

'Mr and Mrs Threadgold, how do you do?' He shook hands with them both.

'Sit yourself down,' said Mr Threadgold. He was a greying, concerned-looking man in a waistcoat, trousers and leather slippers. His appearance set George in mind of an off-duty version of Mr Patchett at Wilkinson's, but he tried not to be influenced by the resemblance.

'Thank you.'

'I don't know what you're used to, George, but I like to know something about the lads my daughter goes about with.'

'I can't say as I blame you,' said George. 'There are some strange people out there.'

'There are indeed,' agreed Mr Threadgold, who seemed unsure how to proceed. George imagined he wasn't as practised at inspecting boyfriends as he would like people to think.

'What do you want to know?'

'First of all, I believe you play the organ for a living. Is that right?'

'Yes.'

'What I don't understand is how you can afford to run a car, doing that sort of job.'

'Do you want to know what I'm earning?'

His inquisitor looked embarrassed. 'I wouldn't dream of asking you that,' he said. 'It's just been puzzling me, that's all.'

'I don't mind telling you. I'm paid twenty-one pounds a week before tax.' He thought the reference to income tax would make him sound respectable and not like someone doing a spot of housebreaking on the side.

'Really?' He sounded incredulous. 'That's more than a thousand a year.'

'Is it? I've never worked it out.'

'It's not the most secure kind of employment, though, is it?'

'Isn't it?' The question had never occurred to George.

'I mean to say, what would you do if that source of work suddenly dried up?'

George's conversation with Mr Handley came conveniently to mind, and he said, 'I'd teach piano.'

'Would you?' Mr Threadgold paused, no doubt trying to think of his next question. Eventually, he asked, 'What did you do before you worked at Wilkinson's?'

'National Service, and before that I was a junior clerk and then bought ledger clerk at Barrett's. They stopped trading while I was serving in the Navy.'

'The Navy?' Mr Threadgold's expression warmed by several degrees. 'I was in the "Andrew" throughout the war. What branch were you in?'

'Communications. I was a radio operator, a "special".'

'Were you? I was an asdic operator. We must have a proper conversation some time.' Turning to his wife, who had remained silent throughout the interview, he said, 'I'm sure we can trust this lad, Edith.'

'Well,' said George, 'if you're satisfied, we'll be on our way. Is there a special time when you want Denise to be back?'

'I think we can trust you to behave responsibly, George.'

'Oh, you can. It's been nice meeting you both.' He shook hands with them again and joined Denise at the door. 'Goodnight.'

'Goodnight, George.'

'Goodnight, George.' Mrs Threadgold added her meek response.

As they walked out to the car, Denise said, 'George, you were brilliant.'

'Not really. Your dad just wanted to know that I was respectable, and I convinced him I was.'

'I'll say you did. What's a "special"?'

'I don't know. What do you mean?' He unlocked the passenger door and held it open for her.

'You told my dad you were a radio operator, and then you said, "a special". I just wondered what that meant.'

'Oh, that.' George took his place in the driving seat before answering her question. 'It means I was connected with Naval Intelligence. In my case, I was trained to read Russian Morse, that's all.'

'Don't say, "that's all", George. You were special and, as far as I'm concerned, you still are.' As an afterthought, she added, 'And you impressed my dad no end.'

'I've had a lot of experience of trying to satisfy the impossible. Believe me, your dad wasn't difficult to please.'

'Well, I was impressed.' As George turned at the top of Highfield Road, she asked, 'Where are we going?'

'Somewhere that's warm, comfortable and friendly.' He smiled at her briefly before returning his attention to the road. 'By the way,' he said, 'I've been meaning to tell you something. You look a treat. You always do, but that dress is really nice.' Her coat lay open to reveal a floral-patterned dress in the warm colours that suited her so well.

'Thank you. I must say this is very nice. I'm not used to compliments.'

'That's just the way I am.'

'You'll do for me, George.'

He indicated right and turned into the carpark of the Gladstone Club, inviting a surprised reaction from Denise.

'This is private, isn't it? Will they let me in?'

'I'll sign you in as a guest,' George assured her. 'It's games night tonight, so we'll be able to have a quiet drink while they're all playing cards and dominoes.' He took her into the bar, where she looked around her in surprise.

'It's very... grand,' she said.

'Not really grand. It's just nicely furnished.'

The steward saw them. 'Hello, George,' he said. 'I didn't expect to see you tonight.'

'We've just come for a drink,' explained George. 'This is Denise. Denise, meet Arnie.'

They shook hands, and Arnie asked, 'What's your pleasure?'

Denise asked diffidently, 'Could I have a Babycham, please?'

'Gin and bitter lemon for me, please,' said George. In his quest for a drink that wouldn't linger on his breath, George had hit on one that fulfilled that purpose, at the same time playing down the strong taste of the juniper berries. He was pleased with his discovery, but Arnie couldn't resist wiggling his lips at him.

Denise asked, 'What's the matter with gin and bitter lemon?'

'It's not what you'd call a man's drink,' George confided, 'but I don't want to breathe beer fumes all over you.'

'You're really thoughtful, George.'

'I'm going to take some ribbing when I come in tomorrow night,' he said.

'That's awful.'

'No, no one means any harm by it.'

From time to time, members came to the bar and greeted George. He introduced Denise, and no one commented on his choice of drink, a fact that Denise was quick to bring to his notice.

'By the time Arnie's told a few people,' he said, 'it'll be tomorrow's headline.'

Convinced that he was unfazed by the development, she became thoughtful. 'What did you mean,' she asked, 'when you talked about satisfying the impossible?'

'When did I say that?'

'It was when I complimented you on impressing my dad.'

'Oh, I see. The man I used to think of as my dad is as close to impossible as anyone can get.'

She digested that information and asked, 'Isn't he your dad, then?'

'No, he isn't. I thought he was, until Norma, my sister, told me the truth.' He went on to explain the relationship, and how Norma had been obliged to divulge the long-held secret. Denise's eyes grew wider as he told the full story, giving him the impression that she must have been a rewarding child at story time.

'So, he was your uncle all along, and you didn't know until last month?'

'Not until after he'd told me about the cats.'

'And that's what led to Janet complaining about you to Mr Patchett.'

'Denise,' he said soothingly, 'let's look at it this way. Leaving Wilkinson's was a good thing for me. It seemed awful to you at the time, but think of what it's led to.'

'Yes.' She brightened up in an instant.

'Would you like to come back for coffee?'

'Yes, let's.'

They went out to the car and drove back to Cheapside.

'I can't get used to this,' said Denise. 'A boyfriend with his own car and his own flat.'

'I've still got my own hair and teeth as well.'

'Don't be daft.'

He unlocked the door and switched the light on.

'I should have paid a call before we left the club,' said Denise, looking uncomfortable.

'You can pay one here,' he told her, relocking the shop door.

'Have you got your own toilet as well?'

'Of course. It beats using a mumble jug in the middle of the night.' He switched the stair light on and left the shop in darkness.

'I suppose it does.' Somewhat embarrassed, she followed him up the winding staircase.

And it's much better than doing it out of the window, particularly in winter.'

'You're daft, George.'

'You're not the only one who thinks so,' he said, 'but you can pay that call now.' He pointed to the bathroom. 'I'll put the kettle on.'

When the coffee was made, he took it to the sofa and joined her. 'I need to get a little table,' he said. 'I'll probably look for one tomorrow.'

'You've got nearly everything here that you need, but how do you manage in that tiny bath?'

'I stand up and pour water over myself. The neighbours can see me, but who cares? I'm just a born exhibitionist.'

'Idiot.' She was looking at him in a way that he'd come to recognise, and he drew her towards him for a lingering kiss.

After a minute, she sighed and said, 'Oh, George.'

'I know. You haven't been kissed like that since last night. We must do it more often.'

'You make fun of me, but when you kissed me the first time, I'd really never known anything like it. Desmond used to do it as if his mind was somewhere else.'

'In the bath with his mates, I suppose.'

'I shouldn't wonder.'

He picked up his coffee and sipped thoughtfully.

'What's on your mind, George?'

'I was just thinking about being with you....'

'What about being with me?'

'And comparing it with sharing a bath with a crowd of muddy, sweaty footballers.'

'George, you horror.'

'But I prefer to be with you.' He kissed her again.

'George?'

'I'm still here.'

'How do you think your stepdad turned out to be so different from your real dad?'

'I haven't really thought about it.' He adopted a thinking pose. 'Maybe they had different parents.'

'Do you think the milkman might have had a hand in it?'

'If he did, he won't be the father of either of them.'

'Won't he?'

'No, you can't make a baby that way. Even I know that.'

'Don't be awful. You know what I mean.'

'Of course I do.' As he bent and kissed her, his hand accidentally brushed her breast. 'Sorry,' he said.

'That's all right. You don't take liberties, do you?'

'Certainly not on Tuesdays. It's not my night for it.'

'You can't be serious, can you?'

'Of course I can. Taking liberties is a serious business.' In truth, he was no different from most lads, in that he felt the urge often, and particularly when he was with Denise. That was the effect she had on him, but there was an inhibiting aura of innocence about her that made him keep those urges in check. He'd never been conscious of the same reserve when he was with Jeanette, but she and Denise were completely different people.

'Well, I think it's one of the nice things about you.'

'*One* of the nice things? Do you mean there are more?'

'Yes, there's the fact that you don't smoke. That's a point in your favour.'

'I tried it once, but it did nothing for me. We used to get duty-free cigarettes and tobacco in the Navy, and some of the blokes used to smoke like mill chimneys just because it was cheap. I couldn't see the point in that.'

'Neither can I. I've never smoked.'

He examined her closely and said, 'That explains it.'

'What?'

'The reason for your shiny, white teeth. You're like someone in a toothpaste advert.'

'Am I?' It was a guileless question.

'Yes, you're pretty and you have eye-catching teeth.' He'd heard an actor say something similar to Betty Grable, except that he hadn't been complimenting her on her teeth at the time.

'Thank you.'

Changing the subject because he was aware of the time, more than for any other reason, he asked, 'What do you like to do, apart from going to the cinema and drinking Babycham?'

'I like dancing.'

He made a mental note of that for later. 'Do you?'

'It's one of my favourite things.' Suddenly, a new light of enthusiasm showed in her eyes. 'I'll tell you what I haven't done for ages.'

'I'm listening.'

'I used to swim quite often, but I haven't done it for ever such a long time.'

'I haven't since the Navy swimming test. Okay, let's go swimming. We could do that at the weekend.'

'All right.' She gave him her innocent, inquisitive look and asked, 'What did you have to do for the Navy test?'

'We had to swim two lengths of a full-size swimming pool, fully-clothed, and then stay afloat for three minutes.'

'I reckon I could do that.'

'Ah, but could you do the second part of the test, the part that separates the men from the boys?'

'What was that?'

'Could you run stark naked through the centre of Plymouth eating a pasty and drinking scrumpy? Many have tried it, but only a few have got past the end of Union Street.

'Idiot. Kiss me again, and then I have to go home.'

17

George and Bernard were taking a break on Wednesday evening, when Alf Harris paid them a visit.

George asked, 'Have you come to take the mickey because I ordered a gin and bitter lemon? Everyone else has.'

'No, it's the first I've heard of it. I've come with good news, actually. The Committee's decided to give you both a rise of ten bob a night.'

'That,' said Bernard, 'is what I call good news. What do you say, George? Another two-and-a-half quid. Think of all the gin and bitter lemon you'll be able to afford now.'

'Bugger off. I don't mean you, Alf. Thanks for telling us.'

'It's no trouble, George, and don't worry about the gin and bitter lemon. It won't be a problem after tonight.'

'Won't it?'

'No, the bar's just sold out of bitter lemon.' He walked off, grinning.

'It's not fair, is it, George?' Bernard was pretending to examine a wire brush minutely. 'All you did was buy your girlfriend and yourself a drink, and you provided your mates with endless merriment.' He was still laughing.

'I wanted a drink that wouldn't hang on my breath, that's all.'

'Quite right. With some epic snogging lined up, you didn't want to put the young lady off by breathing Whitaker's Four X all over her, and I don't blame you. That's why I never drink on nooky night.'

'All right. Before we get started again, what would you suggest?'

'Other than drinking somewhere else where they don't know you?'

'Hell's bells.'

Bernard took pity on him. 'Whisky and soda. Drown the whisky with soda and you'll disguise the smell as well as killing the taste of the horrible stuff.'

'Don't you like whisky?'

'No, do you?'

'I've never tasted it.'

Bernard shook his head at his friend's innocence. 'Try a whisky and soda at the end of the night,' he suggested, 'and see what you think.'

———▶◀———

George found that, taken with a generous squirt of soda, whisky was quite acceptable. He also found, as the week went on, that members were finding other sources of amusement. Even so, he related the story to Norma when he visited her at the nurses' home. He knew she would be sympathetic.

'I think it's rotten, the way men tease each other,' she said.

'It's just the way we're made.'

'It's one of the daftest things about men.' She delivered the observation with conviction, but her thoughts seemed to be elsewhere, because she went on to say, 'I've received an invitation.'

'A wedding invitation?'

'Yes, have you had one?'

'Yes, but I knew it was coming.'

'Don't keep it to yourself, then. Tell your big sister.' It had always been a joke between them, Norma being the elder by just one year.

'I went round there to pick up my books. Carol had already helped herself to the ones she fancied, but that was no loss. Anyway, Elsie was laying into me about being gifted and not needing to practise—'

'What?'

'Yes, she really believes it. She'd been looking through my piano certificates.'

Norma blinked in disbelief. 'The nosey old cow.'

'My thought exactly. Anyway, Carol worked very hard to pass Grade Eight, apparently, and she just scraped through. I wasn't surprised but I was so sick of the nastiness, I suggested a truce, and they agreed. They said they'd invite us to the wedding.'

'Some treat, eh? Still, we ought to go.'

'That's what Mr Handley said. If they hadn't invited us it would have been their fault, and we needn't have worried, but now they have, if we don't go we'll feel bad about it afterwards.'

'David said much the same thing.' Speaking of David made her ask, 'Does your invitation say, "and friend"? Mine does.'

'Yes.' The thought made him laugh.

'Go on, let's hear it.'

'Bearing in mind the way things have been, maybe they should have said, "and second".'

'What?'

'You know. "Ding-ding. Seconds out of the ring. Round Two." '

'Men's humour is lost on me.' Changing the subject, she asked, 'When did you see Mr Handley?'

'The same afternoon I collected the books. I'm starting lessons again.'

'Are you? Good for you. You always enjoyed your lessons with him.'

'I'm going to take a diploma.' Even telling Norma felt like boasting. 'Mr Handley says it'll be another string to my bow,' he explained, 'just in case I find myself out of work. I don't really fancy teaching piano for a living, but it would be better than the dole.'

'Do you have to be qualified to do that?'

'No, anybody can set up as an instrumental teacher, but people take you more seriously if you have letters after your name.'

'That's true. Anyway, good luck, George, and more power to your fingers.' Norma had never been tempted to try the piano. Her childhood inclination had been towards drama, and she'd been quite successful at it.

Returning to a previous conversation, George asked, 'Is David happy to go to the wedding?'

'Yes, he's quite easy-going about most things. Who will you take?'

'I'm going out with a girl called Denise. She's really nice.'

'What is she like?'

'She's pretty and she's good fun, not a bit like Jeanette.'

'Good. It's ten bob and a long ladder to speak to Price now she's trapped Dr Stephenson. Mind you, they deserve each other.' Shrugging off the subject of Jeanette Price, she asked, 'How did you meet her, then?'

'Denise? I worked with her at Wilkinson's. She was engaged to somebody then, but it's all over now.'

Norma's eyes widened at the thought, and then on a more practical note, she said, 'I can't believe you walked out of the job just like that, George.'

'I can, and I've not looked back.' He was enjoying his freedom and the direction his life had taken.

———◆◄———

When he called for Denise, he told her about the wedding invitation.

'Oh,' she said, 'where are they having it?'

'St Matthew's. Elsie was widowed as well, so they can be married in church,' he told her as he started the car.

'Where are they having the reception?'

'Harrison's.'

Denise raised her eyebrows in approval. 'Very nice.' Harrison's coffee house and tearoom had always been considered posh.

'They've been saving up for it for a while.'

'Are you going to be Best Man?'

'No,' he laughed, 'he wouldn't ask me to play the chimney sweep, never mind Best Man. They only invited us because I shamed them into a truce.'

'Dear, oh dear. When is it?'

'The second of next month. They had planned it earlier, but I reckon the cunning old sod postponed it to get the full tax rebate.'

Denise was quiet for a while, presumably thinking about the wedding, because she said, 'I've got a nice frock I can wear, but I'll need a hat.'

'No problem. If you know what you want, we'll find a hat.'

'They don't come cheap, George.'

'Don't worry.'

'I mean, I don't want to let the side down, but I'm not exactly in funds.'

George laughed. 'You won't let the side down. Just wait 't:l you see Carol.'

'Who's she?'

'Elsie's daughter. Let-downs don't come much lower.'

'I don't believe you.'

He pulled into the side of the road outside the swimming pool and parked the car. 'I'll tell you about Carol before we go in,' he said. 'When they put her together, they realised they had the right number of most things: a head, two arms, two legs, and that sort of thing. There was just one part missing. Someone said, "We're clean out of personalities. We used up the last one five minutes ago." Then the foreman looked at the clock and said, "Bugger it. It's nearly home time. Put her together. She'll just have to go through life without." And that's how Carol came about.'

'Poor girl.' Denise opened the door, trying not to smile at the story. 'I wonder how many there'll be in the pool,' she said as they walked to the entrance of the Victorian building. 'It's a cold day for swimming.'

'You'll have to be sure to dry yourself properly,' he warned her. 'On second thoughts, don't bother. I'll come into your cubicle and dry you.'

'You will not. Anyway, they'd chuck you out.'

'Would they? I thought people came here to have fun.'

'We do things differently on this planet, George.'

He stopped at the turnstile and bought two tickets.

'Lads this side, lasses t' other side,' the matron in the box told him.

'All right. We've been here before.'

'I have to tell you whether or not. It's part of my job.'

They walked into the pool area and experienced the familiar din echoed and magnified by the expanse of water.

'See you in a bit,' said Denise, walking around the pool to the other side.

George found a cubicle quickly. Denise had been right about people giving swimming a miss on such a cold day. He changed, used the foot bath, and then passed through the cold shower for good measure before walking down to the deep end and diving in.

He'd just surfaced and swum to the side, when someone tapped him on the shoulder. For a moment, he didn't recognise Denise in her bathing cap, until she asked, 'Did you do your swimming test in a pool like this one?'

'No, it was a full-size pool, about fifty yards, I think.' The Cullington pool was tiny by comparison.

'I'll race you to the shallow end,' she said.

'Okay. If you win, I'll buy you a new hat for the wedding.' Now he'd had time for a quick glimpse, he thought she looked particularly good in a swimming costume, even allowing for the distorting effect of the water.

'That's a safe enough bet for you. Do I have to buy you one if I lose?'

'No, I'll think of something else you can do.'

'I bet you will.'

They positioned themselves side by side at the deep end.

'Ready,' said Denise, 'Go!' They set off, each settling into a front crawl. When George was about halfway, he slowed down to let her catch up.

She asked, 'Are you okay?'

'Yes.'

Looking puzzled, she struck out for the shallow end, reaching it easily before him, but not without incident, because when George arrived, someone was shouting at her.

'What's up?' George half-recognised the lad. He'd known him at primary school, and he'd been unpleasant then. It seemed that five years at the grammar school hadn't improved him.

'Search me,' said Denise.

'She got in my way.'

'It's a public pool, Jacko,' George told him, remembering his name.

'I'm tellin' yer she got in my way.'

'Your manners are untidy, my friend.' George remembered hearing Howard Keel say it in *Showboat*, and it seemed a good time to borrow it. 'You'd better apologise to the lady.'

'Are you going to make me?'

'If I have to.'

That seemed to amuse Jackson until George put him in the arm lock he'd used on Michael Burchett. 'If I stick your head under the water, you won't like it,' he said.

'Leggo me arm.'

'You can apologise in words or bubbles. It's up to you.'

'All right.' Whether the anguished tone was born of humiliation or the threat of being ducked was unclear, but Jackson's apology was no less forthcoming. 'Sorry,' he muttered.

'I should think so.'

'What's happening here?' Alerted by the gathering, the attendant had arrived to exert his authority.

'He was threatening my friend,' George told him, 'so I asked him to mind his manners. That's all.'

The attendant looked hard at Jackson. 'You again,' he said. 'I've warned you before. Get out and get dressed. I want you off the premises.'

'It were his fault as much as mine.'

'I don't believe you. Off you go.'

Meekly, Jackson hauled himself out of the pool and made his way to his cubicle.

'Thanks for sticking up for me,' said Denise. 'There was no need, but thanks anyway.'

'You won the race,' said George, as if the dispute had never intervened, 'so I'll buy you a hat for the wedding.'

'Oh, George, you're lovely.'

'No, I'm not. I'm going to race you to the other end. To your marks, get set, go!'

He reached the deep end and waited for Denise to join him.

'You're awful,' she said. 'You let me win the first time.'

'It was a noble deed,' he agreed. 'I try to do one every day.'

'Were you in the Scouts?'

'Not exactly.'

She looked at him squarely. 'What do you mean by "not exactly"? You must have been either in or out.'

'I was in the Cubs for a fortnight.'

'What happened?'

'I'd rather not talk about it,' he said, adopting a martyred expression. 'It's a very painful memory.'

'You do talk nonsense.'

'That as well,' he agreed, thinking how appealing she looked in her swimsuit.

They skylarked happily until their hour was up, and then they went back to their respective cubicles to change.

George was waiting beside the Brylcreem dispenser when Denise joined him.

She looked at the machine and asked, 'Do you use that stuff?'

'No, I prefer strawberries just on their own.'

'It's hair cream, you clot.'

'I thought it tasted funny.' As he led the way to his car, he said, 'Swimming always makes me peckish.'

'Me too.'

'Shall we go to Harrison's?'

She appeared hesitant. 'If you think they'll let us in. It's a bit posh.'

'Not as posh as it used to be. It's been a while since they threw me out.'

'Okay, then. On the way, you can tell me why you were in the Cubs for only two weeks.'

'Do I have to?'

'The confession will be good for you.' She took her seat in the car, and he closed the door. 'You're ever so nice, opening and closing doors for me,' she said as he got in.

'It's the way I was brought up.'

'Your stepfather got something right, then.'

'It was my mum who taught me good manners. My stepdad still needs to learn them.' He pulled out and drove the short distance to Harrison's Coffee House.

'All right, tell me about the Cubs.'

'You show no mercy, do you?' He gave a deep sigh and began. 'I'd been in the Cubs two weeks. The second time, they were playing a silly game, and I realised I needed a jimmy riddle quite urgently. Now, in those days, I was very shy, and I couldn't bring myself to ask anyone the way to the heads.'

'The what? Oh, I see.'

'So I went outside and had one behind the hut. Unfortunately, Brown Owl saw me, and I was in deep trouble. I was found guilty of indecent exposure and I was dishonourably discharged.'

'I don't believe a word of it.'

'You should ask Brown Owl. She was so shocked, they had to crush one of her powders and leave her to lie down in a darkened tent.' He parked at the side of the road outside Harrison's.

'This is gracious living,' said Denise, getting out of the car.

'They haven't let us in yet.'

'I'm glad I'm not wearing jeans,' said Denise, looking down at her cotton twill slacks.

They climbed the steps and negotiated the revolving door. A grey-haired man in a sober suit greeted them.

'Good afternoon, sir. Good afternoon, miss.'

Good afternoon. 'Have you a table for two, please?'

'We have, sir. Would you care to follow me?'

George followed, bemused because suddenly, people were addressing him as 'sir'.

The man led them to a table by the window and presented them each with a menu. 'I'll leave you to make your choice,' he said. 'A waitress will be with you shortly.'

In the middle of the room, a diminutive, white-haired woman was leafing through a pile of music. She made her selection and placed it on the music desk of a white, baby grand piano.

Denise asked, 'Shall we have the set tea?'

'Yes.' George's attention was on the pianist.

'What kind of tea?'

'I don't know.' He picked up the menu and read, *Lapsang Souchong, Darjeeling, Earl Grey, English Breakfast* and *Tea Room Blend*. 'Let's have the Tea Room Blend,' he suggested.

'Have you had it before?'

'Yes, when my mum brought us.'

The moment arrived, and the pianist began with what turned out to be a selection from *The King and I.*

'Is she any good?'

'No, but she's doing her best.'

The waitress came to the table. 'Good afternoon, sir, good afternoon, miss. Have you decided yet?'

'Yes, we'd like the set tea with a pot of the Tea Room Blend, please.'

'Of course, sir.' She noticed him looking in the pianist's direction. 'Gwen's been with us a long time,' she said.

'You just can't beat loyalty.' He thought he owed that one to Cary Grant, but he wasn't entirely sure.

'The management want to put on a regular tea dance for our older clientele, but poor old Gwen's not really up to it. She's told them, but there's no one else available.'

'What day of the week will it be?'

'Monday, sir, from four until six-thirty.' Perhaps wondering why he was showing interest, she asked, 'Do you know of a pianist, sir?'

'Yes, I'll be in touch with the manager. What's his name?'

'Mr Geoffrey Harrison, sir.'

'Is he one of the original Harrisons?'

'Yes, sir, the last of the line, as it happens.'

George decided not to pry. He had the information he needed.

When the waitress was gone, Denise said, 'It sounds nice. It's a pity it's only for old people.'

'I'll take you dancing, Denise. Don't you worry.' He had it in mind for the following week.

18

The Oak Tree had a private function on Tuesday, so George booked a table for the following week.

In the meantime, he'd written to Mr Harrison and received a reply asking him to attend an audition at nine o' clock on Monday week. That would make two excitements in as many days.

Accordingly, he arrived at Harrison's at eight fifty-five in his interview/going-on-dates suit, and showed Mr Harrison's letter to the cleaner who'd opened the door to him.

'I'll see if he's in his office, love,' she said.

A minute or so later, a large man with sparse, greying hair parted down the centre came out of a room that was behind the cash till.

'George Barker?' He sounded like a man used to wielding authority.

'That's right, Mr Harrison.'

'Come over to the piano. I wouldn't normally consider a pub pianist, but I confess I'm having to cast my net wider on this occasion.'

George ignored the insult and walked over to the piano.

'Haven't you brought any music?'

'I play most dance music from memory, Mr Harrison.'

'Do you, now?' His tone lacked trust. 'I hope you're not one of those pianists who can only play by ear.'

'I *can* play by ear, Mr Harrison, but I prefer to read the music. It's just that I play it so often, I can't help memorising it.'

'All right. Let's hear a waltz.'

'Modern, Viennese or St Bernard?'

'St Bernard. We'll probably be asked for some Old Time.'

George obliged with one of his stock numbers.

'All right,' said Mr Harrison, interrupting him, 'A Veleta.'

Once again, George dipped into his club repertoire.

'The Gay Gordons.'

George played some of 'Cock o' the North.'

'Fair enough, but what about ballroom numbers. Let's say a foxtrot.'

George demonstrated his ability with a foxtrot, a waltz and a quickstep, before Mr Harrison registered his approval.

'I'm hoping to start the tea dances at the beginning of April,' he said. 'They'll be on Mondays from four o' clock until six-thirty and I'm paying four guineas.'

More in response to Harrison's overbearing manner than because of what he was paying, George slid off the stool and stood up. 'I'm sorry, Mr Harrison,' he said, 'I can't do it for that.'

'Why not?'

'Collinson's are paying five pounds, and they're not the only coffee house that's hiring musicians.'

'You set a lot of store by yourself, young man. Four guineas is a good wage.'

'I've shown you that I'm able to do the job, Mr Harrison. If we can't agree, I'll have to go elsewhere.' It was no bluff. George had heard of two coffee houses that were looking for musicians. Harrison's was simply the nearest.

'All right. I'll pay you five pounds, and you can keep any tips. It's up to you to declare your income to the Inland Revenue, and I want total commitment from you, both to me and to the customers.'

George didn't know quite what he meant by that, but it seemed a reasonable demand. 'That's fine, Mr Harrison. I'll be here on the fourth of April, ready to start.' He would also be there on the second, for his stepfather's wedding reception, but he kept that as a surprise for later.

—◂▸◂—

'Did he really call you a pub pianist?' Denise sounded rightly appalled.

'He's a relic of a bygone age.'

'He certainly sounds like it.' They were almost at the Oak Tree when she said, 'You know, George, you tell me you haven't had much education, but you're very articulate.'

'I read a lot. I was always pretty good at English, as well. It was maths that let me down.'

'I'm not brilliant at maths. I only just scraped through O level.'

'But you got the O levels, and that places you apart from me.'

She looked at him in alarm. 'I hope not.'

'I just mean it makes us different.' He turned into the Oak Tree carpark and found a place.

'Does it heck. If you've got ability, and you have, O levels don't mean a thing.'

'Maybe not,' he conceded. 'Maybe it's the shadow of my stepdad that refuses to go away.'

'I shouldn't wonder,' she said, opening her door, 'but I wouldn't want you to be any different from the way you are. So there.'

Her loyalty, like her company, was both welcome and rewarding. He was already conscious that even the thought of her when they were apart seemed to elicit a warm glow that lightened his mood and occasionally hindered concentration. He suspected that he knew its cause, and it pleased him that the feeling was of a different kind from the naïve infatuation he'd felt for Jeanette.

With that pleasing thought, he took her into the Oak Tree, where they chose to forego the aperitif, and went instead to their table. The band was playing 'April in Portugal', and Denise was listening attentively.

'It's a foxtrot,' he confirmed. 'Would you like to dance?'

'Mm. How did you know what I was thinking?'

'I don't know. You're usually easy to read.' He led her on to the floor and they joined the line of dance. He was pleasantly surprised that she moved gracefully and followed his lead without difficulty.

' "Read" is a funny word to use,' she said after a while.

'What made you think of that?'

'You said I was easy to read, as if I'm a book or a paper.'

'I can read your expressions. It's like cricket, when they talk about a batsman being able to read the bowler. It means he knows what kind of delivery he's going to bowl.'

'Oh well, you have the advantage of me there. I've never understood cricket.'

It was a small thing, set against all that they had in common.

The number ended, and they returned to their table.

'We have to decide what we're going to eat,' said George.

'Yes, they do a pheasant *pâté*. That sounds nice, and am I allowed to have the sirloin steak?'

'As well as a new hat? Oh, I think so.'

They gave their order to the waiter, who asked, 'Would you like me to send the wine waiter to your table, sir?'

'Yes, please,' said George.

'I'll leave the wine to you,' said Denise.

When the wine waiter arrived, George ordered a bottle of the *Mouton Cadet*, number forty in the wine list.

'That's just what I meant earlier,' said Denise, 'about education. I can think of a lot of grammar school lads who did French for five years, and who wouldn't pronounce *Mouton Cadet* as well as you just did.'

'I cheated,' he admitted. 'The first time I ordered it, I used the bin number, and then, when the wine waiter referred to it by name, I filed it away for the next time.'

'That takes initiative.'

'If you say so. Would you like to dance?' The band were playing 'Here in my Heart'. 'It's a slow foxtrot,' he prompted.

'Let's. The foxtrot's my favourite. What's your favourite foxtrot number?'

'It's a really old one from the 'thirties. It's "The Very Thought of You". What's yours?'

'I don't know. I'll think about it and let you know.'

They danced close together, an expedient made necessary as well as desirable, because the floor was now quite full.

They returned to their table at the end of the number, and

with professional timing, or more likely a practised eye, the wine waiter brought the wine for George to taste.

'This is lovely,' said Denise when he'd gone. 'When you were at Wilkinson's and you said you were taking that other girl to the Oak Tree, I remember saying how much I envied her.'

'And Janet told you that Desmond didn't take you to nice places because he was saving up to get married.' He still enjoyed the picture of Janet in the communal bath.

'It's history, George. I'm enjoying the present a lot more.' She stood up and said, 'I'll be back in a minute.'

George tried the wine again. It really was very nice, and he resolved to learn more about wines so that he could graduate from *Mouton Cadet* to a wider repertoire.

Denise returned as the waiter brought their starter. They both had the pheasant *pâté*, and it was excellent, but a treat of a different kind came next, as the bandleader made an announcement.

'We have a request, ladies and gentlemen. It's for George and Denise, and it's "The Very Thought of You".'

'Oh, Denise, thank you.' George got up and offered his hand to her.

'It was the least I could do.'

They danced, oblivious to everything and everyone else in the room, such was the effect of Ray Noble's music and the natural rapport between them.

Once more at their table, Denise asked, 'What was she like, the girl you went out with before me?'

'Empty.'

'Empty?' It was evidently a strange concept.

George remembered the way David had described her. 'She's an attractive girl with not much else going for her,' he said. 'Her life's ambition is to marry a successful doctor.'

Denise considered that briefly and said, 'I wouldn't fancy being married to a doctor, not with the telephone forever ringing in the middle of the night because somebody's poorly.'

'That's the life my sister's chosen.'

After some thought, Denise said, 'I think I remember your

sister from school. She was in the year before mine and she was in some of the plays they put on. She was very good.'

'She was in a pantomime at Christmas.'

'Oh, yes, I remember now. You had to play the piano for it, didn't you?'

'The organ, yes. Norma's been in a few pantomimes, always as the principal boy.'

Denise nodded. 'As I recall, she has the figure for it.'

'What's your brother like?'

'Andrew?' She shrugged. 'He's at university, studying chemistry. What can you say about someone like that? He's a swot.'

'He's obviously clever.'

'There you go again, George,' she cautioned. 'You can do things he can't. Doesn't that make you clever?'

'I've never thought of myself as clever. I'm just good at playing the piano and the organ.'

'And you'll soon have letters after your name,' she reminded him. 'Not everyone can say that.'

'I won't want to say it when the time comes.'

'I know you won't.'

The waiter arrived with their main course, which was a pleasant and timely distraction for George.

Denise asked, 'Who else will be at the wedding?'

'It's difficult to say. I don't know any of Elsie's friends, supposing she has any. Carol will be a bridesmaid, of course.' He grimaced, prompting Denise to say, 'Don't be cruel.'

Norma and David will be there, and possibly the Young family from next door. I've known them forever. Their daughter, Sandra, is twenty-two, but her mental age is eight or nine, or so they say. I think, sometimes, she's brighter than she seems.'

'That's awful. What's wrong with her?'

'David calls it "Down's syndrome".'

'Oh, I know what that is. The sister of one of my friends at school has it. You've got to feel sorry for their parents.'

George had often thought that. 'I think it's possible that children with problems are born to the right parents. Either that, or the parents learn to cope.'

'It must still be heart-breaking when the baby's born and they see it for the first time.'

'It must,' he agreed, convinced by then, that there was a great deal more to Denise than the pretty girl he'd noticed on his first day at Wilkinson's. Life was more promising than ever.

Part Two

1

NOVEMBER 1962

Norma poured two cups of tea from the enormous pot in the corner of the nurses' sitting room and carried them to where George was sitting.

'I'm really chuffed,' he said. 'It's a pity David's not here, because I'd like to congratulate him personally.'

'He'll be around, George. You'll see him.'

'When will you move to Manchester?'

'At Christmas. We both have to start in January. You'll come over and see us, won't you? I mean, we'll have our own place after we're married, but you can come over to the hospital any time.'

'Of course I will.'

Sensitive as ever, Norma patted his hand. 'Poor George,' she said. 'Here we are, talking about David's new job and mine, and you're still missing Denise. It's been a while now, but I can tell.'

'I can't deny it.'

'You've been so tight-lipped, I never did find out what went wrong between you. You'd been going out with her for so long, we thought you were set fair.'

'I suppose we were just wrong for each other.'

'Nonsense. You were great together.' She squeezed his hand with sisterly concern. 'It was more than that, wasn't it?'

'Yes,' he admitted, sipping his tea for fortification. Close though his relationship was with Norma, he still didn't find it easy to talk about deeply personal matters. 'She felt that what we had was going nowhere. She wanted to get married and have children.'

'You can't blame her for that. It's quite normal for a woman to want those things.'

'I'm not blaming her for anything. It was just unfortunate, the way things turned out.'

'So, what went wrong?'

He was still reluctant to talk about it, but he made an effort because Norma wanted to know. 'It was my lifestyle, basically. She said she wanted her children to have a dad who came home at night, and not one who spent his evenings playing the organ in a club, so that they never saw him.' He shrugged at the hopelessness of his position. 'It was fair enough, but what could I do? I think she'd have preferred me to be working in an accounts office, like her, but who would employ me after the Wilkinson's episode?'

'It's a shame. I really liked her, and I know you were very fond of her.'

'You just have to put it down to circumstances.' Out of the corner of his eye, he saw Jeanette enter the room. It was evident that she'd seen him, but she poured herself a cup of tea and joined the group in front of the TV set. Norma had also noticed her.

'*Emergency – Ward Ten* still has its audience,' she observed, 'and one member of it came close to failing her final exam.'

'Did she?'

'Yes, Price had to see the external assessor before they'd let her through.'

George made no comment. Instead, he asked, 'Is she still knocking off the house surgeon?'

'Dr Stephenson? No, she sent him packing some time ago. Her latest enthusiasm is a junior house surgeon in Mr Woodhead's firm. He's a gynaecologist, by the way.'

George had to smile. 'She'll be just the thing to come home to after a hard day at the orifice.'

'I imagine she's heard that one many times.' She gave him a searching look and asked, 'You're not fancying a second try, are you?'

'Absolutely not.' A half-forgotten fragment of a song made him say, 'I learned about women from her.' Ingenuous though he was, he really had learned that lesson.

2

JANUARY 1963

Bernard put a copy of *The Daily Herald* on the organ and said, 'Just take a look at that bloke, George. Who'd have thought he'd been spying for Russia since the nineteen-thirties?'

The picture on the front page was of Kim Philby, once a trusted intelligence officer, but now completely disgraced.

'It says he's done a bunk from Beirut, where he was being questioned. What's the betting he ends up in Russia, like the other two?'

'What other two?' George hadn't been following the story, so he was understandably confused.

'MacLean and Burgess.'

'I suppose he'll make a bee-line for Russia if he has any sense, although I must say he's welcome to it. It wouldn't suit me.'

'What do you know about it, George? If it comes to that, what does anybody really know?' Bernard's left-wing politics were no secret at the club.

'You hear about things, Bernard. Only last week, I think it was, they announced that they'd found some blokes guilty of making drawing instruments and selling them at a profit. They put them in front of a firing squad for that. I tell you, that's not the kind of country I'd want to live in.'

'But how do you know it's true?' Bernard was fond casting doubt on official news. He was also ready to scent intrigue where no one else would suspect it.

'The Russians announced it themselves. It was just as if they were proud of it. It was one of those official communiques they talk about.'

'But you didn't hear *them* announce it. You only have the BBC's word for it. For all you know, it might have been cooked up by the government as anti-Soviet propaganda.'

'Well, I know who I'd sooner trust.'

Bernard gave him a pitying look. 'You're like a lot more, George,' he said. 'You just take these things in without question.'

The discussion was cut short when Alf Harris came to speak to them.

'There's not a lot for you to do tonight, lads,' he told them. 'Just start the evening off with a bit of background music and fill in between the guest appearances.'

Bernard asked, 'Who's the guest?'

'Guests,' Alf corrected him. 'It's a group called "Kevin and the Cavemen". I brought them in to please the younger end. I have to try to suit everybody nowadays, and if that means bringing in rock-and-bloody-rollers, then that's what I have to do.'

'Poor bugger,' said Bernard when Alf had gone. 'It's his second stint as Concert Secretary, and now he has to engage those with no talent to entertain them with no taste. Whatever next?'

'Let's listen to them before we knock them,' said George.

They played some of their familiar repertoire for the first half-hour of the evening, while the guests and their technicians set up the complicated audio system behind the curtains. From time to time, members were treated to an occasional expletive as someone encountered a minor problem, having forgotten that the microphones were switched on. Eventually, however, Alf went on stage to introduce Kevin and the Cavemen. There was a vocal response mixed with laughter from the younger members, and a more muted, tut-tut reaction from their seniors as the curtains opened to reveal five young men wearing wigs and fake-fur loin cloths. There was a vocalist as well as lead, rhythm and bass guitarists, and a drummer.

Bernard bent over his drums, laughing silently but helplessly at the spectacle on stage. George was more inclined to wait for the number to begin.

In the event, the first two numbers did little to reward his fairmindedness, and he was thinking of retiring to the bar, when a man he'd noticed earlier came and joined him. He was large, overweight and middle-aged, with an old-fashioned pencil moustache of the kind sported by pre-war film stars. He spoke to George without looking at him.

'What do you think of them?'

George asked warily, 'Are you related to any of them?'

The question seemed to amuse him. 'No, I'm their agent.'

'Have you any more on your books like them?'

The man laughed shortly and said, 'No, and now I've got them on the club circuit, they're on their own.' He seemed about to move away, and then he said, 'Go on, give me your honest opinion.'

'All right. The singer doesn't impress me, the drummer can't keep a regular beat, and if the rhythm guitarist has more than three chords, he's forgotten where he left them. The lead guitarist and the bass player have some ability, but they're with the wrong group.'

'I'll tell you what, young man, you know how to use your ears.'

'It's what I do for a living,' explained George.

The man inclined his head towards the bar and asked, 'Do you fancy a drink?'

As an alternative to Kevin and the Cavemen, the offer appealed, so George left the organ to join the man in the bar.

'What's your name?'

'George Barker.'

'I'm Miles Standish.'

George stared at him for a second and said, 'I don't believe you. Nobody's called Miles Standish.'

'All right, it's a business name. I'm Alfred Fox, really, but keep that under your hat. I have a reputation to maintain.' After a moment's thought, he asked, 'Is yours your real name?'

George nodded. 'It's the only one I've got.'

'What are you going to drink?'

'Orange juice, please.'

Standish looked at him oddly. 'Are you sure?'

'I never drink when I'm working.'

'Very wise.' He ordered a scotch and soda and an orange juice. 'Returning his attention to George, he asked, 'How long have you been in this game?'

'Nearly four years.'

'Have you got a daytime job as well?'

'No, I used to play for a regular tea dance at a local coffee house, and it was all right while it lasted, but that died off with the elderly clientele.'

'Would you be interested in permanent employment?'

'That depends on what it is and what it pays.' George had been conscious for some time of the lack of security in the job at the club, but he wasn't prepared to commit himself at that stage.

Standish handed him a business card. 'Come and see me at my office, George. I know I'll be there on Friday morning. Can you make it then?'

'What time?'

'Eleven-thirty.'

'All right, I'll be there.'

———▸◂———

The recent winter had prompted George to move to a more sophisticated and warmer flat in Providence Road, overlooking the railway station and the Victorian swimming baths that he and Denise had used so often.

Wearing a charcoal grey, two-piece worsted suit, he left the flat and walked down the steps to the Wolsley 15/50 that had replaced the Anglia. He was pleased that he'd been able to move on from his more constrained beginnings, but he still remembered the Anglia and the flat above Albert's shop with a degree of affection. They had been accomplices in his bid for independence.

He drove through the town to the junction with Leeds Road. Inevitably, someone was digging up the road just before the crossroads, but the delay was only slight and he soon found himself on Leeds road.

In what seemed very little time, he was in Wellington Street and then Boar Lane, where Standish had his office, and he nosed in, looking for a parking meter. He was in luck, because a Jaguar was just pulling out. He waited and then stopped ahead of the parking place, ignoring the angry blast from behind him as he reversed into the kerbside. There was half-an-hour left on the meter, and that and George's sixpence gave him a reasonable degree of leeway.

He found the office easily enough; it was to the rear of an exclusive, bespoke shoe shop, and it had a side entrance in Viking Street. He pushed the door open and walked into a corridor with three offices. The door of the first was open, and a smartly-dressed woman with neat grey hair sat at her desk, behind an electric typewriter.

'Good morning,' he said, 'I'm a bit early, but Mr Standish is expecting me at half-past eleven. I'm George Barker.'

She smiled and nodded. 'Take a seat out there, Mr Barker. I'll tell him you're here.'

George followed her finger and found two wooden chairs in the corridor. He sat down, wondering if his visit would turn out to be a waste of time. He knew nothing about Miles Standish Management, and neither did anyone at the club, but that didn't mean an awful lot.

Presently, the door to the second office opened, and a young man came out, looking very unhappy. George heard Standish say, 'I'm sorry, lad, but I've got to be honest. Show business isn't for you. Put all your effort into delivering milk and you'll always know you're doing something worthwhile.'

With something between a sigh and a sob, the disillusioned dairyman went on his way.

Mr Standish came to the door. 'George, good morning to you!' He offered his hand. 'Come in, come in. That was unfortunate, but it's sometimes the kindest way, just to tell 'em.' He indicated a chair that stood beside a Broadwood upright piano. 'Take a seat.'

George sat and waited to be enlightened. So far, all he knew was that Standish was offering permanent employment.

As if reading George's thoughts, Standish said, 'I'll come straight to the point, George. I need an assistant, someone who

145

can share my workload. In the normal way of things, I'd probably have taken my son Nigel into the firm, but the entertainment industry isn't really his thing. In any case, he's happy enough with his advertising agency.'

'I've never done this kind of work, Mr Standish. I've no idea what's involved.'

'I'll guide your footsteps at first, George. One thing I already know is that you can tell good from bad, and that's not something you can be taught. Now, what are you earning at the present time?'

'Twenty-three pounds, ten shillings a week.'

'I see.' Standish thought for a minute and said, 'I'm offering you seventeen hundred a year.' He consulted a ready reckoner. 'That's thirty-two pounds, fourteen and fourpence a week before tax. That's for five-and-a-half days a week, nine 'til five-thirty.'

George blinked. It constituted a rise of more than nine pounds a week.

'Of course, you'll sometimes be required to work evenings, as I did on Wednesday, but you'll get time off for that in lieu.' He folded his arms and sat back. 'What do you think, George?'

'That's very tempting, Mr Standish. It's all a bit sudden, really.'

'Well, I don't expect an immediate decision.' He looked at the time and asked, 'Have you any plans for lunch?'

'I hadn't thought so far ahead, Mr Standish.'

'Miles.'

'Miles, right.'

'Let me buy you lunch while you're thinking about it.'

'Thank you, Miles. I'll probably need to feed the parking meter. It's not far away.'

'All right.' Miles reached for his hat. 'You can do that as we go.'

After a brief word with his secretary, Miles led George into Boar Lane, waited while he topped up the meter, and took him to a restaurant not far away.

The staff welcomed him as an old and valued customer. His attention was taken, however, by a smartly-dressed, elderly man seated at one of the tables. His hair was brushed back sleekly, and he had a prominent, Semitic nose. George thought he recognised him from somewhere.

'Ammy,' said Miles, 'allow me to introduce George Barker. I'm trying to persuade him to come and work for me.'

The waiter asked, 'Would you like your usual table, Mr Standish?'

'Yes, please, but first of all, we'll have a drink with Mr Ambrose. George, I've no doubt you've heard of Bert Ambrose.'

George became aware that he was staring, open-mouthed at a childhood hero, one of the great bandleaders of the golden age and known to musicians of the time as 'The Maestro'. 'I'm sorry, Mr Ambrose,' he said, offering his hand. 'I grew up playing your records.'

'George is a musician,' explained Miles.

'I'm flattered, George. What's your instrument?'

'Piano, really, but I play the organ for dancing and various things in a club.' In his excitement, he was stumbling over his words.

'I'm delighted to hear it. You know, it's unusual for a chap of your age to have heard the music we used to play.'

'My mother brought me up listening and dancing to it,' he said, adding self-consciously, 'and playing it, of course.'

The waiter set down a glass of red wine in front of Mr Ambrose.

'Thank you, Miles. I'm waiting for Kathy to join me. She's been in London, working on her new TV show, but I expected her to be here by now.'

'It's your lucky day, George,' said Miles. 'You've met Bert Ambrose, and now you're going to meet the famous singer Kathy Kirby.'

———— ►◄ ————

Back at Miles Standish Management, George accepted the coffee that Miles offered him.

'What a lunchtime meeting that was,' he said. 'Bert Ambrose and Kathy Kirby.'

'Non-stop excitement,' agreed Miles, 'but have you given any more thought to my offer?'

George had. 'Yes,' he said. 'When would you like me to start?'

147

3

To begin with, George spent most of his time shadowing Miles and learning the role of the agent. As Miles had pointed out, he had the fundamental ability to separate the no-hopers from those who might one day make a career in entertainment, but he had much to learn about the market and about the impresarios who wielded the power. Also, from time to time, his path crossed that of Bert Ambrose, and he listened with fascination to his reminiscences of bygone days.

He was as sad to leave the club as its members were to see him go, but he was enthusiastic about his new career. Increasingly, his new job was taking him away from the life he'd known in Cullington, and he was meeting new people all the time, although one face from the past gave him quite a jolt when he was shopping in Cullington's new supermarket.

He was checking the label on a tin of kidney beans when a voice beside him said, 'You look as if you're doing all right for yourself.'

Recognising the voice even without seeing the face, he said, 'Hello, Janet.'

'What are you doing with yourself these days?'

'I work for a booking agency in Leeds.'

'Oh. Too posh for Cullington now, are you?'

'How can you think that, Janet? As you can see, I make a point of doing my shopping here. Successful though I am, you see, I've never forgotten my roots.' He added, 'I still live here and pay my rates to Cullington Borough Council too.' He was about to bring the conversation to an end and move on, but it seemed that Janet hadn't finished with him.

'I hope you're pleased with yourself,' she said, 'treating Denise the way you did, and after she'd left Desmond for you.'

George wasn't prepared to argue, and especially about something that was none of Janet's concern. Instead, he said dismissively, 'Get out of the bath and get dressed, Janet.'

'What are you talking about?'

'Don't mind me. It's just a little fantasy of mine.'

For a moment, Janet was irate but speechless. Eventually, she said, 'You're disgusting.'

'I'd rather be disgusting,' he told her, 'than too nosey for my own good. As I told you when I left Wilkinson's, you need to start minding your own business.' He carried his basket to the checkout and unloaded it, leaving Janet to think of the retort she might have made if she'd only had the wit to think of it at the time.

A few weeks after his meeting with Janet, he called at the electricity showroom to pay his bill. Both assistants were busy with customers, but George had nothing else to do and he was content to wait. Eventually, the young man who had been helping a couple choose a washing machine came free and he looked enquiringly at George, who said, 'Thanks, but I'll look at these for a bit longer.' He returned his attention to a range of electric kettles and coffee makers, and waited until the young woman with dark hair and attractive brown eyes came free.

She smiled at him and asked, 'Can I help you?'

'Yes, please. I want to pay my bill.' He placed the bill with his cash on the counter.

'Certainly.' She performed a complex manoeuvre on the till and receipted George's bill, handing it to him with his change. 'Is there anything else I can help you with?'

'Yes, I'm looking for an electric coffee maker.'

'A percolator?'

'No, the drip kind, if you have one.'

'We have two. If you like to come this way, I'll show you.' She led him to the far end of the showroom, where he'd previously examined the kettles on display. 'Do you make a lot of coffee?'

'Not really,' he told her. 'I live on my own and I can only drink one cup at a time.'

'This one's good value,' she said, picking up the smaller one. Then, giving him a closer look, she asked, 'By the way, aren't you George Barker?'

'Yes.' He couldn't place her.

'You went out with my sister at one time.'

'Did I?'

'Jeanette Price,' she prompted. 'I'm Lorraine Price.' The resemblance was there. Lorraine wasn't as striking as her sister, but maybe she had other qualities. Remembering how vacuous Jeanette had proved to be, he hoped that was the case. Lorraine was certainly affable.

'I'm surprised you remember me,' he said. 'I only went out with Jeannette for a short time.'

'Don't worry about that,' she said. 'You're not the only one, but I remembered you because I came to the pantomime at the hospital,' she explained. 'That's how I recognised you.'

'Did you?'

'Yes, I really enjoyed it and I thought you were dead clever on the organ.'

'Thank you.' He decided to cash in on his newly-discovered popularity, but first he had to check a few things with her. He asked, 'Have you got a boyfriend?'

'Not at present.' She smiled self-consciously at his directness.

'Have you got your eye on anyone?'

'No.' Her expression changed to surprise.

'Is it your ambition to marry a successful doctor?'

'No,' she laughed, 'that's my sister you're thinking of, and she hasn't managed it yet.' Her tone suggested that she wasn't impressed with Jeanette's aspiration or her efforts.

'In that case, would you like to come out for a drink?'

'All right. When?'

'I suppose tonight's short notice?'

'I'm not doing anything else.' She was amused but still agreeable.

'Where do you live?'

'Mountfield Gardens. Number seventeen. Do you know it?'

'I'll find it. I'll pick you up at seven if that's okay.'

'Fine.'

'And I'll take the coffee maker as well.'

——◆� ◆——

Lorraine sank into the leather-covered passenger seat and gasped. 'This is a lovely car, George.' She ran her fingers over the dashboard and asked, 'Is it wood?'

'Yes, walnut veneer. I'm glad you like it.' Briefly, he remembered Jeanette's reaction when she saw the Ford Anglia for the first time, and then dismissed her from his mind. Her place was in the past, and there she must stay. His current interest was Lorraine, and she looked particularly fetching in a knee-length, wine-red dress.

'Where are we going?'

'I thought we'd go to the Bay Horse in Hindcliffe.'

'Posh.'

'Well, I tried picturing you surrounded by sawdust, spittoons and coarse characters, but it didn't seem to work.'

'I should hope not.' She continued to examine the interior of the car, and asked, 'What do you do for a living?'

'I work in artist management. How's your tap dancing?'

'I can't do that.'

'Singing?'

'I can't do that, either.'

'Conjuring tricks?'

She shook her head. 'No. I'd like to make some of our consumers disappear sometimes, but I haven't succeeded yet.'

'Can you tell jokes or juggle plates?'

''Fraid not. Are you disappointed?'

'No, I'm relieved. It means I can take a night off from talent spotting.'

She gave him an open smile and said, 'You're daft, George, but you're nice with it.' Settling back in the comfort of her seat, she said, 'It's good to be in friendly company.'

It seemed an odd thing to say. He felt he had to ask, 'Is that such a luxury?'

'I was exaggerating, really. When you arrived, I'd just had words with my mum and dad. It happens a lot.' She paused briefly and said, 'I'd move out if I could afford to.'

'How old are you, Lorraine?'

'Twenty-one. I'm old enough to do as I like, but it's the cost, as I said.'

'I had a flat until last month that cost me two quid a week plus electricity. It was above the greengrocer's in Cheapside.'

'Two quid?' It was as if he'd opened up a whole new existence.

'The only problem was that it got very cold last winter, but, to be fair, it was a particularly cold winter. If you're interested, I could speak to Albert, the owner.'

'Would you?' Then, with less excitement in her voice, she said, 'I suppose it would be to furnish.'

'No, it's furnished.'

'That's too good to be true.'

'I thought that when I took the place on.' He told her how he'd escaped from an unhappy home life, and how things had come quickly together. 'It was about the time I was going out with Jeanette,' he said, turning into the carpark of the Bay Horse.

'Everyone remembers going out with Jeanette,' she remarked pointedly.

'I only remember it because it was a mistake.' He switched off the engine and opened his door. 'She wasn't right for me, and I certainly wasn't what she was looking for. You mustn't feel you're in her shadow.'

'I don't, really.' She got out and waited for him before going on. 'It's just that she always leaves an impression.'

'I shouldn't say this to her sister, but the impression she leaves isn't always a good one.'

'Oh, I realise that.' She followed him to the entrance. 'You know,

I've never been here before.'

'Friendly company, the possibility of a flat, and a new experience as well. What else could you wish for?'

'Those three things will do for a start.'

'Let's find a table.' There was a free one far enough away from the bar to be reasonably quiet. 'You grab that table,' he suggested, 'and I'll get the drinks. What would you like?'

'A half of lager and lime, please.'

George went to the bar and returned a few minutes later with a lager and lime and a whisky and soda.

Lorraine asked, 'Do you like football?'

'No, my game's cricket.'

She wrinkled her nose and said, 'I can't take a game seriously that can go on for five days and still not end in a result.'

'County cricket's only three days long,' he pointed out.

'That's almost as bad. No, give me football every time. An hour-and-a-half plus stoppages, and the match is decided.'

'Which team?'

'Huddersfield Town.' Her tone suggested that it should have been obvious. She surprised him then, by referring, completely without warning, to an earlier conversation. 'The argument was about Jeanette,' she said.

'Which argument was that?'

'The one I was having with my mum and dad when you arrived. It happens often.' It was evident that it had also been at the back of Lorraine's mind.

'Arguments about Jeanette?'

'Yes, you see I still haven't accepted the fact that Jeanette is perfect, and absolutely nobody is allowed to criticise her.'

George hadn't come out with the intention of discussing Jeanette, but it was clear that Lorraine had feelings she needed to vent, so he waited for her to go on.

'As I told you before, you're not the only one who only went out with her for a few weeks. It's the normal state of affairs with her. Mind you, the official reason is that it's because the poor girl still hasn't found her perfect man. It couldn't possibly be because it takes them just so long to realise how boring she is, and then, when things begin to go downhill, she decides she's on to a loser and shows them the door.'

'You don't have to convince me, Lorraine. I learned my lesson some time ago.'

'I know you did.'

'Okay. You needed to get it off your chest. That's fair enough.'

'I'm sorry.'

'There's no need to be sorry.' He patted her arm to reassure her. 'Have you any other brothers or sisters?'

'Just a brother. He's only twelve, being an afterthought, but he gets caught up in it as well.'

'Poor lad.'

'Yes.' Lorraine eyed him speculatively and asked, 'Do you get to meet famous people in your job?'

'Not usually. We're at the little-known end of the market, but time will tell.' He suddenly remembered something. 'Actually,' he said, 'I have met Bert Ambrose, the great bandleader.' He added, 'He's an agent nowadays.'

Lorraine frowned. 'I've never heard of him,' she said.

'I met Kathy Kirby at the same time.'

'Kathy Kirby?' Not surprisingly, Lorraine had heard of her. 'Did you really? What's she like?'

'Very nice. She's friendly and easy to chat with.'

'I wish I'd been there.' The movement of her eyes suggested that, exciting though a meeting with a famous singer might be, another abrupt change of subject was on its way. It seemed to be a feature of her personality. 'Kelly Anders wears those tights things,' she announced. 'They must cost her a fortune, but I suppose she's not without a bob or two.'

George could only imagine that Kelly Anders was a pop singer who had so far escaped his notice. 'Are they expensive?' He knew that show dancers wore tights for the sake of decorum, but that was all he knew.

'More expensive than stockings,' she confirmed. 'She wears them because she doesn't like sitting on suspenders, although it beats me why she doesn't fasten the side suspender to the side of her stocking, like most people, instead of the back. Still, it takes all kinds, doesn't it?'

George silently agreed, coping as he was with the mental image of Lorraine in her lingerie. He broke the tension by asking, 'Are you ready for another drink?'

'Mm, please.'

Going to the bar gave him an opportunity to take stock of the situation. So far, he and Lorraine seemed to have little in common, and George was reminded of his conversation with David after the episode with Jeanette. Unlike her sister, however, Lorraine was fun, and that was very much in her favour.

The evening ended, as first dates so often did, with a peck on the cheek and a vague hint of more exciting things to come. George arranged to phone her at work when he'd spoken to Albert about the flat.

4

George listened to a man, possibly in his late thirties, earnestly singing 'Portrait of My Love'. He had a reasonably good voice but little else, and the verdict would inevitably come as a disappointment.

At the end, the man said, 'Of course, it would sound better with a microphone and an orchestral backing.'

George nodded. 'Those things always help.' He wondered how he could soften the blow, and realised that there was no way he could. 'The best I could offer you, Michael,' he said, 'would be to introduce you to the club circuit.'

'I've done club work.' He sounded dismissive, as if he felt he'd graduated from that kind of thing long since.

'It's your best bet,' George told him, 'and even then, you'll find that crooners and ballad singers are no longer as popular as they were. They'll be around for some time yet, but I'm afraid rock and roll is going to sweep all other popular forms aside.'

'You don't understand,' the man pleaded. 'Singing's what I've always wanted to do. I've worked all my life for it, and I just need a break.'

'I do understand and I sympathise, but all the ambition in the world isn't going to make you into a better singer than you are. If you're sensible, you'll take what club work comes along until they're no longer booking ballad singers, and then at least you'll have achieved something.' On a more helpful note, he said, 'Also, if you'll take a tip from me, don't rush into a cover of a song that's been a recent success for a well-known singer, because you'll suffer from the comparison.'

'My girlfriend says that if she closes her eyes when I'm singing, she can imagine it's Matt Monro.'

'That's a very nice thing for her to say, Michael, but not everyone can hear what she hears, basically because none of them is your girlfriend.'

The unfortunate man seemed lost for words, until desperation turned to anger. 'What do you know about it, anyway? You can't have been long out of school. You certainly don't know quality when you hear it.'

'I do, and I've tried to be helpful, but I'm going to have to ask you to leave, because there's nothing more to be said.'

'I'll bloody leave all right. This isn't the only agency in Leeds. I'll go somewhere where they know what they're talking about.'

'You've every right to do that, Michael. Good luck.' He braced himself as the unsuccessful crooner slammed the door behind him. It was unfortunate but inevitable that there was more mediocrity than quality out there. He picked up the phone and dialled the number of the electricity showroom. It was answered promptly.

'Yorkshire Electricity Board Showroom, Cullington. Good morning. Can I help you?'

'Oh, I think so. I'd like to speak to Lorraine, please.'

'This is Lorraine speaking. Is that George?'

'Yes, you sound different when you've got your shawl and clogs on.'

'Well, I thought you were a consumer. I was talking with my business voice.'

'Is that what you call it? Listen, I've spoken to Albert. The flat's still empty, and he says you can have it for two pounds ten a week plus electricity if you want it. It's a bob-in-the-slot meter.'

'A prepayment meter? Fine. Does he really? When can I go round and look at it?' Her excitement was evident from the confusion of sentences.

'Any time when the shop's open. You could go round in your lunch break if you like. I'll give you my number here so that you can let me know how you get on.'

'Just a sec.' There was silence while she found something to write on. 'Okay, what's your number?'

He gave her the firm's telephone number.

'Thanks, George. I mean thanks a bundle! There's a big kiss coming through the phone line. *Mwa!* I'll call you later.'

———◆►◄———

Lorraine phoned at a little after two o' clock, still excited but fairly coherent. 'I've arranged to take the flat,' she said. 'He didn't want a bond, either. He said that any friend of yours is okay with him.'

'Albert's a good lad. When are you going to move in?'

'On Sunday. I've a lot of stuff to move, so it'll take a few trips.'

Then a new thought occurred to her. 'You wouldn't mind helping me, would you? I mean, you could get a lot of stuff inside your car.'

'I suppose I could.' He was quite taken aback by her directness. 'What time to want me to come over on Sunday?'

'Is ten o' clock all right?'

'Yes, I can manage that. I'll see you then.'

She phoned again half-an-hour later.

'Sorry to bother you, George.'

'It's okay. I've no one with me.'

'Oh, good. I just wanted to warn you that my mum and dad might be in a stroppy mood on Sunday when you come over.'

'Don't worry, Lorraine. I've dealt with fathers with shotguns and mothers with garden shears. I'll be okay.'

'I hope so. *Mwa!*'

'*Mwa* to you too.' He felt silly saying it, but the real thing would no doubt make up for it.

———◆►◄———

After a busy week at the agency, it was good to have some free time at the weekend, and George called at Lorraine's house on Sunday, rested and ready for the move. He rang the doorbell, and the door opened to reveal a peevish-looking man, who said abruptly, 'Yes?'

'Barker's Removals.'

'What?' The man peered into the road and, seeing no removal van, asked, 'What do you mean?'

'I've come to help Lorraine move her stuff.'

Realisation dawned. 'So you're the chap she's going out with, are you?'

'Yes. Don't be fooled by the old clothes. I usually wear a suit and polished shoes and I drink tea out of a china cup without slurping.'

'Well,' said Mr Price, 'you look to be an improvement on the last one, anyway.' He inclined his head towards the stairs and said, 'She's up there, getting her stuff together.'

'Do you mind if I go up and give her a hand? She'll need me to carry her cases downstairs.'

He shrugged. 'If you want to. I'm having nowt to do with this nonsense.'

'I got that impression.' George climbed the stairs, wondering if he might find Lorraine's mother in a similarly uncooperative mood, but the first person he encountered was Lorraine. She looked harassed and close to tears.

'Thanks for coming, George,' she said. 'The miserable old bugger wouldn't even carry these cases downstairs for me.'

'That's why I'm here. Cheer up.' He gave her a friendly kiss on the cheek. 'I'll take these two first. Stay there and leave them to me.' He carried the two suitcases downstairs and up the path to his car. They fitted in the boot perfectly, so he returned for the rest of her things, wondering, not for the first time, why women always needed so much luggage.

'There's this case and two cardboard boxes,' she told him.

'I'll take the case and come back for the boxes.' He set off again, watched by Mr Price and probably Mrs Price, who had appeared at the bottom of the stairs. He bade her a cheery 'Good morning', although they hadn't been introduced and were unlikely to be if present form continued.

Finally, and with her goods packed into George's car, Lorraine took her leave of her parents with no outward sign of affection. If George had ever entertained any doubts, he was now convinced that she was doing the right thing.

They'd been on the road only a few minutes when she said, 'I had to pack my sleeping bag. I've no sheets or anything.'

George thought it was a rotten shame, but he said nothing.

'Have you any spare sheets and things, George?'

'Yes, as it happens.' Surprised again, he indicated right and made the turn.

'Where are we going?'

'To my flat. It's where I keep my bedding.'

He pulled up outside the flat. 'I shan't be a minute.' He let himself into the flat and returned with two sheets, two blankets, pillows and pillowcases. 'There,' he said, piling them in the back. 'They're from my spare bedroom. They'll tide you over until you get organised.'

'Oh George, I feel guilty now.'

'You're not the one who should feel bad, Lorraine. Anyway, friends help each other, don't they?'

'Yes, more than bloody relations do, sometimes.'

When they arrived at the flat, George carried everything upstairs while Lorraine set about unpacking. When she was finished, she looked in the direction of the sink and cooker, and sighed hopelessly. 'You've done all this for me, and now I can't even give you a cup of tea,' she said.

'Why not?'

'I haven't got any tea or milk. I was in such a hurry to move, I didn't think about those things.'

'I'll tell you what. If you make sure the kettle and teapot and mugs are clean, I'll nip out and get some bits and pieces.'

'Where?'

'The Indian shop on the corner. You'll find it's very handy.'

He walked down the street to the shop, exchanged greetings with Mr Patel, and returned with tea, coffee, sugar, milk, biscuits, butter and bread.

'There,' he said, turning out the contents of the bag, 'you can even have toast for breakfast tomorrow.'

'I'm hopeless,' she said, 'and you're lovely, doing all this.' She held out her arms in a gesture of wonder at the humble collection of groceries on the table.

'Are you all right for soap, toothpaste, shampoo and all those things?'

'Yes, I packed those things. I suppose I'm not completely useless.'

'You might struggle a bit in that bathroom,' he said thoughtfully.

'Yes.' Now that the initial embarrassment was gone, she was able to show interest in other things. 'How did you manage in that microscopic bath?'

'It's easier for me to take you through the process than to describe it. Take your clothes off and I'll demonstrate.'

'What?' Realising it was a leg-pull, she smiled and wrapped her arms round him. 'If you could manage in that bath, I'm sure I can.'

'Yes, the problem will be when we get into it together.'

'I can never tell when you're joking,' she said, looking confused.

'Who said anything about joking? After all that heaving and unpacking, I daresay we're both ready for a bath.'

'Will you settle for a kiss just for now?'

'I suppose so. It's not guaranteed to get both of us clean all over, but it's worth a try.'

They kissed properly for the first time, and Lorraine emerged after a while, breathless and faintly embarrassed.

'I'm not the sort to rush into things,' she confided. 'I thought I'd better let you know.'

'I'll bear that in mind.' Looking suitably solemn, he said, 'We are going to have that bath together, aren't we? I've been looking forward to it, but if you don't want to rush into it, I'm happy to wait ten minutes or so.'

'Be serious for once. I told you that because I thought you should know, and then you're not making plans and being disappointed.'

'I appreciate that, I really do, and if anything does develop, it'll be when you're on the starting blocks and not before.'

'Thanks, George.' She kissed him again to seal the contract.

'Mind you, there is one thing I'd really like, but that's only if you can see your way to it.'

'What is it?' She eyed him doubtfully.

'I'd really like that cup of tea you were talking about. I'm absolutely parched.'

Relieved, she said, 'Of course. Tea or coffee?'

'After hard, manual labour, it has to be tea.'

'Okay.' She took the things over to the cooker and filled the kettle.

'While you're doing that, let me give you the itiner-whatsit for the rest of the day.'

'Have you planned it?'

'I plan everything. Listen, when the pubs have been open for a bit, I'll take you for a drink and a snack. Then, I'll go back to my place to wallow in my full-size bath and change into something civilised, and then I'm going to take you to dinner to celebrate your new flat. How does that sound?'

'To be honest, I don't usually like it when someone else organises me. I prefer to do it myself, but today's different, and it sounds as if you're going to spoil me to death. I still don't believe all this is real. I think I'm going to wake up in my old room, with all the problems that went with it.'

'No, you're not,' he said, putting his arms round her. 'Your new life starts here, just as mine did.'

'Did you have problems like mine, I mean with your mum and dad?'

'No.' He let her pour the tea and accepted his, appropriately in one of the original mugs, before going on. 'My mum was great, but she died seven years ago, and I found out recently that my real dad was killed early in the war.'

'Oh, no.' She left her chair and joined him on the sofa, ready to dispense sympathy and comfort.

'The problem for my sister and me was our stepdad.' He went on to tell her about the arguments that had led to his moving out.

'It's incredible,' she said, 'how parents can get it so wrong.'

'Some make a good job of it.'

She nodded her agreement. 'They should give lessons to the dunces.' After considering that possibility, she asked, 'What's your sister like?'

'Norma's great. We've always got on well together. She was a staff nurse on the Children's Ward, but she's at a hospital in Manchester now, and she's married to a doctor. He's a good hand too.'

'She managed it, then.'

'Yes, but it happened quite naturally. They'd known each other for four years or more when they got engaged.'

That made her smile. She said, 'Jeanette's been trying to find the ideal man since she started her training. She'll get desperate soon, and throw herself at the first medical student that comes her way.'

George still had difficulty in fathoming the workings of Jeanette's mind. 'What's so marvellous about being married to a doctor? Hospital doctors have to work long hours, and they're usually on call in the middle of the night.' He heard about it often from Norma.

Jeanette doesn't think about the details. She just thinks it'll help her up the social ladder.' She frowned suddenly. 'Anyway,' she asked, 'why are we talking about her?'

'You mentioned her first. I was only being polite.'

'You are polite, George. I'm just beginning to discover that you're all kinds of things I like.'

'So, if anybody mentions my criminal past, I hope you won't be too disappointed.'

'You're daft as well.'

'Good. Let's go to the pub and get something to eat.'

5

By day and occasionally by night, George was learning the agency business, whilst in his spare time he was learning a great deal about Lorraine. He'd already noticed, in conversation, the way she could change the subject with absolutely no warning, and soon, he discovered that, whilst reluctant to rush into things, she was quite determined when she made up her mind on a course of action, and as she'd already told him, she liked to take control. It was a trait she demonstrated three weeks after moving into the flat. It was a Saturday night, and they'd been out for a drink.

He asked, 'Your place or mine for coffee?'

Without hesitation, she said, 'Yours, definitely.'

'Fine, if that's what you want.'

'You have a proper coffee maker,' she reminded him.

He was happy to do it that way. It would be no trouble to run her home afterwards, so he drove her back to his flat.

He made coffee, and they sat together, talking about nothing of any importance. Inevitably, they were soon in each other's arms, a situation that George found pleasing and frustrating, roughly in equal measures, but he'd kept his word and would continue to do so for as long as Lorraine remained disinclined or even hesitant to cross the threshold of innocence.

After some time, she surprised him by saying, 'I'd like to stay the night, if that's okay.'

'You're always welcome. There's just one tiny hitch.'

'What's that?'

'The bedding from the spare room is all at your flat.'

164

She was unperturbed. 'I meant with you in your bed.' she explained.

Suddenly, the evening had taken an upward turn. He asked, 'Have you had a change of heart?'

'Mm, I said I didn't rush into things, but we've been going out together for three weeks now.'

'Long enough,' he concluded. Only one question remained. 'By the way,' he asked, 'are you a virgin?'

'No.' She looked at him uncertainly. 'No, I'm not. Are you disappointed?'

'Disappointed? No, I'm relieved. It means I don't have to spend time teaching you the theory, and then taking you step by step through the process.'

'You're daft, George.'

'I know. Everybody tells me that.'

'By the way,' she said, standing up, 'there's no need for you to use a whatsit.'

'A whatsit?'

'You know, a contraceptive. I'm fully equipped.'

George considered the news. 'That's how the estate agent described my kitchen,' he said. 'I imagine you're not talking about plumbing.'

'It's a kind of plumbing,' she said, following him to the bedroom. 'I went to the Family Planning Clinic and told them I was getting engaged, and I wanted to be prepared for the great experience.'

'What did they say?'

'The woman I saw told me not to build up on it, because the experience is never all that great. She said it was an overrated pastime, but she gave me a thingy and showed me how to fit it. I need to use your bathroom for that.'

'Be my guest.' He imagined the 'thingy' to be the kind of thing Denise had used.

While Lorraine busied herself in the bathroom, he checked that his bedroom was tidy. Lorraine wasn't exactly house proud, but that was no reason why he should let his standards slip, and he wanted everything to be right.

With the covers straight and the pillows plumped up to his satisfaction, he waited for Lorraine to join him.

When she appeared, she sat on the bed and began unfastening her stockings, breaking off to say, 'Don't stare at me when I'm undressing.'

'Sorry.' He turned away and hid his eyes.

'Aren't you going to take your clothes off as well?'

'Only if you promise not to stare.'

'There's no need to be sarcastic.' There was a swishing sound, and she asked, 'Where can I put my dress?'

'I'll get you a hanger.' He opened the wardrobe and found one, handing it to her with one hand whilst covering his eyes with his other.

'You're allowed to look at me,' she told him impatiently. 'Just don't stare.'

He parted his fingers to peep and saw that she was down to her bra, pants and suspender belt. He proceeded to undress.

'I've only ever done it twice,' she said, as he joined her. 'Like the woman at the clinic said, it wasn't all that great, but I thought, with you being so nice, you'd probably make it nicer. Do you know what I mean?'

'You expect a lot.' As he kissed her, his hand moved to one breast, which was firm and pleasing. It was a fleeting impression, however, because she caught his hand and returned it to him.

'Don't do that,' she said.

'Sorry.' Moving downward, he asked, 'Did you manage to fix the thingy?'

'The what?'

'The plumbing they gave you at the clinic.'

'Yes, it's *inside*.' She enunciated the word carefully, as if it were something precious, to be revered, and George thought that was quite appropriate.

Again, however, the sensation was short-lived, and he felt his hand being grasped and moved to a neutral corner. 'Don't tickle,' she chided.

'Sorry.' It was evident that some clarification was needed. 'Lorraine?'

'Mm?'

'Which parts of your body am I allowed to touch?'

'Don't touch anything with your hands. Just lie there and cuddle.'

'Will you tell me when the moment comes? I'd hate to miss it and cause offence.'

'Are you being sarcastic again?'

'In a gentle sort of way,' he admitted, 'but it's your body when all's said and done, and it's up to you what happens to it.'

'I've never liked the bike shed business, all that groping and fiddling around.' Having stated her repugnance, she asked. 'Have I put you off?'

'Only temporarily, I hope. It should be okay when the time comes.'

Happily, it was, although George found that the experience lacked a great deal.

Strangely, however, Lorraine's impression was of a different and contrasting kind.

'George,' she said, 'I knew it would be better with you.'

'Did you?'

'I never realised it was possible to... you know,' she whispered, '*come more than once.*'

'Didn't you?' Disillusionment and the lateness of the hour had overtaken him, and he was vaguely aware that she was speaking again, but sleep beckoned more invitingly.

----◆I◆----

In the relaxed drowsiness of waking, Lorraine initiated matters again, confirming for herself eventually that George had taken sex to a higher and more rewarding level than she'd previously known. It was true, as she pointed out at breakfast, that she wasn't particularly experienced, but the revelation of the previous night and that morning was no less dramatic for that. She was so taken by the experience that it was some time before she realised that George had so far had little to say, and his reticence on the subject prompted her to ask, 'What's the matter, George? Have I said something that's upset you?'

'You haven't upset me.'

'You didn't enjoy it, did you?' It was almost an accusation made in total disbelief.

'It was okay.'

'Only okay?'

'Remember what the woman at the clinic told you.'

'That was rubbish. What's this about? Do I turn you off, all of a sudden?'

'No, you don't. You're pretty and you have a lovely figure. It's all there, but you just expect it all to happen like a bolt out of the blue, and that doesn't work for me.'

'But it was great last night and this morning. What was wrong with it for you?'

'It just doesn't work for both of us.'

'Rubbish! There was nothing wrong with it.'

'If you insist.'

Clearly exasperated, she said, 'I still can't see what you're driving at.'

'All right. Let's just accept that what's good for you doesn't work for me. You and I are....' He remembered the word he needed. 'We're not entirely compatible, at least where sex is concerned.' He decided to be completely open with her. 'Also, the fact that you need to be in control of everything makes it all very one-sided.'

'Look, if you're working up to finishing with me, you're going a funny way about it. You might as well come straight out with it now. Have you found somebody else?'

For a moment, he was tempted to invent a conveniently fictitious third party, but he opted for the truth. 'No,' he said, 'there's no one else, but this business has caused the kind of upset that's basically impossible to undo, so it's probably the best thing if we split up, anyway.'

———◄►———

She refused his offer of a lift home, preferring to walk, and pointing out waspishly that it was something she knew she could get right. For his part, George remained as patient as he could be. He told her she could return his bed linen in her own time.

He thought it sensible to pay future electricity bills by post, thereby avoiding unpleasantness at the showroom.

He saw neither her nor his bed linen again.

6

MAY 1965

George had enjoyed his 'luxury' flat in Cullington, but he had no wish to live in rented accommodation longer than he had to, so as soon as he was able to demonstrate to the building society that he'd been employed for the requisite length of time, he bought a small house in Fearnley, just twenty minutes' drive from the office. With half the purchase price in the bank, he encountered no difficulty securing a modest mortgage.

He now spent very little time in Cullington, going there only to see old friends, who included his erstwhile neighbours, the Young family. Sandra was still at the ice cream factory, and still complaining because she wasn't allowed to sample the product. George saw little of his stepfather and Elsie on his visits, and he'd long since stopped feeling guilty about that, as they seemed to be driven by their jealousy of his success.

His Wolsley had also served him well, but the time came for him to buy something newer, and he now had a Singer Gazelle. Friends ribbed him about his old-fashioned tastes, reminding him that most young men in his position ran sports cars, but George wasn't prepared to sacrifice comfort for speed, especially when he spent so little time on roads made for fast driving.

At the agency, he'd built up a successful clientele, and Miles had rewarded him generously for his efforts.

One source of annoyance for George was that Nigel Fox called occasionally at the office to see Miles, and when he did, he seemed more interested in the work of the agency than in his father's welfare. George found him impossible to like, and found his presence intrusive. Physically, as well as personally, he was completely different from Miles, who nevertheless welcomed him and tolerated his meddling behaviour.

Away from the office, life was good for George, who had a new girlfriend. He'd met Rachel at a party given by a client, a magician and illusionist, who worked under the name 'Leger de Main', and he found her immediately attractive, with the kind of dark looks and appealing eyes that reminded him, at least physically, of Lorraine. Happily, she shared none of Lorraine's characteristics. It had become his habit to check a new girlfriend's credentials before asking her out, and he was more than happy with Rachel's. He remembered particularly his initial conversation with her. He'd just helped her avoid the crush in the crowded room, by getting her a drink.

'Thank you,' she said. 'You're very kind.' It was then that he'd really noticed her deep, brown eyes.

'I'm George Barker,' he told her, 'Roger's agent.'

'Whose agent?'

'Leger's. His real name's Roger Morley.'

'Good grief. I thought I'd come to the wrong party. I'm Rachel Ronaldson, by the way. A friend of a friend.'

'How marvellous,' he said. 'Your initials purr.'

'No one's ever told me that.'

'I'm surprised. Are you seeing anyone currently?'

The question made her smile. 'No one in particular.'

'Do you favour sex without foreplay?'

Her smile disappeared. 'As a strictly brought-up Catholic,' she said, 'I have to say that I don't know what you mean. However, as a free-thinking human being, I couldn't even contemplate sex without foreplay. It would be like an opera without an overture.'

'*La Bohème* hasn't got an overture,' he pointed out.

'It's a very passionate opera. I think we can excuse it for being in a hurry.'

'I can see we agree about the important things. Would you consider joining me for dinner one evening soon?'

Her smile reappeared. 'Which evening do you have in mind?'

'Next week. Pick an evening, any evening. This is a conjuror's party, after all.'

'Tuesday. Let me give you my address.'

It was at that moment that the idyll began.

———◆◄◆———

They saw each other three times in the next two weeks. The third time, they went back to George's house.

'You make excellent coffee,' she said.

'Thank you, but the difference is in the buying rather than the making.'

'You're very modest. A lot of men would have claimed they had a secret method or something equally bogus.'

'I've never been able to do that. Honesty has been my downfall on occasions, but I'm not going to change now.'

'I should hope not.' She made herself more comfortable on the sofa and asked, 'How did you come to be an agent, George?'

'Quite by chance. I was playing the organ in a club, and Miles, my boss, came one night to watch a new turn, and he invited me to his office and offered me a job.'

'I'm sure there was more to it than that. He must have recognised potential.'

George's natural modesty asserted itself. He said, 'It's possible, I suppose. He's very perceptive.'

'Do you enjoy working for him?' Considering Rachel was employed in her father's business and must lead an interesting life, she seemed more interested in George's.

'Very much. It's funny, you know. He looks like a wide boy, but he's as straight as a die. He keeps talking about retiring, but I hope he's going to stay around for a while. His son, Nigel, is forever hovering around, and I suspect he'll eventually take over the running of the agency.'

'Doesn't the prospect appeal to you?'

'Not really. It's more an impression than anything concrete, but if he took up acting, he could give a fair portrayal of Daniel Quilp.'

She smiled grimly at the description and asked, 'Do you do a lot of reading?'

'More than I should.'

'How can you say that?'

'It takes up so much of my time and makes me feel guilty and self-indulgent.'

'Enjoy it, George. That's why it's there. Far too many people are put off reading when they're at school and they have to do it as a discipline, but you apparently don't have that impediment.'

'I didn't go to that kind of school,' he confided. 'They just encouraged us to enjoy reading.'

'Good for them.' Reverting to a previous topic, she asked, 'How did you come to be playing at the club?'

'It was my job. I'd worked in an accounts office, but it wasn't for me, and I wasn't qualified to do anything else.'

'Nothing at all?'

'Oh, I tell a lie.' He'd almost forgotten about the diploma. 'I have a diploma in music,' he said. 'I'm a Licentiate of the Guildhall School of Music, believe it or not.'

'I knew there was more to you than met the eye.'

'Do you really think so?'

'I do, although what really matters to me is that you're obviously a very nice man.' She had a look in her eye that was sending him signals, so he drew her gently towards him. They were evidently the right signals, because she joined him readily in a long, searching kiss.

After a while, he asked, 'Shall we go upstairs?'

She nodded silently and followed him, stopping on the landing. She asked, 'Where's the bathroom?'

'There.' He pointed to the first door on the right before switching on the light in the bedroom.

She joined him after a short time. 'Just making things safe,' she said reassuringly. She allowed him to take her in his arms again in a kiss of exquisite delay, before sitting on the bed to take off her shoes and release her stockings, which she draped carefully over the back of a chair.

George took her dress and arranged it neatly on a hanger.

'You're a wonder, George.'

'I'm told I live in an ideal world. Whether it's true or not, I like things to be as good as I can make them.' Then, realising he might have inadvertently set up an expectation, he said, 'We'd better both keep our fingers crossed now.'

He finished undressing and joined her in another prolonged kiss.

'When we met,' she said eventually, 'you asked me something about foreplay. What was it again?'

'I asked you if you preferred sex without it, and you gave me the answer I wanted.' He explained between repeated kisses, 'I knew... someone once, who... was strongly opposed... to it, but that was... a long time ago.' He returned his attention to Rachel's generous breasts. There was the possibility they would possibly prove cumbersome in later life, but for now, he was concerned only with the present and the glories it bestowed. Meanwhile, beneath the covers, Rachel was making her own introductions.

Presently, they joined each other in the ultimate coalescence, and at least for the moment, the world seemed ideal.

———— ►◄ ————

Later, they lay together in the darkness, talking.

He asked, 'Am I right in thinking that Catholics don't practise contraception?'

'This one does,' she assured him. 'Actually, it's something of a grey area nowadays, for married couples. Some priests are quite pragmatic about it, although none of them condones sex outside marriage.'

'So, you're living on the fringe, as they say.'

She turned her head to whisper theatrically, 'Let's just say I'm not as devout as my father would like me to be.'

After a spell, she asked, 'What are you, George? Such is my lack of interest in sectarian matters, I never did ask you, but now that the subject has come up, do tell.'

'Lapsed C of E. Due to my mother's influence, I joined the church and was confirmed, but since her death, I've drifted away.'

'I'm sorry, George.' She kissed him softly out of sympathy.

'As for my stepfather, he's officially a Methodist, but in reality, he's a godless bastard.'

She laughed. 'He's not your favourite person, then.' Becoming almost serious, she said, 'Simply being a protestant would make him a godless bastard in my father's eyes.'

'Really?' George was genuinely surprised. 'I thought we'd come a long way since the Spanish Inquisition.'

'Not at my father's house,' she assured him. Then, encircling him with her long legs, she said, 'That's enough talk about man-made taboos. I don't know how we got on to the subject in the first place. Let's do something that comes naturally.' She kissed him temptingly.

'Okay, you've persuaded me.'

They repeated the experience with occasional variations that only served to enhance something they'd believed incapable of improvement, and George was conscious of a completeness that had been absent from his life for more than three years.

7

In June, George took a week of his annual holiday to look up old friends. First, he called on Mr Handley, who was teaching. His old teacher ushered him to an armchair.

'I'll be free in ten minutes,' he told George.

For the remainder of the lesson, George listened to a very creditable attempt at the Clementi sonata that Carol had attempted after the pantomime.

'She's only been working on it a couple of weeks,' Mr Handley told him after the girl had left. 'She's very keen.'

'I was more impressed with her than I was with the daughter of the woman who married my stepfather,' said George. 'When she played it, I thought her right foot was paralysed.

'Oh, dear.' Mr Handley chuckled. 'When you referred to her in that way, it sounded like "The House that Jack Built".'

'I know. I can't think of a better way to describe her, without being rude, anyway.'

'Wasn't she the one who wanted your piano?'

'That's right, although the mischief-maker behind that was her mother.'

Mr Handley shook his head at the memory of it. 'You went through a rotten time, George. I'm glad things have looked up for you.'

'Thanks, Mr Handley. They really have.'

As one memory led to another, Mr Handley said, 'Tell me, how is Norma these days? I was rather fond of her, even though I saw less of her than I did of you.'

'She's married now, and living in Manchester. Her husband's a registrar at the hospital. As a matter of fact, I'm going over to visit them later in the week.'

'Good for you, George. Please give them my regards. I don't know your brother-in-law, of course, but I wish him well.'

'Thank you, Mr Handley.'

'Now, George,' said his host, 'what is it like, handling all those people, when, let's be frank, not all the music of today appeals to you?'

George had no need to think about his answer, because he'd been asking himself the same question. He said, 'People are talking nowadays about the "music business", and that's what it is, a business. It's the reason why some people in the world of pop music are becoming rich, and I have to admit that, in a small way, we are a party to that. There's still variety out there, but the writing is on the wall, and there'll come a time when the only pop music that gets recorded will be the kind that sells. Even the demand for it is being manipulated at a very high level.'

'Yes, but how do you cope with that?'

'I'm coming to that, Mr Handley. When I audition a new turn, I ask myself two questions. Is it good enough by its own lights, and can I promote it? It doesn't matter to me if it's lead, rhythm and bass guitars making what for me is an infernal row with drums in fierce competition. If the group does it in a way that audiences accept and it's therefore the kind of thing I can sell, I'll give it a chance. Then, at the day's end, I'll go home and listen to Walther Gieseking playing Ravel, or Colin Davis conducting the LSO. I might even play the piano myself. It'll remind me that there are still people who can read dots, interpret and perform music for the joy of reproducing something that's beautiful, rather than simply lucrative.'

Mr Handley nodded. 'I think that's a fair answer,' he said. 'You haven't sold your soul, as I feared at one time. I think you've found the right balance, George.'

———— ►◄ ————

His next visit was to the Young household, stopping en route to buy four ounces of dolly mixtures before the shops closed.

As usual, Mr Young was at work; he was a maintenance electrician and he worked long shifts, but Mrs Young was pleased to see him. Sandra, as ever, was overjoyed.

With the ritual chin-kiss accomplished, she proceeded to tell him off for his absence.

'I've been worried to death about you, George,' she said. 'Five years, and not a word from you. I'd given you up for dead.' Sandra made a habit of picking up words and phrases and using them, although not always appropriately.

'I hope not, Sandra. I came to see you six months ago.'

'Well, it were a long time.' Eyeing each of his pockets in turn, she asked, 'Have you brought me some dolly mixtures?'

'Sandra,' said her mother, 'it's not nice to ask George like that. You should always wait for him to give you them. Anyway, he might not have had time to call at a shop.'

George said, 'Hold out your hands and close your eyes, Sandra.'

'Did you buy some?'

'Just hold out your hands and close your eyes properly.' He waited until her eyes were fully closed, and then dropped a bag of dolly mixtures into her waiting hands. 'You can open your eyes now,' he told her, quite unnecessarily, but it was part of the ritual. The dolly mixtures then provided the usual distraction, enabling George and Mrs Young to catch up on each other's fortunes.

'Tell me about Norma's wedding,' said Mrs Young.

George hesitated, knowing from experience that women could spend hours discussing a wedding, whereas he would normally sum it up in two or three sentences, however enjoyable it might have been. In this case, however, he made an effort. 'It was a very happy affair,' he told her, 'and not just for Norma and David. There was a lot of good feeling there.'

'Even from them two, next door?'

'Yes, they were on their best behaviour.'

Mrs Young gave him a meaningful look, but went on to say, 'I heard you played the organ. Is that right?'

'Yes, the church didn't have an organist at the time, so they arranged for me to do it. It solved another problem as well. You see, we didn't know if my stepdad and Elsie would be there, and Norma wanted me to give her away. I'd have done both if it had been necessary, but they turned up, and he gave her away, so there was no ill feeling about that.'Mrs Young was looking at him strangely. She said, 'You called Arthur your stepdad just then.' She left the rest unsaid.

'Yes, Norma told me the truth. It was around the time I moved out, when Elsie got rid of the cats.'

Mrs Young bowed her head. 'Your poor mum,' she said. 'She was a lovely person, and that miserable bat next door isn't fit to take her place.' Visibly forcing herself to think of other things, she asked, 'What hymns did they have?'

George couldn't help smiling at the perpetual feast the wedding presented. 'The usual ones,' he said, ' "Praise My Soul" and "Love Divine". She came in to "The Arrival of the Queen of Sheba" – Norma calls it "Matron's Rounds" – and they left to the good old "Wedding March".'

'I like a traditional wedding. You can't beat—'

A shout from Sandra interrupted her observation. 'T' washing's come off t' line!'

They went to the back door and saw that one shirt had been blown off the line. The rest of the washing was intact.

'They're dry enough to come in,' said Mrs Young, picking up the casualty.

'I'll give you a hand,' said George.

Next door, Elsie was doing the same. She caught sight of George as she was dropping her washing into a basket.

'Oh, it's you. I wondered who that flashy car belonged to. I might have known.' It seemed that the good feeling at the wedding had evaporated already. 'You must be doing all right for yourself, with a car like that. What are you doing now?'

'I'm still in the same job.' He took a business card from his wallet and handed it to her.

'It's all right for some,' she said, peering at it. 'What's this LGSM when it's at home?'

'Oh, my boss insisted on that. I wouldn't have bothered, myself.'

'Okay, but what does it stand for?'

' "Licentiate of the Guildhall School of Music". In my case, it's a piano teaching diploma.'

'Oh, I see. Our Carol's starting to take pupils. I won't tell her about this, though.'

'No.' He took back the card. 'Anyway,' he said, 'I hope she gets plenty.' To avoid ambiguity, he said, 'I mean pupils.' He couldn't see anything else coming her way in a hurry.

'Well, I'll tell Arthur I've seen you.' It sounded like the opposite of an invitation, but George didn't care.

'You do that, Elsie.' He went in to re-join Mrs Young and Sandra.

Mrs Young asked, 'Did she tell you about Carol?'

'About her taking pupils?'

'No, she failed her exams at the college place, and she's working at Carter's Dry Cleaners now.'

'That'll be a joy for their customers.'

'I take mine to Denham's.' Looking at the clock, she said, 'Will you stay and eat with us, George? There's plenty.'

'Yes, please. I'd like that.'

It seemed to George that the two adjacent houses couldn't have differed more. One was filled with goodwill and generosity, and the other was a place of envy and resentment. He preferred to dismiss the latter from his thoughts, at least for the time being.

———◆�▸◄◆———

George had arranged to visit Norma and David when they were both off-duty, a process sufficiently involved that it reminded him of Jeanette and her ambition to marry a doctor. She really hadn't given it sufficient thought. He wondered idly if she'd found her dream partner, because if she had, he felt sorry for the unfortunate victim.

It was good to be at the dinner table with Norma and David. The close relationship between George and his sister had always been special, and his friendship with his brother-in-law was an added blessing.

'We're thinking of putting on a revue,' David told him. 'Apparently, there's a lot of talent among the hospital staff, so it should be fun.'

'There's more to life than drudgery,' observed Norma.

'When they told me about it at first, I was a bit wary. It was the word "revue" that did it. I'd experienced far too many reviews to be enthusiastic, but then, someone explained the difference and the nature of the thing, and I realised that it was harmless.'

'I'd like to come to that if I'm allowed,' said George, 'except I'm not volunteering to play the piano this time.'

'That's a shame,' said Norma, keeping a straight face. There are two or maybe three nurses who might be worth more than a second look.'

'Never again, Norma. I learned that lesson the hard way.'

'Oh, yes. I wonder if Price ever found her man.'

'It's funny,' said George. 'I was thinking about her recently, although not with any degree of fondness.' The wine was having a relaxing effect on him, and he was more inclined than usual to confide. 'I went out with her sister Lorraine for a few weeks,' he told them. 'In fact, she took over my old flat.' Remembering the incident, he said, 'She still has some of my bed linen.'

'A few weeks. As long as that?'

'Yes, David. They breed them difficult in that family.'

'Wait a minute,' said Norma. 'How did she get hold of your bed linen?'

'I lent it to her. She left her parents' house in a hurry, and they were no help. Apparently, they have no time for anyone but Jeanette and they spoiled her to death.'

'She always gave that impression,' said Norma.

David was keen to hear more. He asked, 'Why did you part so soon?'

'We weren't compatible.'

'It's a Price characteristic,' said Norma. 'Her sister was a rolling disaster. What did you fall out about?'

'Oh, just... things.'

'George, you're more articulate than that. What things?'

'Oh, there was her need to control everything, and... things I shouldn't discuss with my sister.'

'I see.' Norma adopted a disapproving tone. 'Someone's been a naughty boy.'

'Someone will be twenty-six next month, Norma. Celibacy is a lot to expect.'

'I suppose so.' She relented and gave him a forgiving smile.

In the softly-lit room and after several glasses of wine, he decided to end the mystery. 'It was a difference of approach,' he said. 'I like things to be gradual, good for both concerned, and above all, to happen naturally.'

'You were born a gentleman,' said David.

'On the other hand, Lorraine favoured the main course without the *hors d' oeuvres*, or the opera without the overture, as someone recently described it.'

'Funny girl,' said Norma.

David waited for him to go on.

'It was her choice, and I respected it, but my lack of enthusiasm triggered an argument that got out of hand, and we broke up.' He shrugged off the story by saying, 'It was ages ago.'

'As you said, you respected her choice,' said David, 'and you were right to do that, but if she showed no respect for yours, you're the innocent party.'

Suddenly, the candles seemed to glow more brightly. George said, 'Thank you, David, I've only just realised that I needed to be told that.'

'He's only a phone call away,' said Norma, 'if you're lucky and he's not attending to an emergency. Anyway, how's your love life now?'

'Pretty good.' He was looking forward to seeing Rachel again.

8

George was busier than ever at the agency, as the number of would-be performers continued to increase, and Miles was delighted with the new accounts that resulted. He demonstrated his approval by raising George's salary to two thousand pounds a year.

Meanwhile, he and Rachel saw each other frequently. They had much in common and there was plenty for them to do. They went to the theatre, to restaurants and the cinema. Because of Rachel's restricted upbringing, she had never learned to dance, and once more, George assumed the role of teacher, so that they could take advantage of the few remaining dance venues in the area. Rachel was an able pupil and quickly learned the waltz, the foxtrot and the quickstep, all in George's sitting room. They were short of space, but as George pointed out, most restaurant dance floors were tiny, anyway.

One night, when they were at his house, they'd been dancing to a record of the New Mayfair Dance Orchestra. As the current track ended, Rachel tapped him on the shoulder and said, 'We need to talk.'

'Do we?'

'Yes, come and sit down.'

He lifted the pick-up arm and switched off the record player. 'What's the matter?'

'Come and sit down.'

'All right.' He took the armchair opposite hers.

'We mustn't get too keen on each other,' she said.

'I don't know about you, but I can't switch my feelings on and off.'

'I mean it, George. You've always known there's no future for us.'

'I can't see why. History's full of parents who've disapproved, forbidden, been defied and consequently woken up disappointed. Some have even been known to get used to the idea and learn to live with it.'

She gave him a patient look. 'My father isn't a good loser,' she said. 'That's because he never gets any practice at losing. He's also a vindictive old tyrant, and anyone who crosses him lives to regret it.'

'What are you telling me, Rachel?'

'Simply that our days together are numbered. He's already making noises about wanting to meet you.'

'I'm not proud, and I'm not cowed either. I'm happy to meet him, either on his turf or mine.'

Her patience was beginning to fail. 'I can't make you understand, can I?'

'Understand what?'

'That, unless you can disguise yourself as a devout Catholic, you don't stand a chance. I know that, because I've lived with his brand of bigotry all my life.' Consciously relaxing a little, she said, 'Let's not talk about it now. Let's just enjoy the time we have left.'

He asked resignedly, 'What do you want to do?'

'You. Let's go upstairs.'

'All right, you've talked me into it.' He led the way to his bedroom, but stopped on the landing to ask, 'What's the worst he could do?'

'Don't ask, George. Just trust me.'

They undressed and joined each other as they had so often over the three or so months they'd known each other, but Rachel's message seemed to give their coupling a new and unwelcome poignancy from which they knew there would be neither relief nor return.

---◆�►---

They met again the following Saturday, at the Art Gallery operating in its dual role of recital hall, to hear a pianist recently arrived from Poland. Perhaps not surprisingly, the programme consisted of music by Chopin, Moszkowski and Szymanowski, an arrangement that pleased them both.

It was an excellent recital, and they were both in a cheerful mood when they left the building. They stood for a while at the bottom of the steps, deciding what to do that evening, when Rachel looked over George's shoulder and said, 'Oh, hell. That's torn it.'

'What has?' He turned to see where Rachel was looking.

'My father. He must have come looking for us.'

Instinctively, George put out an arm to protect her, but she stepped away.

'Don't touch me, George. We're supposed to be casual friends.'

'I don't believe this is happening.'

'Trust me,' she advised. 'Now, walk away from me. Behave as if you're going home alone.'

Out of concern for her, he did as she asked. Resisting the urge to look over his shoulder was difficult, but as he reached his car and unlocked the door, he half-turned to see them walking away together. As far as he could make out, Rachel was looking far from happy.

He drove home feeling sour on the one hand that Rachel's father could be the ogre and bigot that he was, but at the same time he was conscious of a sense of inevitability, because, despite his earlier optimism, Rachel had convinced him that their relationship was doomed. The tangle of emotions caused his stomach to tighten in sympathy, so that, when he reached home, he couldn't even think of eating.

He sat, ruminating over the problem but without coming close to a way forward. While he was based in Leeds, they couldn't even elope to a place where her father would never find them. That kind of thing worked in novels of a certain kind, but in harsh reality, the idea died at birth.

One mystery he'd never fathomed was what Mr Ronaldson could actually do to them. He knew that the family business was a kind of investment house, and that Rachel had hinted vaguely at some unnamed facility on his part to make life impossible, but George knew no more than that. The agonising continued until almost eight o' clock, when the phone rang. He was reluctant, at first, to answer it, as if ignoring it would make bad news disappear, but common sense emerged, and he picked it up.

'Hello.'

'George, it's Rachel.' She sounded awful.

'What happened?'

'We have to stop seeing each other. I tried telling him we were only friends, but he…. You don't know what he's like.'

'What can he do, Rachel? You're over twenty-one, so he can't put you in a convent. What is there to be afraid of?'

'You don't understand, George. He's so powerful in this city, he could ruin you.'

'Well, let him. I've had worse things—'

'George, stop and listen. It's not just you.' Her voice caught for a second, as if she were about to descend into tears, but she managed to go on. 'He could ruin the agency as well,' she said. 'He has the power to do that. He's even threatened it.'

'As a true Christian would, I suppose.'

'Oh, George, it's gone beyond argument. We have to stop seeing each other. It's as simple as that.'

He was silent for a few seconds, and then he said, 'It's seems we've no choice.'

'No we haven't.' It was little more than a whisper. 'Remember me, George. I'll never forget you.' Her last word came out as a sob, and then she put the phone down.

With a feeling of unreality, George poured himself a whisky and soda. He didn't know why, because he didn't like it all that much, but it was there, and he felt that he needed a drink.

He sat down with it, and the phone rang again. His mind raced. Maybe it was Rachel again. He wondered wildly if maybe something had happened to make everything all right. Maybe she'd decided to defy him after all. He picked up the phone.

'George Barker.'

'George Barker, eh? My name's Ronaldson. My daughter has just spoken to you on the telephone.'

Knocked flat again, George said, 'That's right.'

'Well, I've no doubt she asked you nicely, but I'm telling you straight. Don't come near her again, don't phone her or write to her. It's finished. Do I make myself clear?'

George said wearily, 'I knew that even before you stuck your finger in the dial. You could have saved yourself the trouble, unless you get your kicks doing this kind of thing.'

'Now, listen to me, young man—'

'No, let me say one last thing.' Even though he was defeated, George was determined to make his point. 'When I went to confirmation classes, I learned about a loving, forgiving, all-embracing God. I know you learned about a very different one, but I'll tell you this, I prefer mine to yours any day.'

He left it at that. He was so angry, he didn't trust himself to say any more, and he was about to put the phone down. when he realised that the line was already emitting the dialling tone. Rather than hear him out, Ronaldson had hung up.

———▸◂———

'It was inevitable,' Miles told him, 'and the young lady was right about the influence he wields in the Silver City.' He leaned forward confidentially, as if not wishing to be overheard. 'As a matter of fact, he owns this building and several others. Not only that, he's the backing behind several investors.'

'I'm not a vindictive chap, Miles,' said George, 'but I could wish all kinds of misfortune on him for what he's done to Rachel and me.'

'He's a Herod,' said Miles, dropping a small tablet into a glass of water, 'and his kind make so many enemies, they usually come to a sticky end.'

'Are you all right, Miles?' George was watching the tablet disintegrate in the water.

'Yes, I'm fine. I just have to take one of these little aspirins a day, just to thin the blood out.' He added, 'Just as a precaution.'

Then, returning to the original conversation, he put a sympathetic hand on George's sleeve and said, 'What you have to do now, George, is to get on with your life. It won't hurt forever, and you're not thirty yet.'

'I'm twenty-six,' George reminded him.

'Well, that only adds weight to my argument.'

9

George took his employer's advice and immersed himself in his work, some of which he found particularly rewarding. There was still much quality to be found; ballads were holding on gamely against the inevitable advance of the commercial recording, and some artists were even producing entertainment for the older market.

On the other hand, he'd noticed a new posturing element creeping into commercial pop music, which he saw, at best, as a distraction. It was more than a distraction, however, when novice performers adopted it as part of an assumed persona. He had a taste of it early in December, when he auditioned a group called No Exit. They had chosen to perform a song written by their lead vocalist, a bumptious youth called Mick Ball. George sat through a playing of the song and proceeded to interview Mick.

'What gave you the idea of calling the group "No Exit"? I know it's a sign over a door, but what was the appeal?'

'Well, it makes you fink, dunnit?'

'Does it?'

'Yeah.' Mick seemed surprised by the question. 'When you fink about it, it makes you fink.'

'I'll take your word for it, Mick.'

'We've been finkin' of changin' it.'

'Ah, so it *has* made you think.'

'Yeah, the last agent we talked to suggested changin' it to "Egress". I fink he fort o' that 'cause people like animals.'

George had to break the news. ' "Egress" is another word for "Exit", Mick.'

'Gerraway. Is it?'

'Cubs' honour. I think maybe he was having a bit of fun at your expense.'

'Yeah, well, I fort of changin' my name an' all.'

'To what?' George suspected that his answer might be interesting.

'I fort of "Rick Stacker".'

'I suppose it might go down well in farming communities.'

'Yeah?'

'It might, but changing names is all about improving your image, isn't it? Don't you think you should do some work on your music first?'

It was as if George had accused him of gross indecency. 'What are you sayin'? That last agent said we wasn't good enough, but he didn't know what he were talkin' about.'

'Calm down. I'm just saying that you have no lead guitar, you have two playing basic chords, so at a pinch, I suppose you could call them rhythm guitars, and your bass is barely keeping up with the beat. Your drummer's not bad, but he's limited. Basically, you all have a lot of work to do.'

By this time, all five were eyeing him with open resentment.

Mick said, 'So what are we supposed to do, then?'

'Get a lead guitar, you two on rhythm guitars need to learn some more chords, and your bass and drummer both need a lot of practice.'

'You don't need to practise when you've got talent.'

George took a long breath. 'Even when I was a kid, I used to practise for two hours a day. When I was working for my diploma, I did at least four.'

Mick shrugged. 'Yeah, well,' he said, 'maybe you had to do that 'cause you haven't got no talent.'

George stood up and said, 'I can't help you if you won't help yourselves.'

'Are you saying we're no good?'

'Let's say you have a long way to go. Now, I have other people to see, so I must ask you to leave.' He picked up their letter and took it to Miles's secretary, Joan, for filing with the other rejected acts. As he did so, he overheard Mick say to one of the group, 'That's anuvver agent what don't know his arse from his whatsit, his elbow.' Then, as if his judgement required explanation, he added, 'He don't know talent when he hears it.'

The group eventually packed their equipment and headed for the exit. George heard one of them say, 'I told you "Egress" was a fuckin' stupid name.' Another one said, 'Anybody got any dosh? Yeah? Let's get pissed.'

George said, 'It was a shame you had to hear that, Joan.' Because she always acquitted herself in a dignified manner, he'd always thought of her as living in a state of naïve maturity. She was invaluable, however, and regrettably, soon to retire.

She smiled. 'Hear what, George? I wasn't listening.'

'It's just as well.' Recalling the group's attempt at their audition song, he reckoned it would have been better if he hadn't been listening either.

It was a familiar, sorry tale, but there were also turns that made the job seem worthwhile, and one came shortly after the audition with the hapless No Exit. Her name was Linda Westmacott, and she sang 'Losing You', a song made popular by Dusty Springfield and others, but Linda gave it a fresh, new sound that George thought he could sell.

'You need a stage name, Linda,' he said afterwards.

'Do I?' It was a naïve, innocent response.

'As names go, "Linda Westmacott" is as good as any, but you need one that's short and memorable, that audiences will respond to immediately.'

'Do you really think I have a future?' Her absence of pretentiousness was a tonic after No Exit's loutish posturing.

'If I didn't think so, I wouldn't be talking to you about a stage name,' said George, leafing through the Equity directory. Having found the appropriate page, he asked, 'How does "Lyn West" sound? It's available if you want it.'

'What do you mean? How is it available?'

'There's no other performer with that name. Are you a member of Equity?'

'What's that?'

'It's the union that represents, singers, actors and models, and you can't work professionally if you're not a member. That's why I had to check that there was no one else called Lyn West. Equity insists on its members having unique names.'

'Oh.' She seemed unsure.

'Is that a problem?'

'Well, you see, I'm already a member of Nalgo, and I don't know if I can be in two unions at the same time.'

The question had never occurred in the past. 'Would you like me to check?'

'If you don't mind.'

George picked up the intercom and buzzed Joan. She answered immediately, as usual.

'Yes, Mr Barker?'

'Joan will you find the number, please, of the National and Local Government Officers' Association, and then put them through to me?'

'Certainly, Mr Barker.' Joan always addressed both Miles and him formally in front of clients.

'Now, Linda,' he said, 'where do you work?'

'At the Town Hall.' She added modestly, 'I'm only a clerk, really.'

'That's what I was when I left school.'

'Were you?' She almost gaped, as if unable to believe that the influential, all-powerful agent had once been a humble clerk.

The phone rang, and George picked it up.

'Nalgo are on the line for you, Mr Barker.'

A short conversation with someone in the Membership Secretary's office answered the question. Linda could be a member of as many unions as she wished. So, with the preliminaries dealt with, George wanted to hear her in front of an audience.

'Let me make a phone call this evening,' he said, 'and I'll be in touch.'

———◆◆———

His phone call was to the Gladstone Club, and he discovered that the Concert Secretary was Hubert Townend, an old acquaintance.

'What can I do for you, George? You're not wanting your old

job back, are you?' His tone suggested that such a development might not be unwelcome.

'No, I'm trying to place a new turn, just so that I can see how she goes on with a live audience. I suppose you're booking well ahead.'

'I am, but I've had a cancellation. What does this lass do, George?'

'She's a singer, very similar to Dusty Springfield. She's a nice-looking lass and she's good. When's your cancellation?'

'Next Saturday. Any good?'

'I'll get back to you and let you know.'

———— ►◄ ————

Linda was available for Saturday evening, so George picked her up and took her to the club.

'I'm ever so nervous,' she said.

'Of course you are. It's only natural. Mind you, I auditioned a group this week, and they weren't at all nervous. I don't think they'd turn a hair if they had to appear at the London Palladium in front of the Queen.'

'Don't you?'

'No, I don't,' he said, turning into Whitehall Road, 'but they're as likely to get that gig as they are to find a phone box on Saturn, because they haven't an ounce of ability between them.'

'Oh, I see.' Realising he was being less than serious, she smiled back at him, and he wondered how she would cope with life in the night clubs, because that was where she would begin if the evening's try-out went according to his wishes.

'Linda,' he asked, 'do you know anyone in London?'

'Only my cousin. He's at university there.'

'Oh, what's he doing?' George knew absolutely nothing about university education, but he had to show interest.

'Dentistry.'

'That could be handy.'

'Yes, and he works in his spare time as a professional wrestler.'

'You're kidding.'

'No, I'm not. He once threw Umi Guliz out of the ring and knocked him out cold.' For a gentle soul, she imparted the news with some pride.

'He'll be very handy.' A cousin who could get the better of a thug like Umi Guliz would be adequate protection for an innocent girl.

Reverting to their original conversation, he said, 'When you go on stage tonight, just keep telling yourself that the members, who'll be your audience tonight, are all on your side. They *want* you to do well.'

'Oh, I hope so.'

He avoided further reference to nerves for the remainder of the journey, by asking her about her life generally. He learned that she'd done well at school and succeeded in getting a good job at the Town Hall. Her ambition, however, had always been to sing professionally, and now that she was over twenty-one, she was finally able to follow her inclination. Where most girls of her age were looking for the right man, Linda was far more interested in a singing career.

Before long, they reached Cullington, and George took the familiar route to the Gladstone Club, where he found members only just arriving.

He introduced Linda to the Secretary and to Hubert Townend.

'You'd better come and meet the organist,' said Hubert. As they entered the Concert Room, he said to George, 'I only hope he's up to it. He's not in your league, not by a long chalk, but we have to take what we can get nowadays.'

They found the organist sorting through a pile of music. He was very young and he appeared nervous when Hubert brought George and Linda to the organ. There was no sign of a drummer.

George asked, 'Doesn't Bernard play here nowadays?'

'No, his missis got fed up with being on her own all the time and she gave him the hard word. It was her or the club.'

'A tough decision,' said George.

'This is Mark, our organist,' said Hubert. 'Mark, this is Lyn West, this evening's vocalist. I'll leave you two to sort things out between you.' He beckoned to George, who shook his head. He wanted to make sure Linda was happy and settled.

'I've put these in order,' said Linda, handing him her music. 'I sing them in the original keys. Just play as written. I don't muck about with them at all.'

Mark opened the first number, and his face registered his alarm. 'I can't play this,' he said. 'It's in five flats.'

'How many flats are you used to?'

'No more than three.'

It was Linda's turn to be alarmed, but George gave her waist a squeeze and said, 'Don't worry, I'll speak to Hubert.' He looked around the room and caught Hubert's eye. The Concert Secretary hurried over.

'What's the matter, George?'

'Mark's got a bit of a problem with Lyn's dots. Would it be okay for me to play for her, and Mark can play in between.'

'Of course it would, George.' Hubert rolled his eyes discreetly, and George got the impression that the problem occurred more often than he would have preferred.

'That's settled, then, Lyn. Do you want to give the first number a quick run-through?'

'Is it all right to do that?'

'Of course it is. Just take your time, flower,' said Hubert. 'There's only a few here, but if you do a bit now, they'll feel they're getting extra value for their money.'

'Okay,' said George, 'stand beside me, and we'll have a go at "Stay Awhile". Are you ready?'

'Yes.' It was almost a gulp.

With Mark watching somewhat abashed from the front row, George played the four-bars of introduction, and she began tentatively at first, gradually gathering confidence until she was singing with obvious enjoyment.

As she reached the end of the song, there was a clatter of applause from the members dotted about the auditorium, and one woman said, 'Very nice, love. We're all looking forward to hearing you sing on that stage.'

Seeing the delight on Linda's face, George kept quiet about the fact that the woman was Hubert's wife Mary.

———◆I◆———

The evening was the success that George wanted it to be. By the time Linda finished her third song, 'I Only Want to Be With You', the audience was captivated.

It was an excited client that George drove home later that evening, but he only half-listened to her eager chatter. The evening at the club had reminded him of another time when he'd been recovering from a broken relationship, and he realised that the awful hurt he'd felt at losing Rachel was becoming easier to bear. He hoped she was finding that too.

10

George spent Christmas with Norma and David, and that involved attending the hospital's Christmas Revue. Despite it being something of a busman's holiday for him, he enjoyed the production, which included a dance troupe trained and led by his sister, and he was as proud of her as ever.

'We could have used you on the piano, George,' she said after he'd congratulated her. 'Mr Jeffries is ever so willing, but he's a bit limited. You'd think a surgeon would be cleverer with his hands, wouldn't you?'

'No.' David dispelled the myth out of hand. 'Cleverness is the province of the physician. We do the brain work and leave the surgeons to do the plumbing and joinery.'

'You can imagine a similar conversation taking place in a parallel household,' said Norma. 'At this moment, some surgeon will be telling his family that he and his colleagues spend most of their time putting right the physicians' mistakes.'

'It helps them maintain morale,' said David. 'Anyway, I know I'm changing the subject, but how's the love life, George?'

' "Diplomacy" and "directness" are on the same page in David's dictionary,' explained Norma. 'It was an easy mistake for him to make.'

Relaxed as ever in the company of his sister and brother-in-law, George made no demur. 'If you're really interested,' he said, 'I'm happy to tell you about it.'

'Only if it's lurid and dramatic,' said David.

'Don't be horrible,' his wife told him.

'I don't know about lurid,' said George, but it was certainly dramatic.'

'From your use of the past tense, I get the impression you're between affairs.'

'That's right, David. 'It was great while it was allowed to go on happening, but let's say the term "star-crossed" springs to mind.'

'Hold it there.' Norma held up her hand. 'Go easy with the literary allusions, George. David thinks Shakespeare was an early case of Parkinson's disease.'

'I know what star-crossed lovers are,' protested David. 'Don't let this nit-picking sister of yours interrupt you again, George. I'm fascinated.'

George told them about Rachel, how they were so well matched, and how the only shadow over the relationship was the vague but insistent threat of her father's intervention. He described Rachel's final, wretched phone call and then her father's browbeating edict.

'I've nothing against his church,' he said, 'nothing at all, but I can't stand bigots and bullies of any persuasion.'

'Poor George.' Norma patted his hand across the table. 'It's not fair. You have absolutely no luck with women, and none of it's your fault.'

'Don't write him off,' said David. 'He's only twenty-five.'

'Twenty-six,' George corrected him.

'My mistake.' David grimaced and said, 'You're right, Norma, time's running out.'

'I'll throw something at you in a minute.'

George didn't mind. Time spent with his family was just as it should be: a priceless luxury and a cushion against unpleasantness.

———◆◈◆———

Because Christmas Day had fallen on a Saturday, the following Monday and Tuesday were public holidays, and George used the time, as before, to look up old friends. Naturally, he spent time with the Young family, much to Sandra's delight, and with Mr Handley. He also made contact, quite by accident, with Janet Firth from Wilkinson's. He would never have described her as an old friend, but he was prepared to be civil. He saw her leaving the cemetery gates, and he remembered how she used to put flowers on her mother's grave. He stopped to offer her a lift.

'Oh,' she said, 'hello, George.'

'Hello, Janet. Did you have a good Christmas?'

'It was quiet, but nice. How about you?'

'Very nice, thanks.'

Eyeing the car, Janet said, 'You're evidently doing all right for yourself. Where are you working now?'

'You asked me that last time we met, Janet, and I'm still working for Miles Standish Management. Anyway, where do you live?'

'Just outside Beckworth. It's good of you to offer me a lift, George, but it'll take you out of your way.'

'It's no trouble. It'll give us time to catch up on what's been happening at Wilkinson's.'

She took her place in the passenger seat. 'Since you left, let me see. Quite a lot's happened.' She stopped to think. 'You know Denise got married, don't you?'

'No, but we haven't seen each other since we split up.'

'Yes, well, she did. She married a senior member of staff, the accountant, actually, but that needn't concern you. Let me see, who else did you know?'

'Young Neville.' George stopped at the bottom of Mount Street, where he'd once skidded and come off his bike. He'd never forgotten that episode, because it was the night he made his first date with Jeanette. He dismissed it from his mind and turned left into Beckworth Road.

'Oh, Neville left a year or two ago, to work for his uncle somewhere.'

'Good for him. I hope he's happy. The poor little sod suffered enough at Wilkinson's.'

'Oh, you've just reminded me. Michael Burchett came back, you know.'

'After National Service?'

'Yes. Well, he only did a month or so before he was discharged. They said he was suffering from anxiety and depression, but it wasn't long before he was full of himself again. I can't say as I ever warmed to him, not after he shut Neville in the stationery cupboard.'

George nodded grimly. 'I wouldn't be surprised if he worked his ticket. Either that, or he couldn't take the rough army life.'

'Aye, well, you two never got on, did you?'

'Only because he wouldn't stop tormenting little Neville.'

Janet evidently went on remembering, because she said, 'He never qualified, you know. Michael, I mean. He kept failing the same exams time and again.'

'Economics and Statistics, as I recall.'

'I believe so.'

'So he was only clever by his own standards.' The traffic lights at the junction with Bradford Road turned amber and then red, so he stopped.

'You were daft, George, the way you went on. If you'd kept your nose clean, you might still have been there.'

'At Wilkinson's? I'm glad I'm not. Anyway, I'd have upset old Patchett sooner or later, and he always took Michael's side when we had a disagreement, whether he knew the whole story or not, so the writing was on the wall.'

'Well, Michael's leaving, anyway.'

'Who are the new misguided employers?'

Janet looked thoughtful. 'I did know, but I've forgotten for the moment, I'm afraid.

As they continued on their way, she said, 'They've got a really nice girl doing your old job now. Your replacement never really settled.'

'Somebody else with a bit of sense, then.'

Janet ignored the observation. 'The new girl, Patricia,' she told him, 'is engaged to a nice lad, a trainee manager at the Co-op Outfitters.'

'That's handy. He'll get her wedding dress cheap and collect the divi on it as well.'

Janet ignored his flippancy and said, 'She's ever such a nice girl.'

'Somebody else for you to watch over, Janet?'

'I don't know what you mean, and it's left at the next turning.'

'I bet you're forever warning the lads off, telling them she's spoken for.' He made the left turn.

'And left again, and it's number fourteen. Of course I tell them. Somebody has to.'

'Not everybody takes betrothal as seriously as you do, Janet.'

'You're right there.' She gave him a suspicious look, but evidently decided that his remark had been sincere. 'Just here, George. Thank you for the lift.'

'You're welcome, Janet. Give my regards to the other inmates, and all the best for the New Year.'

'Thank you. A Happy New Year to you too.'

She got out, and George drove off, satisfied that he'd done his good deed for the day. It seemed that Janet hadn't wasted any time before finding another virgin to watch over. He recalled those earlier days at Wilkinson's and hoped Denise was happy.

11

By the end of February, George had taken to opening up the office. Miles had done it in the past, but he'd been warned by his doctor to lead a less-demanding life. Reluctantly, he'd agreed, and was taking on a much reduced workload.

He arrived one morning, and came to see George straight away.

'Come into my office, George,' he said. 'I've something to tell you that'll interest you.'

George joined him, and Joan came in shortly afterwards with coffee for them both.

'Thanks, Joan.' Miles could scarcely contain himself. 'Do you remember last autumn, when you and Noel Ronaldson's daughter had to split up?'

'I'm not likely to forget it in a hurry, Miles.'

Miles looked guilty. 'You're not still grieving about it, are you?'

'No, I'm okay, but it was a blow at the time.'

'Well, do you remember me telling you that someone who goes through life making enemies usually comes a cropper in the end?'

'Yes, I do.' It was clear that Miles was working up to a major announcement, so George let him do it in his own time.

Miles had an opened newspaper on his desk and he tapped it gleefully. 'Ronaldson,' he told George, 'has been charged under the new Race Relations Act. He's accused of discriminating against a local Jewish firm on the grounds of race and religion. It's open and shut, apparently. There are witnesses and everything. Ronaldson's goose is as good as cooked.'

Miles had been right to say that George would find the news interesting, but he needed to know more. He asked, 'How will this affect him, Miles?'

'To begin with, it'll hit him where it hurts, in the pocket, because he'll have to pay a huge fine. As well as that, though, his own church has turned against him.'

'How does that happen?'

Miles explained patiently, 'The priest had to give a press interview. He said very little, but he had to speak out against racism, and he's not alone. Several other clerics have taken up the shout. On top of that, the Jewish business community have frozen Ronaldson out, so you could say he's as popular as a pork butcher at a *bar mitzvah*.'

George took the paper to read the story for himself, after which he returned it to Miles, saying, 'It looks as if you're right, Miles. He's going to get his just deserts.'

'What did I tell you?' Looking more serious, he said, 'There's just a possibility that he'll put this building, among others, on the market, and we'll be at the mercy of whoever buys it. If the worst happens, though, we'll move in with Nigel, so that exit is covered.'

The thought of sharing an office suite with Nigel Fox had no appeal for George, but he kept that to himself. 'You know,' he said, 'the ultimate irony for Rachel and me is that this happened too late.'

'Couldn't you two get together again?'

'I really don't think so.'

———◆◀———

A few weeks later, George was in a restaurant off the Headrow. He'd been entertaining the owner of a new night club, and his guest had just left in response to a phone message. As George paid the bill and got up to leave, his eye fell on a couple several tables away, although it would have been more accurate to say that he recognised one of them. The man's identity was a mystery, but his companion was Rachel.

George made his way over to them. The man looked surprised until Rachel spoke to him, and then he stood up to greet George.

'George,' said Rachel, 'it's wonderful to see you again.'

'And for me.' He bent to kiss her cheek.

'Let me introduce my *fiancé* Nicholas Symonds. Nicholas, this is George Barker, a dear friend of mine.'

The two men shook hands, and George said, 'Congratulations to you both. I'm delighted.'

'Thank you. You possibly heard the news about my father, George.'

'Yes,' he said, 'it must be very embarrassing for you.'

'To some extent,' she agreed, 'but it means that Nicholas and I can be married. Even before the case goes to court, my father is a spent force.'

———◆|◆———

Seeing Rachel was a surprise, but even more surprising was the knowledge that, pleasant though it was to see her again, he was no longer a slave to her memory. He was genuinely delighted for them, and for her especially, in view of the awful circumstances of their parting. He felt that she deserved the happiness that was hopefully coming to her.

He'd put the matter from his mind, regarding it as a compartment that was now closed, and so it remained until the hearing at Leeds Crown Court, when, in spite of an elaborate and lengthy defence, Noel Ronaldson was found guilty as charged and ordered to pay a heavy fine and court costs.

George could only imagine how the verdict might have affected Ronaldson, but he was surprised, two days later, when he received a phone call at home from Rachel.

'I thought I'd tell you, before your employer learns officially, that my father is no longer with us. I found him in his bed after he'd taken an overdose of some medication he was on.'

'Oh, Rachel, what a shock that must have been.' He was careful not to offer the usual platitudes.

'It took me by surprise, yes, but as you know, he was never what you or I would call a loving father. In fact, his actions demonstrated quite the opposite.'

'Even so, it creates hellish problems for you.'

'I have an excellent solicitor,' she assured him, 'and that's what I want to talk to you about. You see, it may be necessary to liquidate certain assets to pay the fine and meet my father's legal fees, which are considerable, but I want you to know that I'm going to avoid, if at all possible, selling Clare House. It was one of the threats my father used against you, and I'm determined not to let it happen.'

He was struggling. 'I appreciate that, Rachel, but I don't really understand what the problem would be.'

'The most likely purchaser,' she explained, would be Rendle and Hulme.'

'The shoemakers?'

'That's right. They'd give a lot to be able to extend their premises to the rear, and that would necessitate the eviction of Miles Standish Management. It's a prime sight, and I know Miles Standish values it enormously.'

'I see your point now, Rachel, and I'm very grateful.'

'It's the least I can do. You and I have gone our separate ways, but I'm happy to do this for old times' sake.'

———◆◆———

Miles was similarly grateful when Rachel spoke to him the next day.

'The will has yet to be proved,' he told George, 'but, effectively, Ronaldson has left his estate to Rachel.'

'Good.'

'Is there still no chance of you two getting back together?'

'Miles,' said George, 'you're like an old woman with your matchmaking, and no, there's no chance, because she's engaged to someone else.'

'I just want you to be happy, George.'

'I appreciate that, Miles. I'm quite keen on that myself, but I have work waiting for me.'

'Before that,' said Miles, we have to organise Joan's retirement party.'

'And we have to do it quietly,' George reminded him, 'or it will no longer be a surprise party.'

'I've organised the outside caterers,' said Miles. 'I did it from home. How are the invitations coming along?'

'They've been sent,' George assured him, 'R.S.V.P. by mail to my home address.'

Organising a surprise party for a secretary and book-keeper was quite difficult for obvious reasons. An additional problem was that Joan's husband Harry, who was also invited, was an inveterate chatterbox He had been sworn to secrecy.

In the event, the party was such a surprise that Joan spent the first few minutes in tears.

Miles asked, 'Did you really think we'd let you go without marking the occasion?'

No one ever found out what she'd expected, because when she finally regained coherent speech, her attention was diverted in a number of directions. The important thing, however, was that she was sublimely happy.

Harry then felt prompted to tell her about all the elaborate preparations that had gone on in secret.

'It's just like pulling the cloth off a parrot's cage,' observed George, thankful that Harry would be Joan's problem after 6:30.

It was evident that his employer's attention was elsewhere, because he said, 'That girl from the caterers has been giving you the eye ever since she arrived.'

George had noticed her. She was particularly attractive, with dark hair and an impish smile.

'I think you're home and dry,' said Miles.

'Forget it, Miles. I'm enjoying a period of celibacy.'

'*Enjoying*?'

'I know, and there will come a time when I'll forsake the monastic way of life, but let me decide when that will be.'

'All right, but have some more champagne, or I'll think you really are a lost cause.'

George placed his hand over his glass. 'Better not when I'm driving.'

'In that case, George, take a bottle home. You've earned it.'

'Thank you, Miles, I shall.' Mindful of his duties, however, George picked up a bottle and circulated, topping up his guests' glasses as he went. Everyone except Julie, the new office junior, was drinking champagne. She was only sixteen, so she had to be satisfied with orange juice, although George made sure she had enough bubbles in her glass to drink to Joan's health and happy retirement.

The girl from the outside caterers looked hopefully in his direction, but he wasn't to be tempted.

Back with Miles again, he asked, 'What's the new secretary like?' He'd been out of the office when Miles interviewed her.

'Very good, I think. She's sensible and she knows her stuff. Good secretary book-keepers are like gold, so it was a stroke of luck that I found her.'

'I have complete faith in your judgement, Miles,' said George. 'If I know your recruiting skill, I'm sure she'll be an excellent choice.'

'I think so. Her name's Mrs Kershaw, and she'll be in on Monday morning. Can you be here to meet her when she arrives?'

'It'll be a pleasure, Miles.'

———◆◆———

George was usually at the office by eight-thirty, and he had things to do on Monday morning, so it was no effort for him to be there in good time.

He was working on a press handout when he heard the outer office door open and close. It was almost eight forty-five. There was the sound of confident footsteps on the corridor, and he knew they belonged to Julie. A moment later, she greeted him.

'Good morning, Mr Barker. How was your weekend?'

'Good morning, Julie. It was very welcome, thank you. How was yours?'

'Okay, thank you. I finished with my boyfriend.' She made it sound like a highlight of the weekend.

'Oh?'

'Yes, he was being a pain in the neck. Can I get you some coffee?'

'Yes, please, Julie. That'll be very welcome.' As an afterthought, he said, 'The new secretary will be arriving shortly. I expect she'd like coffee too.'

'Right-oh, Mr Barker.' She said uncertainly, 'I wonder what she'll be like.' The new secretary would be her supervisor.

There was a knock on the outer office door, and George said, 'I think you're about to find out, Julie. Go and let her in, will you?'

'Right-oh, Mr Barker.'

Julie was a truly promising trainee and one of Miles's expert acquisitions.

Half a minute later, Julie announced, 'Mrs Kershaw's here, Mr Barker.'

George looked up and stared in disbelief.

The newcomer smiled and said, 'I suppose I should call you "Mr Barker" now.'

'Denise,' he said. 'What a surprise. What a wonderful surprise.'

1

It seemed that the surprise was entirely George's, as Denise explained.

'I learned you were here when I came for my interview and saw your name on your office door. I was quite taken aback, but I don't think you were expecting me.'

'I wasn't, but I'm delighted to see you again.'

'I'm just as delighted, George.' Her manner had developed in the last few years from girlish innocence to easy sophistication, but he still recognised the Denise he remembered so fondly.

Julie emerged from the kitchen with a tray. 'Where would you like your coffee, Mr Barker?'

'In Mrs Kershaw's office, I think, Julie.'

'Right-oh, Mr Barker.'

Denise smiled as she left. 'Isn't she lovely? I think I'm going to enjoy working here.'

They found their coffee in Denise's office. Tactfully, Julie was busying herself elsewhere.

Denise hung up her coat, and George saw that she was wearing what he always thought of as October colours, the ones that suited her best. Forcing himself not to stare, he asked, 'How did you make the transition from ledger clerk to secretary?'

'Secretary *book-keeper*,' she corrected him. 'For various reasons, I needed a complete change, so I went back to night school and learned touch-typing and shorthand. It was quite an experience, being in a class of sixteen-year-olds.'

'It was very enterprising of you, though.'

'No, George, it was self-preservation.' Accepting a cup of coffee, she asked, 'How long have you been here?'

'I started shortly after we… the last time we saw each other.'

'That must be one, two, three….' She struggled to count the years.

'Nearly four years.'

'Has it really been as long as that? I told Miles at the interview that we knew each other. I asked him to keep it under his hat that I was starting here, because I wanted to surprise you. He was remarkably game about it, considering I'm new.'

'You've surprised me all right. He told me he'd appointed a Mrs Kershaw, but the name meant nothing to me. Did I ever meet your husband?'

She shook her head. 'He was the accountant at Wilkinson's. He joined the firm after you left.'

'That explains it.'

She smiled. 'I remember your departure vividly.'

He was conscious that they had a lot of catching up to do, but for the moment, he was unsure of his ground. She was, after all, a married woman. He asked, 'Am I allowed to take you to lunch so that we can have a proper chat?'

She smiled in a way that was pleasingly familiar. 'Same old George,' she said. 'Of course you're allowed. I'd like that.'

'Oh, good.' Moving on, he said, 'I saw Janet Firth at Christmas. She told me you were married but that it needn't concern me, that Michael was leaving Wilkinson's, and that there was a new girl who's recently got engaged and who needed her protection.'

'Oh, she would. The poor girl can't walk into the next office without Janet shadowing her. She has my sympathy, quite literally.'

'Janet's in the wrong job. I'm sure she'd get more satisfaction guarding a sultan's harem than she does from keeping the nominal ledger at Wilkinson's. I used to think of her as a human chastity belt.'

Denise smiled at the recollection.

'When I saw her a few years ago, I told her again to mind her own business, and when she got stroppy, I told her to get out of the bath and get dressed. I explained that it was a little fantasy of mine, and she didn't take it as a compliment.'

Denise looked blankly, and then remembered. 'The bath at the football club,' she said. 'Of course. I remember now.'

Later, at the restaurant, they continued to swap experiences, and eventually, the matter of Denise's marriage cropped up, simply because George could ignore it no longer.

'I'm naturally pleased for you,' he said, looking at her wedding ring. 'Your husband gave you what I couldn't. Did you get the children you wanted as well?'

'No.' She fingered the ring self-consciously and said, 'I don't know why I still wear this, although it's sometimes useful. The fact is, though, our marriage didn't work.'

———•┤•———

It soon became evident both to George and Denise that something remained of the feelings they'd shared earlier, but Denise cautioned, and George reluctantly agreed, that to rush into a helter-skelter liaison would be foolhardy. As Denise pointed out, they couldn't ignore the interval of four years and expect things to be exactly as they remembered them.

'For one thing,' she said, 'we can't be sure that we remember them as they actually were, and some of the things we remember may no longer exist.'

'I know. It's a shame, but there it is.' They'd been out for the evening and had returned to Denise's house in Beckworth.

'What's a shame?'

'I've caught myself thinking, lately, about how we used to go swimming and then to Harrison's, and how old man Harrison had to treat me as a customer and not as the cringing lackey who played the piano at his tea dances. Happy days.'

'You were never a cringing lackey,' she said, 'but Harrison's is a case in point. So are the swimming baths.'

'What do you mean?' It was late, and he was beginning to lose the thread of her argument.

'Harrison's Coffee House was bought last year by a group

based in Manchester, and the old swimming baths became a carpet warehouse. They've built a new, Olympic-size pool at the sports complex. That's two things that are no longer as we remember them.'

'And the places where we danced are either disappearing or being turned into something else.'

'Not only that. They've pulled down the Regal Cinema in Cullington. It's waste land now.'

How could they? 'We went there on our first date.'

'Don't despair, George.' She patted his hand. 'The future may yet be an improvement.'

Her observation encouraged him to say, 'As a matter of fact, I'm a member of Ferne House Golf and Country Club. Miles and I use it for entertaining.'

'I didn't know you played golf.'

'I don't play very well. I leave that to Miles, but eating, drinking and dancing are another matter, and the club has an excellent restaurant with a sizeable dance floor.'

'I can see you move in elevated circles nowadays.'

'It's no posher than the Oak Tree,' he assured her. 'Do you fancy it?'

She looked doubtful. 'Is it the one near Skipton? I'm wondering about getting home afterwards.'

'It is, and I can put you up at my place.' He held up both hands. 'No strings.'

————◆◀◆————

The band at Ferne House was actually a quintet, comprising piano, alto saxophone, clarinet, double bass and drums.

'We used to have a full band,' the waiter told George somewhat wistfully.

'I know, but don't apologise. They're doing a fine job.'

'Thank you, sir. I'll leave you with the menu and wine list.'

When he'd left them, Denise asked George, 'Have you ever considered handling band musicians?'

'No, I'm afraid the dance band has had its day. What we see

here is a gallant remnant of the rear-guard.' Nodding at the menu, he said, 'Feel completely free. If you fancy the sirloin steak, go right ahead.'

'How did you know what I was thinking?'

'I know you of old, and, whatever you say, some things never change.'

When the waiter returned, George ordered for them both. 'And a bottle of the *Chateauneuf du Pape*, the 'fifty-nine, please.' He pointed to bin number twelve on the wine list.

'Certainly, sir.'

'George,' said Denise in mock-admiration, 'you're more sophisticated than ever.'

'So are you in a subtle kind of way.'

'Everyone has to grow up some time, and subtly is the way to do it, I'm told.'

He had to agree. 'Would you like to dance?' The band had just started 'Around the World'.

'Let's.'

He led her on to the dance floor, and the past came to life once again as they waltzed effortlessly in unison. He could tell from her delighted expression that she was similarly aware of something happening, and they enjoyed the number to the end, which came far too soon for both of them.

'That was lovely,' she said.

'It was a luxury.'

'Oh?'

Before he could explain, the waiter arrived with the wine, which he tasted and found to his satisfaction.

Denise returned to their conversation by asking, 'What made that dance a luxury? It seemed an odd way to describe it.'

He shrugged. 'Having the perfect partner.'

'Perfect?'

'I don't want to dance with anyone else, and that makes you the perfect partner for me. Also, I didn't need to teach you to dance.'

'Has that been a pattern recently?'

'To some extent.'

She nodded, understanding. 'I see now why it was a luxury,'

she said, sipping her wine. 'By the way, is there also something special about this vintage? You were very particular when you ordered it.'

'Something very special. I don't know one vintage from another, but nineteen fifty-nine was the year we met.'

She smiled slowly. 'It was a nice gesture.'

'I can't disguise the way I feel.'

Denise's response had to wait, because their first course arrived, and then George imagined she'd put it to the back of her mind when she looked around the restaurant and said, 'You can see the prawn cocktail's still riding high in the charts.'

'That's why I never ask for it.'

'I'm not surprised.'

Eventually, she said, 'Don't be in too big a hurry, George. Neither of us is going anywhere.'

'I still think I was the biggest fool to let you go when I did.'

Smiling, she shook her head. 'You didn't let me go, George. I made the decision, so I was the fool.' Suddenly, conscious that the conversation had become somewhat intense, she brightened and asked, 'What do you imagine your stepfather and his wife would say if they could see us now?'

'The usual, I imagine. The first thing Elsie says to me when we meet is, "You look as if you're doing all right for yourself." She always makes it sound like an accusation, as if I'm doing it at their expense. As for my stepdad, he can just about manage, "What do you want?" '

'I'll never forget meeting them at their wedding. They were like naughty children making a huge effort to behave themselves.'

That re-awoke the memory for George as well. 'I'm surprised you remember the wedding,' he said.

'It was a major event. You bought me a new hat.'

'Ah yes,' he sang in a passable imitation of Maurice Chevalier, 'I remember it well.'

'I still have the hat.'

'You're kidding.'

'No, I'm not. It's a lovely hat, even though I couldn't wear it with anything I've got now, but it meant a lot to me at the time.'

'Did it?'

She gave him a patient look and said, 'You've forgotten, haven't you?'

'Throw me a prompt,' he suggested, maintaining a straight face.

'Cullington Baths, remember? We had a race. You said that if I won, you'd buy me a hat for the wedding.'

'You left me standing.'

'You cheated and let me win.'

'Ah yes,' he sang again, 'I remember it well.'

'George,' she said, 'if we weren't in public, I'd throw something at you.'

'Dance with me instead.' The bandleader had just announced 'Blue Moon'.

'Okay.' She allowed him to lead her on to the floor.

For the next three minutes, they moved together, lost in the music and the joy of each other's proximity.

Afterwards, Denise disappeared to adjust her make-up, although George could see nothing out of place, and he sat alone in thought.

It seemed to him that they had been given that rare luxury, a second chance, and one part of him wanted to hold her close so that they would never be parted again. It was vital, though, that he didn't spoil things by appearing too eager, although one important safeguard was already in place, and that was his assurance that the offer of his spare bedroom came without strings. It was a binding promise, because he never made an undertaking lightly. It was a lesson he'd learned in early childhood. His mother had always insisted that 'promise' was a special word, and he'd never forgotten that lesson.

Denise returned, and a minute or so later, the main course arrived. After the waiter had gone, George said, 'I can't detect the slightest difference in your make-up, but I never thought there was any room for improvement, anyway.'

'Thank you, George. I've missed your compliments.'

'Couldn't you find anyone to stand in for me?'

She shook her head. 'No, I couldn't. I don't know anyone else with your combination of appreciation and sincerity.'

'Now I'm the one being complimented.'

'I'm only giving credit where it's due.'

They chatted easily through the main course. The food and wine were good and the band was unintrusive, at least until the bandleader made a surprise announcement.

'We have a request, ladies and gentlemen. It's for George and Denise, and it's that Ray Noble masterpiece, "The Very Thought of You". Take your partners for a classic slow foxtrot.'

'Denise,' said George, 'you remembered.'

'Ah yes, I remembered it well.' Laughing, she followed him on to the floor.

◆◆◆

'With all your warnings,' said George, 'what prompted you to make that request?' They were driving home, and the road was quiet and peaceful.

'I was being nostalgic. I don't see why you should have that all to yourself.'

'I don't, though, do I?'

'No, but I'm being careful. I've just emerged from one failed relationship, and I don't want another.'

He left Skipton and joined the A65. 'Are you really afraid it could fail?'

She hesitated. 'I don't think I am, really. It's just the negative state of mind these things leave behind.' It was clearly difficult for her to express her exact feelings, because she said, 'Let's not talk about it now.'

'Okay. What do you want to talk about? Or would you prefer silent companionship?'

'Isn't that what old people get up to in their quieter moments?'

'I don't know. They tend to keep their domestic pastimes to themselves as a rule, and I'm not inclined to intrude.'

'There's something I've been meaning to ask you.'

It sounded important, so he kept quiet and waited for her to enlighten him.

'You said earlier that the day of the dance bands was over and you couldn't see yourself handling that kind of musician.'

'Sadly, but there it is.'

'Where do you see popular music heading?'

He slowed down to drive through Addingham and said, 'Yet more loud noise with pretentious but meaningless lyrics relieved occasionally by banal platitudes.'

'Nothing good, then?'

He thought again. 'I'm not so sure. I think there may yet be a niche in popular music for quality.'

'What kind of quality are you talking about?'

'Performers of quality. Competition for openings in classical music is so fierce that a great many musicians and singers simply fall by the wayside.'

'I can see that, but what has that to do with pop music?'

'It's an alternative market for them. I think there's a future for classically-trained artists in what Billboard magazine calls "Easy Listening".'

The idea was beginning to appeal to Denise. 'Kenneth McKellar was classically trained, wasn't he?'

'Yes, he specialises in traditional Scottish songs, but it's the same idea.'

'There's Herb Alpert and Sounds Orchestral.'

'Horst Jankowski. Remember "A Walk in the Black Forest"? That's a recent one.'

They spent the remainder of the journey exploring the possibilities that easy listening had to offer. George had regarded it previously as a passing thought that might one day reward closer examination, and it had never occurred to Denise, but now it seemed very much a way forward.

While George was making coffee, Denise asked, 'When are you going to put the idea to Miles?'

'I'm not.'

'I don't understand.'

'Miles is considering retirement. His doctor's advised him to change down a gear. When he does retire, the likelihood is that his son Nigel will take over.' He poured coffee into two mugs.

Denise was overcome with curiosity. She asked, 'Are you saying that would be a bad thing?'

'I hate to paint a bleak picture when you've only been with the firm a short time, but yes, I think it would.'

'And you don't feel inclined to share your ideas with him?'

'You'll meet him soon enough, and then you'll draw your own conclusion.'

They took the coffee into the sitting room and sat down.

'I must say,' said Denise, 'you're always so fair-minded – some would even say too trusting – so there must be something awful about this Nigel character for you to take against him.'

'Well, don't let him spoil the evening.'

'No, let's not.'

Even so, George's curiosity was ignited. 'What was that,' he asked, 'about being too trusting?'

'Oh, I think it's generally agreed that you'd have given Dr Crippen the benefit of the doubt.'

'Actually, my brother-in-law once told me the same thing. He also said that I expected others to live by my standards, and that it was a recipe for disappointment.' He smiled self-consciously. 'I think that sounds pompous. It's saying there's something special about my values.'

'I think there is. I think you live by a set of ideals, and that's not a criticism.'

'No?'

'Far from it. Who told you that you lived in an ideal world? Was that your brother-in-law as well?'

'No, my sister, and I'm surprised you remembered that.'

'I remember a great deal more than you think. Actually, there's nothing wrong with it, just as long as you don't confuse your ideal with perfection.' Then, bringing the conversation to a close, at least for the time being, she stood up and asked, 'Where's the bathroom?'

'Off the landing and next to the spare room, where you left your overnight things.'

'Thanks. Back in two shakes.'

George was beginning to wonder. Maybe he had seen his ideal world as a perfect one. If he had, it was the ultimate naïvety for a man approaching twenty-seven. Maybe he was destined to suffer a string of disappointments simply because he expected too much from life. The danger had to be considered, and he gave it some immediate thought.

When Denise came down, she looked like someone who'd made a discovery; in fact, she demonstrated the fact by saying, 'Your bath is enormous.'

'It's only six feet long, and there's the shower, if you prefer that.'

'I'm not complaining, but do you remember the tiny bath in your flat above the greengrocer's? You joked about it. Of course, you joked about most things.'

'I thought we were supposed to be avoiding memory lane.'

'We were, but you've worn me down, George.'

He hadn't been aware of it, but it was good news.

'It's late,' she said. 'Will you unhook me?'

'With pleasure.' It was another familiar reminder. He unhooked the fastening of her dress and ran the zipper down to where it ended, at her waist.

'Are you coming?'

He nodded and followed her upstairs. When they reached the landing, he asked, 'Have you everything you need?'

'Not yet. Are we really going to sleep in separate rooms?'

'You wanted to take things slowly. That's why I said, "No strings".'

'And you're a man of honour.' She kissed him slowly and softly. After a minute, she asked, 'Will you let me pull the strings tonight?'

———◆◄———

Denise had chosen to sleep on the side George usually favoured, so she had the benefit of the bedside table, which was where he placed a mug of tea, relegating his to the floor beside the bed.

She stirred when he resumed his place, and opened her eyes, blinking in the light that filtered between the curtains.

'Good morning,' he said. 'There's tea on the table beside you.'

'You wonderful man. Good morning.' She levered herself into a more upright position, casually causing the sheet to slip down to her waist, and reached for her tea. 'You know,' she said, reviving herself with a first sip, 'last night's trip down memory lane was anything but a disappointment.'

'I'm in complete agreement,' said George, 'and it was all the better for being completely unexpected.'

'Yes, you had the look of a man taken by surprise.'

She took another sip and closed her eyes in ecstasy. Then, pulling the covers aside, she swung her legs over the side of the bed and stood up. 'Back in a jiffy.'

George sat up, drinking tea and marvelling at his luck. For his relationship with Denise to be rekindled the way it had was the most glorious thing of all, and he could scarcely believe it. He was still trying to convince himself of his good fortune, when she returned.

'George,' she said, 'that bath is far too big for one person.'

'Just what I was thinking.'

She slipped in beside him and snuggled up to him.

'Actually,' he said, 'the bath is so big, we could get into it and probably squeeze Janet Firth in with us as well. I wonder if she's up and about yet. I could maybe get her on the phone.'

'Don't you dare.'

They laughed about it until Denise changed the subject by reminding him of an earlier conversation. 'What do you intend to do about the idea you had last night? I mean, if you're not going to introduce it at Miles Standish Management, where are you going to use it?'

'I can't do anything yet. Ideally, I'd like to start my own agency, but I need more cash before I can do that. I need the capital to finance things while I'm building a clientele, and that has to be done from scratch.'

'But you're very good at that. Miles says so.'

He shook his head dismissively. 'It takes time to become established. I have contacts among the night clubs and concert venues. I also know a few people in radio and TV, but clients are another matter. Also, I don't want to go into competition with Miles, and I'd never dream of pinching his clients.' Tiring of the subject, he said, 'Let's leave it for another day. We shouldn't be talking business when more urgent matters need our attention.' He kissed her at some length to make his point.

Eventually, she was able to ask, 'What urgent matters do you have in mind, George?'

'The first,' he said, distributing his kisses more widely, 'is a pressing need to revisit memory lane.'

'And then to wallow together decadently in a deep bath with lots of bubbles.'

'Yes, we'll need that.'

13

George's office door opened, and when he looked up, he saw Nigel in the doorway.

'Sorry, Nigel. I didn't hear you knock.'

It seemed that irony was lost on his visitor, who ignored the remark and asked, 'What's new, George?'

'Nothing, as far as I'm aware.'

'Oh.' Nigel looked around the office, as was his way, and said, 'I just thought I'd ask, as you're supposed to have your finger on the pulse.'

'It's beating quite normally, Nigel. Have you a particular reason for coming to see me? I ask because I'm rather busy.'

'I'm just generally interested, but I'll leave you to work.'

'Thank you, Nigel. Goodbye.' He looked down again and continued reading the press notice he'd been given after a client's theatre debut.

An hour or so later, there was a knock on the door, so he knew it wasn't Nigel again. He said, 'Come in,' and looked up to see Denise, who looked concerned.

'Hello, Denise. What's the matter?'

'I don't know that there's anything you can do, but I think I should tell you what's been happening. I had Nigel Fox in my office earlier.' Her expression told him that the visit had not been a pleasant one, although that was no surprise.

'Snap.'

'I don't know why he came to see you, but he asked me – no, he demanded – last year's final accounts and balance sheet, and when I told him I'd need to consult Miles, he got quite shirty. It's

222

difficult to describe exactly. I can only call his attitude disdainful and threatening at the same time. I have to say, it was reminiscent of my ex-husband warming up for a tirade, and I don't need any reminders of that.'

'I'm sorry, Denise.'

'It wasn't just me. He upset Julie as well.'

'Will you bring Julie to me, please, Denise? I'd like to speak to you both.'

He waited, knowing he could do no more than appeal to Miles, but he was determined to show both Denise and Julie that someone was batting for them.

Denise knocked out of courtesy and pushed the door open.

'Come in, both of you, and take a seat.' Julie's eyes were reddened, and tears were forming again. He pushed a box of tissues towards her and said, 'There you are, Julie. Help yourself.' Turning to Denise, he asked, 'What happened?'

'He told Julie to give him the list of clients, and when she couldn't lay her hands on it immediately, he told her she'd have to buck up her ideas if she wanted to have any future with the firm. More than anything, it was the nasty way he said it that was so offensive.'

Between sobs, Julie asked, 'Is he... going... to buy the agency?'

'I'm afraid he doesn't need to, Julie. Believe it or not, Nigel is Mr Standish's son, and he'll take over soon enough.' He corrected himself. 'Far too soon, for my liking.'

'I'd rather... leave... than work... for him.' Her youthful innocence made her determination all the more real.

'You'd leave a big hole, Julie, because you're an excellent worker, but I wouldn't blame you if you did.'

'Would you... give me a refer... ence?'

'You can count on me for a glowing reference.'

'Thank you, Mr... Barker. I don't... want to ask Mr... Standish in the circ...'

'In the circumstances, Julie, I quite understand.' Addressing them both, he said, 'I'll certainly speak to Mr Standish.'

———◆◆◆———

As George had anticipated, Miles was embarrassed, and that made for an awkward meeting.

'I realise this is a sensitive matter,' said George, 'but, for the sake of staff morale, I had to bring it up.'

'I'm sorry, George, but I really am in a cleft stick. Let me try to explain.' He looked defeated even before he began.

George said nothing, but simply sat back and listened.

'You've possibly wondered why Nigel and I are so different. The fact is that, because of a bungled operation, my late wife was unable to have children. She was also unable to function fully as a wife.' He was clearly uncomfortable, but he went on nevertheless. 'Nigel was the result of a liaison with an ex-client, who is no longer alive, and therefore whose identity is irrelevant as far as this conversation is concerned.' He paused, and it seemed right for George to comment.

'I don't think less of you, Miles. Quite the reverse, in fact. I admire your honesty.'

Miles smiled gratefully. 'You're making it easier for me, George.'

'Good.'

'The fact is, George, that having behaved the way I did, I felt all the more responsible for him, and I really have tried my hardest. I helped him into work, and when he seemed unable to hold a job down, I set him up in the agency that he has now.'

'I gather it's not entirely successful.'

The defeated look returned to Miles's features. 'That's an understatement, George,' he said. 'It's going down the pipes. He's lost the members of his team who knew the business, and without that expertise, he can't possibly continue.'

'So that's why he's been taking an interest in our books.'

Miles nodded. 'At least, when I have him under my roof, I can exercise some control over his behaviour, but I'm sorry if the arrangement causes difficulty for you and the staff.'

'I'm a big lad now, Miles. I'm more concerned for the staff.'

'I'll speak to him about that, George.'

'Thank you. When will he move in?'

'As soon as he can wind up Get Ahead! and re-assign the lease on his premises.'

———◆◆——

'He told me certain things in confidence, and I have to respect that, but basically, he feels responsible for Nigel's future and wellbeing, even after being repeatedly let down.' They had eaten at Denise's house, and she had just opened a second bottle of wine. 'I'll have to throw myself on your mercy tonight,' he said, looking at the wine.

'I'll take pity on you. First, though, what are we going to do? I mean about Nigel.'

'There isn't much we can do except keep an eye out for jobs, because it's inevitable that when the agency is in his hands, it'll go the same way as Get Ahead!'

'It's a funny name for a business that's going into liquidation,' she observed, topping up their glasses.

'Not so funny for Miles. He provided most of its capital.'

'Poor Miles.' It was clear that she meant it.

'I've been wondering about something,' he said, 'although tell me to mind my own business and I will.'

'Tell me what you've been wondering, and let me decide.' She snuggled more comfortably against him.

'You said that Nigel reminded you of your ex-husband.'

'Yes, he does, because cruelty is second nature to both of them. I divorced Alan on the grounds of mental and physical cruelty.'

'Oh hell.'

'Most of the time, he was careful to hit me only where it didn't show. I mean, it wouldn't have looked too good if I'd gone into Wilkinson's wearing sunglasses. He couldn't very well tell everyone I'd joined the Roy Orbison Fan Club.'

George could think of nothing useful to say, so he said what he was thinking. 'If you see him when we're on our travels, you will point him out, won't you?'

'Why?'

'So that I can return the compliment, and then *he* can go to work in sunglasses.'

'I'm tempted, George.'

'Did he admit to all this?' George was a newcomer to the divorce process.

'He had to. Our neighbour from next door came round to complain about the noise – his wife was a nurse on the night shift and she needed her sleep – and he saw Alan using me as a punch bag. He was only too happy for me to name him as a witness.' Looking up at George again, she said, 'I don't know why I hesitated with you, George. You and he couldn't be more different.'

———◆◆◆———

During the next few weeks, George, Denise and Julie found job opportunities less than plentiful, but they continued to keep an eye on the papers, hoping for a change in their fortunes. Those same newspapers suggested that employers were reluctant to invest at a time when a succession of by-elections had left the British Government with a majority of one seat. Companies were waiting for the General Election scheduled for the end of March before committing themselves to further recruitment. Meanwhile, however, an event took place at the agency that focused everyone's mind on the present.

George was in a meeting with Miles, when his employer seemed suddenly preoccupied.

George asked, 'Are you all right, Miles?'

Miles stared at him urgently. He was struggling for breath, and George could see perspiration forming on his forehead. He picked up the phone and buzzed Denise.

'Hello.'

'Denise, call an ambulance, please. I think Miles is having a heart attack.' He put the phone down without waiting for a reply. Miles had slumped back against his chair.

There was a framed photograph of his late wife on his desk, and George held it in front of his employer's nose and mouth. A second or so later, there was no misting on the glass. Miles had stopped breathing.

George pulled down his tie and unfastened his top shirt button before pulling him on to the floor. Pushing his chin upward, he pinched his nose and applied mouth-to-mouth resuscitation.

The door opened, and he heard Denise say, 'An ambulance is on its way. Can I get you anything?'

George broke off just long enough to say, 'No,' and then continued to resuscitate.

After a while, it was evident that Miles was never going to breathe again, but George nevertheless persisted with the procedure until the ambulance arrived.

14

The atmosphere after the funeral was one that George would have been happy to forget, had that been possible, but the memory remained with him for several weeks afterwards. Nigel was characteristically abrasive and seemed completely untouched by his father's passing, a fact that was noted by several clients and business associates.

Denise remarked, 'I wonder if he realises just how unpopular his behaviour makes him.'

'I doubt it. I think he's incapable of any kind of self-appraisal.' George had come to regard Miles almost as a father figure, and he deeply resented Nigel's attitude towards him.

There were also practical concerns to be addressed, and they included the running of the agency until probate was granted, when Nigel could legally assume ownership. George naturally took control as far as he could, with Denise's willing assistance, the two often working late. It seemed wrong to George that Denise should be working as hard as he was, but she seemed to find jobs that needed to be done. One evening, he found her going meticulously through the clients' files, making notes as she went along, and in his preoccupied state, he could only marvel at her dedication to the job.

Thankfully, Julie had been successful in finding another position and had almost worked her notice when the next fateful event occurred.

Without warning, Nigel turned up at the agency. George was in Denise's office when he arrived.

'Good morning,' he said.

Surprised, George, Denise and Julie returned his greeting.

Nigel turned to Julie and asked, 'Have you found out yet where the client list is kept?'

She looked at him uncertainly, but answered, 'Yes.'

'A result at last. In that case, take it to my assistant. You'll find him in George's old office.'

George looked at him squarely. 'My *old* office?'

'Yes.' With his customary, sardonic expression, Nigel said, 'Come with me.'

George imagined for the moment that he was being taken to Miles's office, but he was not to be accorded even that courtesy. Instead, Nigel stopped in the passageway to speak to him.

'It's only natural that I should bring my own people into the business,' he said, 'and that means there's no longer a place for you. In any case, I could never see you and I working together. You'll be paid up in lieu of notice, of course, and I'll give you a reference.'

'Save yourself the trouble, Nigel. No one in the business is going to take any notice of a reference written by you, and I certainly don't need your help.' He inclined his head towards his office and asked, 'I imagine I'm allowed to remove my personal belongings?'

The sardonic smile lingered. 'Go ahead. You'll find my assistant in there. I believe you and he have already met.'

Convinced by now that nothing else would surprise him, George walked along the corridor and pushed the door open. There, behind his desk sat Michael Burchett, his antagonist from the Wilkinson days. Janet had said he was leaving Wilkinson's, and now George knew why.

'Well,' said Burchett, obviously enjoying the situation, 'if it isn't the secondary modern sailor boy.'

It was equally childish, George knew, but he had to retaliate. 'Michael "Bird Shit",' he said, 'the wimp who's too soft for the army, so he torments helpless kids.'

'I worked my ticket, Barker.' He made it sound like a worthy achievement.

'It amounts to the same thing, Bird Shit. Just move aside while I empty my desk. I must say, you and Nigel Fox are a matching pair. What's your function in his nasty circle?'

'I'm his accountant.'

'Do you call yourself that on paper?'

Burchett smirked. 'Who said anything about being qualified?'

As George leaned over to pull out the lower drawer, he noticed the client list on the desk. 'I signed up most of those clients,' he said. 'Do you honestly believe they'll stay with you?'

'They've no choice, Barker. They're under contract.'

'As I said, you and Fox are two of a kind. Neither of you is fit to be in business, and certainly not this business.'

'Oh, but we are, and this is a thriving business, as you know.'

'And one you can't even begin to understand.'

The smirk persisted. 'Talent scouts can be hired as well as fired, Barker. We just prefer it if the talent scout is someone other than you.'

'And devious shits who pose as accountants can come to a sticky end, especially when they keep the wrong company.'

He returned to Denise's office and found Nigel in the doorway. Michael Burchett had also emerged to watch the proceedings.

'You're not going in there, George,' said Nigel. 'I won't have you helping yourself to the firm's documents.'

Over Nigel's shoulder, George saw Denise looking angrier than he'd ever known her. Julie looked scared as well as angry.

'Listen, Nigel, I want your undertaking that you'll deal fairly with Mrs Kershaw and Julie.'

'Mrs Kershaw will remain in her post, George. I'm going to need her assistance.'

'Don't worry about us, George,' Denise told him.

'No, there's no need,' said Julie. 'I'm off, now. Good luck, Mr Barker, and thank you for the reference.' She pushed her way past Nigel and made for the stairs.

The smirk continued. 'Well,' said Nigel, 'who needed the silly child, anyway? I've got all the staff I need for now.'

'You can stick your job, Mr Fox,' said Denise. 'I wouldn't work for you at any price. Wait a minute, Julie, I'll give you a lift home.'

Suddenly, Nigel looked anxious. 'You can't leave,' he said.

'Watch me.'

'I need you here.' It was a demand rather than a plea, but it was no less urgent.

'But I don't need you.'

'You've got to sign a new bank mandate before you go.'

'The account's in the executors' hands. They make the decisions about any changes. Hadn't you realised that, you crook?'

Nigel tried another approach. 'Don't think you'll get a reference from me, Mrs Kershaw.'

'Why would I want a reference from someone who's earned the contempt of everyone who knows him?'

They left together, leaving the interlopers wrong-footed and visibly worried.

Once outside, Denise asked, 'What now?'

'When you've taken Julie home, come back to my place,' said George. 'I'll do some shopping on the way, and then we can have lunch and see if we can find a way forward.'

'It sounds good to me.' Denise was looking remarkably cheerful for someone who had just forfeited her job.

'I'll see you back there, then. Goodbye, Julie, and thanks for all your hard work.'

'Goodbye, Mr Barker. Thank you too.'

———◆◄◆———

George had prepared lunch, and the wine was sufficiently chilled by the time Denise arrived.

'What a morning, George.' She stopped to kiss him. 'For a sweet little thing, Julie was angry enough for all three of us, and who could blame her?'

'Just stand here for a minute.' He wrapped his arms around her and enjoyed his first moment of peace since early morning.

'As hugs go,' said Denise, 'this one was sorely needed.'

'Mm.' Words were superfluous. Eventually, he kissed her and said quietly, 'I love you.'

'I'm glad to hear it, because I'm just as potty about you. I may even be a weeny bit pottier than you are.'

'Impossible.'

As he released her, she asked, 'What have you been up to in my absence? I see you've prepared lunch.'

'I've done more than that.'

'Go on, then. I'm all agog.'

I've made two phone calls, one to the firm's solicitors and the other to Ronaldson Securities, who own Clare House.'

'Pour us a drink and fill me in.'

George took the bottle of wine and poured two glasses. 'I think you'll agree I'm not a vindictive chap,' he said.

'Out of all the adjectives in the dictionary, "vindictive" is among the last anyone could ever use to describe you, and that's got nothing to do with "v" coming so near the end of the alphabet.'

'Even so, I've tipped off the executors that Nigel has taken possession of a business that's currently subject to probate.'

'Good,' said Denise, accepting a glass of wine.

'Also, I've told my contact at Ronaldson Securities that I'm no longer employed by Miles Standish Management.'

'Who's your contact?'

'Rachel Ronaldson, an ex-girlfriend who, I hasten to add, is now engaged to be married to someone else.'

'I wasn't worried. What's the story there?'

George tried the wine and gave it an approving nod. 'Ronaldson's had a liquidity problem even before they were hit by a hefty fine and considerable legal expenses, and they have to sell some of their properties. We needn't go into that, but Rachel held off selling Clare House while I was employed there. She did it as a special favour for old times' sake, but now I've been fired, she can go ahead and sell it to Rendle and Hulme, who've been after it for some time.' A newcomer to intrigue, he smiled faintly and said, 'So far, then, Nigel will be unpopular with the Probate Registry, and before long, he'll be evicted from Clare House.'

'Also,' said Denise, smiling comfortably, 'you and I are the only surviving signatories registered at the bank, so he can't transact banking business of any kind.'

George nodded his appreciation. 'It's just a shame I couldn't grab the client list before Bird Shit collared it. I suppose I can do something from memory, but it's going to be awkward without the contract expiry dates.'

'He was another unpleasant surprise. It's a pity you didn't get a chance to lock him in the stationery cupboard with a rubber snake.'

'Happily, he'll go down with the sinking ship, along with Nigel.'

'Hopefully, but I shouldn't worry too much about the client list if I were you, darling.' Her tone betrayed the fact that she'd been saving the best news until that moment.

'Why not?'

'Because I have a shorthand copy of it with contact details as well as the contract expiry date for each client. I made it when we were working late after Miles's death, knowing that you no longer owed the firm a scrap of loyalty.'

George was momentarily stunned into silence.

'Actually, several contracts will soon be due for renewal.'

'I know.' Suddenly, he found his voice and he was able to register his delight. 'I remember signing them. Denise, you are bloody wonderful!'

'No, I'm just more devious than you are, although I must say, you're beginning to get the hang of it.'

'Will you be my partner in the new agency?'

She hesitated, considering his offer, and said, 'I hope I'm going to be rather more to you than that.'

'So do I.' He held out his arms and drew her into a glorious hug. 'I can't believe it,' he said. 'One minute it's desperation, and then….' He found it impossible to describe.

'It won't be perfect, George. Nothing ever is, but I think we can look forward to something that's as close to ideal as anything ever can be.'

THE END